I0654557

Table of Contents

Prologue

Judgment passed long before the trial began.

The coarse concrete scraped my knees as I struck the ground. Cold air wrapped around me, its chill biting my nose. The hairs on the back of my neck stood and tingled.

They're watching.

We hadn't done it. No, but we're still ruled guilty.

I blinked away the tears blurring my vision. I must be strong, especially today. At least, for my family.

The last votes were held. It was final.

Mom and Dad were thrown forward first, their shouts filling the vast silence of the room. But those cries were in vain. Mercy wouldn't be given to them. Not to anyone.

We knew that.

Sparks flew around their figures, covering them like a blanket. It lasted minutes, days. I could not discern. Time froze, and the screams blended, coursing in my ears and through the atmosphere.

As the sparks receded, I saw my parents' backs. Their backs were bare. Their wings gone. No longer were they Ikris, and neither will my brothers nor I be.

I shut my eyes tightly, shaking and clenching my teeth. Zackarius rested his hand on my shoulder. *It will be okay. As long as my brothers are with me, it must be alright.*

It was our turn.

Sparks cloaked my skin, coating me until I felt

nothing. The change was timeless, a blink of emptiness. One—that wasn't complete. Electricity lingered at the edge of my vision. Something rested in its place, fighting to escape and flourish, but hiding as it failed… until darkness.

I walked to the exit, my breath short. Anyone would call this the end. But I refuse to let it be the end of my story…

Cold stung my eyes and I blinked. Did I lose something? Why did it feel like I'd woken from a dream I couldn't quite remember? What's happening?

They shoved my brothers and me to the exit.

One of the captains muttered under her breath so softly I could barely hear, "May lightness protect them—and what I've done be worth it."

Chapter 1

IZZIE

No matter how cautious we moved, how exact we followed, she found us.

Shards of glass crunched underfoot like brittle bones as I raked my fingers through my hair, unknotting it. Bugs scuttled over the paint, peeling from the walls, where broken picture frames dangled loosely.

Across from me, my twin brother Kyle tugged at the loose carpet, exposing rusted nails beneath. He hid our meager belongings underneath the floorboard, his greasy blond hair shining against the dim light. He wore an old collared shirt with a small stain at its edge and a hole in the back.

I gave him my small pillow and straightened my torn long-sleeved shirt. I repeatedly glanced at the door, moving to put myself between it and Kyle. There were a few items we were allowed to have, such as clothes and shoes. If she caught us with something not on the list, we'd pay the price.

Not just from her but from her friends. They all watched. Her. Us. They made sure we never told anyone or attempted to escape, threatening to kill the other twin if we tried. Even if we did, we had no one to run to. Not the law, not the government. They didn't care. My 'mom' and her friends had powerful connections. They made sure the authorities turned a blind eye as long as one of us showed up at school each day.

My breath grew ragged. *Who would want to help us?*

The TV ran in the background, a news lady mumbling words I barely made out. "Magic users... accused of mass destruction across the southern regions. Nemesis, the self-appointed guardians… pledge to protect us, using any means necessary."

I stiffened, clenching my trembling fingers. *The Nemesis pledged to protect us, so would they help us with her if they fully knew what she's done? Or is that another lie?*

The creaking in the floorboards grew louder. I met Kyle's gray eyes, his irises rimmed with gold held a trace of horror in them; but it was mainly acceptance. He messily replaced the floorboard, his frame shrunken inward.

The woman, *Mom,* stumbled into the doorway. Her shoulders slumped, and a smile twisted on her lips. A strong stench of weed and alcohol emanated from her. Her words enchanted people.. But not to us. We knew better.

"My friendssss… come today. Better be— good," she slurred, eyes darting behind her. She held a glass bottle in one hand and a strange modified gun in the other, scanning us for a few moments with dull eyes and a puzzled face. Slowly, her brows furrowed, and she raised her arms. "Areee you trying to escape? I told you and you don't listen!" She slammed the bottle against the doorframe, breaking it in half, and entered. I flinched, squaring my shoulders as Kyle crawled over to me. "You have no idea what sacrifices

5

were made for you to have this life, you ungrateful brats! You would've been dead!"

Years ago, she loved us. She'd play with us in between her drunken states, make dinner, and buy us clothes. And then it became worse when she began smoking pot, mixing with the alcohol. Her frame and hair grew significantly thinner and paler. She dyed her hair dark brown instead of the old blonde, and numerous wrinkles painted her face. But the largest change was her voice, going from sweet and soothing, to low and husky.

"I'mmmm your only family," the woman drawled. "Who are you looking for? Who would you go toooo?"

I forced myself to nod, my whole body tensed. These situations have become common in recent years. Fighting back only made it worse. I shifted to hide Kyle more. "We won't do anything. We'll be good. I promise."

Straightening, the woman smiled, raising a hand. "Like I believe youuuu, idiot." I braced myself, but she twisted away. She exited the room, shouting over her shoulder, "If I catch you, then you'll wish you were dead."

Kyle brushed my arm with his. When she was out of reach, he muttered, "Our dad may be dead, but we have siblings. I-I think. Remember that memory I told you of that boy with silverish hair and glowing eyes?"

"Of course. I believe you." I glanced at him, forcing my shoulders to relax. "One day, when we escape, I will make sure we're safe. Then we can find our lost family and never let her hurt anyone again."

With a deep breath, I stood. *When that day comes, I will be ready for it and whatever choices it may bring.*

Chapter 2

IZZIE

TWO YEARS LATER

Two years, and we still weren't free. I told myself he'd be okay. But deep down, I wasn't sure if that mantra would ever become true.

Wreeee-Urrrrr. The swings creaked in the park I passed, echoing through the empty street. The sunlight reflected off the buildings, enhancing their colors almost magically. But there was nothing magical about today. Magic was always something distant, whispers, news reports of far-off events, or rare sightings. Except for what *'Mom'* could do. And my twin brother, Kyle, sat stuck at home with *her*.

It's so wrong... I paused, my heart skipping a beat. *I hope she doesn't hurt him.*

Sweat streaked down my face and back, drying my mouth as the hot sun beat down. Adjusting my frayed backpack, I leaned forward, relieving the ache in my back and catching my breath as pain shot up my leg—a pain from last night.

Slowly, I climbed the hill to my school. *Only three more years.* I sighed, using my partially ripped sleeve to wipe my face. A kid rang a bell behind me, zooming past on his bike.

I continued to the metal doors, placing my hands in the pockets of my jeans. I weaved past growing crowds of people and through the doors, where a gust of wind hit me, cooling my face. I stumbled to my right into a hallway full of lockers, locating mine at the far end where my two friends stood, laughing.

"You're joking!" Kate snorted, playfully shoving Laral.

Laral wiped the tears from her eyes before they found mine. "Oh, Izzie! You're here!"

I nodded, opening my locker as she continued the story about her dog and ex-boyfriend, with Kate chiming in from time to time. I shoved my bag inside and went to close the door, but I paused upon seeing it shaking. No, not the bag, the school.

It stopped moments later with no damage. I spun, searching my friends' faces. Everybody's faces. Nobody moved or seemed to be fazed. An uneasy sense rested on my shoulders. *What? Am I imagining things? Must've been hit in the head too many times... But I could've sworn...*

"Izzie? Hello?" Laral flicked her hand in front of my face. "Are you daydreaming again?"

I blinked, shaking my head. "Oh, sorry. I dozed off for a second. What did you say?"

"Well," she continued her story, strangely delighted. Her blonde bun bounced up and down as she explained with her hands, but the words became a jumbled mess.

"Oh cool, yeah," I mumbled throughout, deciding to

dismiss the shaking from earlier.

"Don't dismiss it," a soft, fleeting voice breathed in my head.

Rubbing my head, I pressed my lips together. *Am I hearing and seeing things?*

My friends giggled. I smiled, folding my arms, my eyes darting to the clock on the brick wall. *Can't be late for Sign Language again. Not after what happened last time with that wom- 'Mom.'*

Kyle and I took it to communicate in secret, without our 'mother' hearing us or waking her up. She knew we had it, but she didn't care unless we got a bad grade, missed a class, or were late. Then we would pay.

Kate sighed, reclaiming my attention. "You don't care about what we're talking about, do you?"

"Huh?" I met her fierce gaze. "Sorry, I got distracted." A low rumble overtook the ground. The hairs on my neck stood as the air thickened with a metallic tang. A loud crash overtook the school, and this time, everyone noticed. Screams exploded throughout the hallways. People ran, papers and dust flying everywhere.

So it wasn't my imagination. Why did I notice it before anyone else? That sinking, ominous sensation... A mix of relief and dread churned in my stomach.

"What the hell was that?" Laral cried, tilting her head up and backing away.

The screams of my classmates grated through my ears. My heart pounded. *What if something happens to my friends? My brother? Is Kyle safe at home?* I gulped, my skin becoming warm and my breath quickening—what if I'd

9

missed something? *I should have mentioned the first quake.* A shiver snaked up my spine, and I backed up.

Shaking... people frantic.. beeping... blue lights... I pressed both my hands to my face. *I can't go back there.*

Another loud snap followed the first. I staggered as a person collided with me before they scrambled away and disappeared beyond the doors.

Cracks spidered across the walls and ceiling, right above where Laral and Kate were. My instincts screamed at me. I barely had a second to think.

"Laral! Kate!" I shouted, lunging forward. I pushed them as hard as I could as the ceiling began to give way. It felt like time slowed as the ceiling buckled and came crashing down, blocking my view of them as they stumbled back.

Clouds of dust mushroomed with a sharp scent of metal and chalk, stinging my eyes and burning my lungs. I coughed, pressing my hand to my mouth, and squinted through the thick cloud.

"Laral? Kate? You okay?" My heart raced as I saw nothing beyond it and lifted my head towards the open gap. A gigantic creature, about ten meters high, filled the frame. Its pale, grayish rubber skin gleamed in the sunlight, with four gray, furry paws.

One of the cat paws dropped inside, scooping rubble. The hybrid creature brought it close to its seal-like face, peering at it with a cloudy black eye.

With a loud bellow of rage, the hybrid chucked it back and leaped into the remains of my school, shattering another wall. Its tail, barely visible as it waved, appeared fluffy like a cat's. I backed against a locker and crouched, watching it sweep its head from side to side.

By now, I seemed to be the only one standing in the practically vacant school. Laral and Kate were hopefully gone, too.

What is that thing? It's searching for something... What's it looking for?

A low, clear voice cut above the seal-cat creature's roaring, "Seriously? A high school? You got anything better to do than terrorize kids?"

I tore my eyes from the creature to the man standing beside it, his dark brown hair tousled and a sword gripped firmly in his hand. He stood tall, yet barely as big as the hybrid's paws.

What is he doing? He's going to get himself killed!

I shifted my stance, squinting to examine him more closely. His shifting gray-blue eyes were like Kyle's, rimmed with gold, yet his face was framed by sharply defined features. He wore a faded loose flannel button-up and jeans, his skin notably tan.

I rolled to the balls of my feet, widening my stance. *I don't stand a chance against the thing, but if I—*

"Come on Mike, it's a chimera. It's not like it thinks for itself." Another voice cut in from my right.

I scanned the area for the source. Another man emerged from the rubble, making his way to the dark-haired man's side. This one shared the same shade of hair with similar facial features, though he was shorter and had light brown-rimmed gold eyes instead of gray. He wore a dark yellow rain jacket with a dagger grasped tightly at

11

his side.

"It's stupid, yes. But that doesn't make it any less dangerous," Mike responded, angling the sword.

A third figure approached adjacent to the seal-cat creature's tail, advancing silently. His pink-tipped blond hair was disheveled. Dirt smeared his rounder features, accentuating his dark gray-blue eyes, also weirdly rimmed with gold. He had on a black jacket and jeans.

The seal-cat focused on digging inside another room, its claws glinting, unaware of the men's presence.

From the left, a fourth man appeared, rounding the wall. His dirty blond hair and features resembled those of the third man, and he wore athletic wear with a tattoo on his arm and black leather wristbands. "Keep talking, guys. Maybe it'll get bored and leave."

They all look eerily alike. Is it a coincidence or are they related? I squinted. The latter seemed to be more plausible. Perhaps brothers or cousins. The fourth particularly resembled my twin with his blond hair. *Could they be related to us? No, that's crazy and coincidental, yet...*

Kyle mentioned we had siblings, though I can't remember them. 'Mom' said he's making it up, but I know Kyle believes it, so I do too. Even if the chances are slim, and it turns out these men aren't, I have to find out for us. Then maybe, if it turns out they're not, I can retrieve Kyle, and we will be free to search for them together.

I grabbed the edge of the crumbled wall. The seal-cat roared, standing on its back legs, drool stretching from its mouth.

The men stood in a combative stance and

12

positioned themselves around it. The first one, Mike, gestured to the man beside him and ran forward with his sword. Jumping then jumping again on *nothing* in mid-air, his sword flashed and struck the seal cat's face. It screeched, thrashing its head. The second man rounded to its back leg, slicing it with his dagger, while the third and fourth worked around its backside. Their movements were fluid and purposeful, as if they didn't need to communicate.

This is my chance to get out. I took a few steps out of the cover and then froze, my body locking up. *No, no, come on...* I tried to move, to duck, to do anything, but my legs refused to budge. Every second made my heart beat harder.

If I died here, Kyle would be left alone with her.

The seal-cat stomped and snarled, twisting back into the hallway. Its eyes glinted sharply, finding me. An electric orb formed before its nose, sizzling the air.

Where'd those guys go?! My muscles tightened, holding my body hostage like a deer caught in headlights. *Why can't I—*

It spat it at me, the electric orb rapidly increasing in speed and size. I stood nailed in place, my feet stuck as if encased in cement.

This is it. I'm done. I'm sorry I couldn't save you, Kyle.

"MOVE!" a sharp voice commanded in front of me.

I clenched my teeth, curling my hand into a fist. *I can't,* I thought. *Don't you think I've tried?*

Then my feet shifted, an invisible force shoving me out of the way, pressing me to the side and behind the rubble as the ball whizzed past and exploded another wall.

I rubbed my eyes, shifting my hair from my face. *A*

gust of wind knocked me out of the way... At the seal cat's side stood Mike, holding out his hand. I blinked, narrowing my eyes on him, catching my breath. *He saved my life with magic. Why?*

It seemed unlikely, but I was sure of it. Even if magic was rare and dangerous—hunted to the brink of extinction. Even if those who had it had no choice but to hide. *So why would they so plainly reveal it? Even to save a stranger's life?*

Shaking my leg out, I got to my feet and dusted off my jeans. I lifted my head, locking eyes with the seal-cat chimera. Its unsettling gaze searched over me as I stared back, unflinching. A voice forcefully shoved into my head, slowly, like running through water.

"Where is it? Tell me where it is and I will leave you alone."

I had to focus to keep my expression neutral, but my hands trembled. Clenching them, I pressed my arms to my sides. "What do you want?"

"Don't act coy," it snarled. *"Hand it over."*

"I don't know what *it* is."

The seal-cat creature swung its head at me, claws extending from its paws. *"Pathetic human! You have the stupidity and the audacity to lie to me? I'll just have to kill you to get it myself!"* It swung at me, spitting furiously.

My mind blanked. Again.

The dirty blond-haired man from earlier ran, beating the chimera in seconds. With insane speed, he wrapped an arm around my stomach and practically flew us outside. Once we were in the middle of the front parking lot, he let go, keeping an arm out to steady me.

14

"Don't come back inside," he said lightly, briefly meeting my eyes. His brows furrowed. *Why do I feel like I know him? Did he feel it too?* A subtle light flashed across his eyes. He spun and I reached out an arm.

"Wait!"

The man vanished in a blur.

Isn't magic supposed to be dangerous? I mean, that's what the news reported.

Despite having it herself, that woman told us about it every day, would beat it into memory. That if we ever had it, the world would lock us up and kill us.

A roar echoed from the school, snapping me from my thoughts. Parts of the seal-cat monster emerged from the roof only to disappear again.

Whoever they were, these guys were brave or *really* idiotic to confront the creature.

Taking a deep breath, I turned to leave.

Cold bony hands wrapped around my arm, nails digging into my skin. I twisted to see a woman as she both pulled then pushed me onto my back. "Get out of my way, girl!"

"What the heck?" I yelped, catching myself with my hands.

She strutted past me, towering over six feet. The woman was beautiful yet hideous at the same time, with captivating eyes, a small nose, and way too much makeup. She held a three-foot scepter, detailed with black and silver dragon scales along the staff and two clear glass crystal balls held by tight claws hanging at the ends.

"What was that for?" I asked sharply, my hands stinging. "Who are you?"

"Just stay out of my way! I don't have time to deal with you." She turned to dash for the entrance, her long white lab coat spinning around her.

It caught my eye, a dark purple 'NDH' outline with golden thread on her sleeve. It was the same one that man wore in that beeping, sterile room with blue lights. The only person I've seen my 'mother' willingly work with. The one who she was afraid of, despite portraying otherwise.

She seems to have an association with the monster. Or men. I'd guess the monster, and in that case, I guess I have to keep her away from them. Return the favor, if I can.

"Wait!" I shouted as the woman began running.

She slid, clearly agitated, and twisted to face me. "What? I don't have all day!" The woman folded her arms with the staff clenched tightly in one hand, tapping her foot like an impatient child.

"There was a large flash coming from the forest over there, minutes ago!" I pointed. "That seal-cat creature was chasing after someone. They left minutes ago, but if you hurry, you might be able to catch up."

A large crash erupted behind me. I flinched, my smile dipping.

Narrowing her shiny brown eyes, the woman tucked a strand of golden-tinged brown hair behind her ear. "You lied to me. I obviously know where my creation is and where it's fighting. However, why would you—" Her eyes seemed to widen and grow darker as she cut herself off. "Wait. You know them, don't you?"

16

I slid back. "No! No, nothing like that. I was——"

"Oh, I'm right." She straightened her back, her smile becoming psychopathic. Twisting the middle of the staff, two hidden blades extended from its body with a *shing*, angled at the ground. "Why else would you try and protect those with magic from me?"

"I'm not," I tried to continue, but cut off as she pointed the blades at my throat.

"What exactly are you to them anyway? Friend? Coworker? Girlfriend?"

"What? Gross, no! I don't even know who they are! I literally just met them."

She laughed with a snort. "I'm sure you don't. Oddly enough, you look like some of them as well!" Shifting her back to me, she tucked one sword between her arm and side and lifted a strange device to her ear from her pocket.

"Reiner? Reiner my dear, please come in. Yes, I got 122… somehow she's with them. I can't figure it out! Oh, don't worry, of course, dear. I'll keep her until you send someone darling. Bye now." The woman hung up, turning and throwing her hair over her shoulder. "Oh dear, I forgot to give you my name. I apologize, that's so rude of me. You can call me… Jane."

I scrambled to a crouch and then to my feet. *I need to find Kyle.*

Jane smacked her lips, the corners perking. "Oh, no I can't have you leaving yet. We barely got acquainted!"

A small modified harpoon gun poked out from her lab coat, springing a net out. I registered what happened too late as it landed over me, immediately sticking to my skin. It knocked me to my knees and hands, an electrical spike coursing through the net and my body. Sparks of slicing pain followed hot in pursuit.

Jane replaced her gun, smirking. "That'll teach you to lie to me. But what do I expect from those in the clan XXS?"

I squinted, following the net where a few feet away lay a small code box. Far enough that I can't get it even if I ignored the electrocution.

I'm sorry, Kyle. I got myself into this mess and you'll pay the price for it. I wish I could protect you.

The woman, Jane, chuckled as she went inside. As the door shut, it began to rain in cold, large drops.

I breathed hard. The world felt too loud, too sharp, and far away. I pressed my forehead to my arms, wincing. My hand brushed the jagged edge of my jeans where the bottle had hit me.

"You're not strong enough to protect anyone," her voice echoed in my head.

I wanted to scream. Instead, I closed my eyes and imagined Kyle's face. His hands fidgeted with a pencil. The tiny smile he gave when he was proud of me.

Of those days, hiding our meager belongings under the floorboards. Where I would always place myself between him and her. But I would no longer be there. And he'd... he'd...

"I'll come back for you," I whispered, tightening my grip. "I swear."

18

Chapter 3

MIKE

The choice wasn't easy, but it was the only one he could make.

In the middle of the parking lot curled the girl, wearing a ripped shirt and jeans. She reminded Mike of the faces in his dreams—faces he couldn't place. Almost as if a veil was blocking him in. Saving her was a risk; yet he couldn't leave her. If there was a chance she was one of them or not... how could he live with himself if he let another innocent life die? No, protecting humans was always the right call. No matter the cost.

. . .

IZZIE

I closed my eyes as freezing drops of water streaked down my arms and neck. Being so lightweight, I almost forgot about the electric netting covering me. The muscles in my body ached and tingled, my breaths ragged gasps. I couldn't feel my fingers.

Kyle's face constantly appeared behind my eyelids. The way he always waited for me before opening a can of soup he stole.

A sob caught in my throat. The kind I couldn't let

out. *What would it be like if I don't make it?* If Kyle never knew what happened. If my last words to him had been "I'll be back for dinner," instead of "I love you."

I clenched my jaw. *I won't give up. My twin needs me. I still have time.* The metallic taste from earlier lingered on my tongue.

So much for trying to be useful. I shivered, glancing around the oddly deserted street. *Seriously, where is everyone? Where are the authorities?*

"Hey, Luke! I think I found a fish caught in a net!"

I jerked my head up, wincing from electricity burning my skin. A tingling sensation spread all over my skin. Two of the men from earlier approached me, one with the dark yellow jacket and dagger and the other with the tattoo and dirty blond hair.

"Seriously, Ryan? That's not funny," the guy who saved me retorted. *That must be Luke.* He stopped a few feet away, arms folded. "You know the net hurts like hell if you move."

I glanced at the dark clouds as the rain lessened to a sprinkle. My breathing slowed, and the road felt rougher, yet my body shook and my head pounded.

"Well, she does look like one." Ryan stepped close to me and crouched, tilting his head. "Need some help, little fishy?"

I smirked and flicked my eyes to the pad, careful not to move where my body touched the net. "If it wouldn't be too inconvenient for you, that would be nice."

"Stop teasing her," the pink-tipped blond-haired man snapped, alerting me to his and the dark brown-haired man's presence. He squatted at the pad, clicking a few buttons. It sent out a low beep, electrocuting me again. The man fell backward, cursing.

The dark-haired boy, Mike I recalled, looked at him with concern. "Hey, you okay?"

"Peachy," he muttered, rubbing and shaking his hands before moving back to his knees. Rain continued down, already soaking his light blue jeans and black jacket, which covered a thin button-up shirt.

"Who designs this trash? If they spent half the time innovating instead of torturing, this wouldn't even exist," Ryan groaned from the side, rolling his eyes.

The blond-haired man with a chain necklace pushed at the buttons again, and it beeped happily. The netting around me disintegrated into a fine powder, the box light going dead.

I brushed off the powder from my half-torn sleeves and got up, doing the same to my pants. "Thank you— again," I stammered, the tingling over my body strengthening. The men were all soaked as the rain kept coming, and the dirty blond, Luke, slightly swayed with bags under his eyes. "If—I may ask—Who *are* you? What-what was that thing? Why'd you end up here? Why'd you save me?"

"Oh, right." Luke gave a half smile directed at Mike, scratching his head. "By chance, you didn't see us—"

Ryan elbowed him in the side, cutting him off. The man with pink-tipped hair glared at him.

"How could I not?" I breathed, weaving my fingers through my dark hair, unknotting it. "You used it on me."

21

In fact, if they weren't in front of me, I'd think someone was playing a sick joke. Or I made it up. My fingers felt numb. I stepped back, replaying the hybrid attacking, the wind knocking me over, and Luke, who ran out of the school at lightning speed to save me from the seal-cat creature.

Mike lowered his head, refusing to meet my gaze. His eyebrows drew together and his lips pressed into a straight line.

Luke raised an eyebrow. "Did you see anyone besides me? Are you going to report us?"

"She better not," Ryan scoffed, running a hand through his hair. "We saved her, *thrice.*"

My throat tightened. I glanced at the smoky ruins of my school. *That's true, but it didn't make sense. Why would they bother saving me?* I wiped a streak of ash off my cheek and clenched my fists, an image of my brother's face popping into my mind.

Agh, if I don't go back home, she will hurt him. I could almost hear his shallow breath. *And he'll worry about me.* The sting of past bruises throbbed faintly under my skin. I *had* to go back to tell him what happened, and find a way for us to get out. Anything, as long as he was safe.

And yet, for the first time in years, a strange calm crept over me, loosening my knotted shoulders and slowing my breaths until they came steady and even. I wasn't running. I wasn't hiding. Whoever they were, they didn't let me get hurt.

The ground tilted slightly as I refocused on them, feeling lighter than I had in years. Almost dizzy. I recognized how their eyes and two of their hair colors

22

matched Kyle's, yet it differed enough that they couldn't be our family.

Could they? And could they help me save him?

"I would not worry about it," the blond-haired man reassured, patting Luke's back. "She knows we saved her."

I straightened, retaining my composure.

Giving a small nod, Mike faced me. "Sorry about that. We have to be wary."

"I get it," I said and rescanned the remains of my school. "And you don't have to worry. I won't rat you out. I owe you after all." I ripped the rest of my right and left sleeves off, dropping them onto the street. The men slightly smiled at me, except for Ryan, who rolled his eyes.

"Well, it was nice to meet you. My name's Mike Hyphenx. These are my brothers Ryan, Zack, and Luke." Mike gestured to the rude one, the one with pink tips, and the dirty blond one. He glanced at the forest and gently rubbed a small cut on his cheek. "Sorry to cut this short, but we need to get going. Reinforcements will be here soon."

"Wait, can you answer my questions first? Are you in danger? What happened to you guys and that monster inside? I didn't hear or see much," I asked, stumbling over my words. "Did you fight that woman—Jane? She said something about a group called XXS. What is XXS? Are you guys even safe right now?"

"They are gone. We are safe for now," Zack answered absently. He crouched, sifting through loose rocks in the road with his hands, picking one up only to toss it back.

"For now?" I repeated, my voice involuntarily

wavering. Lightning flashed in the distance, forcing birds to squawk and fly out of a nearby tree.

I shifted my weight, glancing at the men. A strange warmth curled in my chest—unfamiliar yet oddly known. Why did it feel like I'd been here before?

"We have siblings, I think," Kyle said.

That feeling, these men, my family, XXS, the creature, Jane—the reason everyone thinks magic wielders are so dangerous. I had to figure it out. I have to know.

This must've been the chance I've been waiting for. I should go with them. I got to. They might be the only option I have to rescue Kyle.

"Where do you live? If it gets us going, we can take you home," Luke suggested while bouncing on his toes, repeatedly glancing over at the street.

"What?" I replied, shaking my head. "Home? No, I don't want to go home."

Part lie, part truth. My brother was there, but so was my 'mom'. Home was the place that contested with hell. That woman didn't deserve to be called that. To be called my *mom*. But Kyle... *I-I can't leave him, can I? Not with her...* What if it's the only chance I have?

"I have so many questions. Who are you guys? Why are people after you?" I paused to catch my breath. "Why'd you save me? Can I join you?"

Ryan's jaw dropped. He ran his fingers up his face. "You're a kid. That's a stupid idea. It would be considered kidnapping! No, no, absolutely not!"

Frowning, Mike placed his hand on Ryan's shoulder. "Yeah, I'm with him on this. I get you're curious and got guts, but we can't let some kid come with us. It's too dangerous, especially for someone without powers. What we can do is make sure you get home safely or leave you to wait until help arrives. But coming with us isn't an option."

I narrowed my eyes. "I under—"

"At least she's not trying to kill us," Luke interrupted. "Also, didn't Nemesis capture her in an electric net? That's usually meant for people with powers. And the Morph attacked her too. They wouldn't do that without a reason."

I inwardly flinched when he said Nemesis, half-expecting the woman to appear and slap me. When no one came, I took a sharp breath.

"Actually—" I tried.

Ryan rolled his eyes, which I swear is the only thing he did, shrugging off his dark yellow jacket and letting it fall to the ground. "The Morph attacks anything it sees within its range. She was just stupid enough to still be there. As for the net, Jane probably thought the girl was with us."

"Yeah," I agreed slowly. "That lady thought I was one of your friends after I tried to stop her from going to you."

"You tried to stop her?" Ryan facepalmed. "Do you have a death wish?"

"I was trying to help, to repay you."

"And now they're after you, too," Mike sighed. Sirens blared in the distance, steadily growing louder. All of them straightened. "Look, I'm sorry, we can't take you. Stay here and tell the authorities what happened. They'll get it sorted out and cleared up with Nemesis, make sure you're safe, and get you home. But we have to go."

The brothers darted off into the forest, right of the parking lot, which happened to be directly away from the approaching sirens and lights. Left on the ground lay the dark yellow jacket Ryan wore, with a bulge in the pocket. I crouched, picking it up and taking out a dagger.

Nemesis? No, I can't. Blue and red lights flashed off the street and homes, growing brighter. *Okay...* I bounced on my toes. *Guess I'm doing this.* I clutched the dagger, dropping the jacket, and took off after them, sprinting across the road and into the dense oak forest. *Kyle's going to hate me. This might be a mistake, but this might be our only chance.* I jumped and picked my way over roots and bushes, straining to follow or hear any sign of where they'd gone. *I can't shake the sense... Where do I know them from?*

Hours flew by, and the rain eventually eased and stopped. With no sight of them yet, I sighed and wiped my nose. I leaned against a tree and looked over my shoulder, unable to see anything but the dense forest and overgrowth. I could return, but I'd made it this far already. And the world of hurt I'd be in...

"Do you think they're following us?" a voice said faintly. I froze.

"If she told them about us, definitely," another voice responded.

"Maybe it would've been a better idea to have brought her with us," the first voice said again and sighed.

"You're joking, right?"

"It's not kidnapping if she said she wanted to come!"

"That's not how the law works!"

Finding a large bush, I ducked behind it and peered through the wet foliage. On the other side, obscured by a tree, I barely made out Mike walking away. Behind him trailed Ryan, Zack, and Luke.

"Oh crap." Ryan stopped, patting his sides. A scar on the edge of his lip pulled downward as he frowned. "I left my jacket."

"Ah dude, seriously?" Luke sighed, throwing his hands out.

"We can't go back to get it now," Mike pointed out.

Ryan lifted his hands. "I know that!"

Zack exhaled, pinching the bridge of his nose as he paced. He kicked a rock, sending it skidding into the ferns across from me. A low growl rumbled in response. He stiffened, head snapping up, a curse slipping from his lips.

"You're arguing probably attracted it," Luke said and glared at Ryan, widening his stance.

"My arguing? Do you hear yourself?" Ryan retorted, shifting his weight back and forth.

Mike gasped, rubbing his forehead while the other growl responded again. Its owner bounding out from the bushes, with long scaly brown legs supporting a fairly large body. Stringy fur pulled back as it snarled, blood dripping from its muzzle.

Trampling over the grass, the bear with scales barreled straight to Luke. He sidestepped out of its way in a blur, hands low. A bright light streaked past him toward it. Floundering out a growl, the scale-bear staggered, smoke swelling at its side.

Zack held out his hand, eyes glowing bright white.

27

The scale-bear slowly reclaimed its balance, swinging its head to Zack, whimpering, and then charged again. *What did he do to cause that smoke?*

The wind picked up, whistling and battering my hair. Mike threw out his hand and the wind mimicked, picking up the scale-bear and yeeting it over the trees. My gaze lingered where the bear vanished, leaves still waving.

Zack collapsed to his knees. He clutched his chest, his face pale. Ryan instantly arrived at his side, kneeling and taking his brother's arm. "You already used your power today. You haven't had enough time to recover, especially with the rain." His mouth kept moving, but I couldn't discern more.

White light burst and flooded around them, flowing over and between Ryan and Zack like waves. The brilliance and brightness made me squint. Words couldn't explain the connection. The atmosphere lightened. In a blink, it ended, fading to normal, clouded daylight.

Ryan stumbled back, flinching, and fell to the ground, fists resting on his legs and eyes shut. Blood ran down his nose, and the smell of vanilla wafted through the air. Mike ran to Zack while Luke helped Ryan back to his feet, who brushed the mud off his pants and shirt.

Still on the ground, Zack brought his hands to his chest. They trembled, small enough that the detail was almost easy to overlook.

"Are you guys good?" Mike squatted beside him. "The creatures Nemesis let loose are becoming more common, but you need to be careful."

Zack coughed, giving him a small smile. "Yeah, I'll be fine."

28

Chapter 4

IZZIE

I shifted in the wet hedge, scratching my nose. If they caught me now, I'd never convince them to help me.

In the clearing stood the brothers in a semicircle, with Mike facing the mountains. He propped his hand on his chin. "It's about time for us to head back to XXS."

"Not yet." Zack shook his head beside him. "There is still the flash drive we have to retrieve."

At the edge, Luke tossed a small pebble into the air and caught it absentmindedly. The black leather bracelets on his wrists bounced, his movements casual, yet he kept glancing back toward the forest as if he expected something to emerge at any moment.

"We can't keep running!" Ryan exclaimed, pacing back and forth. A deep crease carved between his brows. "They're going to find us, especially if we keep messing around."

Luke smirked, shrugging one shoulder. "Relax, man. We've dealt with worse."

Ryan stopped pacing and leveled a glare at his brother. He quickly glanced into the forest where some leaves rustled. "This isn't a joke. Every time we run, they get closer."

"Guys." Mike straightened, his gold-rimmed eyes scanning the group, resting on each of them for a moment before landing on Ryan. "We're not getting anywhere by arguing. We'll start by regrouping."

By the edge of the clearing, Zack crouched and brushed his fingers against the damp earth, eyes distant.

Luke clicked his tongue, tossing the pebble higher, his tone light. "What's the point of surviving if we're not even going to live a little?" He caught the pebble again, spinning on his heel to face Ryan. "Besides, we saved a girl, didn't we? That counts for something."

Ryan crossed his arms, shifting his weight back and forth. "Great. Now Nemesis thinks she's one of us and we're all walking targets."

Luke's grin faltered. He quickly chuckled as he tucked the pebble into his pocket. "Relax, man. If they come, we'll handle it—like we always do. And she's not helpless. She'll sort it out."

Zack sighed, rising slowly. "That girl. Something is wrong. I get the sense she's scared of something and it's not the Nemesis. We need to consider this more carefully."

"Maybe she's hiding something," Ryan muttered. He glanced toward the forest again. "She shows up out of nowhere, and Nemesis is at her school? That's convenient."

Luke rolled his eyes. "Not everything's a conspiracy, Ryan. Maybe she's just unlucky."

"Or maybe she's bait," Ryan shot back. His gaze shifted toward Mike. "Think about it."

Mike scratched his head, his lips pressed into a thin line. "She's not our problem anymore. Nemesis is. Zack's right. The flash drive is still out there and we need to get it."

My stomach twisted. I pressed my back against the bark. "I'm not some kid you can ditch," I muttered to myself. The leftover rain dripped off the leaves above, a rhythmic patter that did nothing to soothe the tension knotting in my shoulders.

Ryan yawned, stretching out his arms.

"I think it is time we got to sleep and recharge." Zack nodded, a rasp bleeding into his voice. " This day was a lot to handle."

His brothers agreed, with Luke heading to the bush where the bear came from. Two trees hung at its side, which kept the ground fairly dry. He waved them over.

"Did everyone get enough food and water?" Zack asked as they settled amongst the leaves and grass.

Luke nodded, patting him on the back, and they settled down, soon falling asleep.

They must've been out here for a while to sleep that easily. At least Kyle and I had a roof over our heads, though the living conditions aren't great. I suppose out here isn't too different from the cold tile flooring.

I breathed in sharply and found myself dozing off at my hands, thoughts whirling in my mind over and over. These people were being chased. So many things could go wrong, yet they kept each other safe. They took care of each other.

Could I be wrong in believing they'll help me?

The pain in my leg ached. I yawned. *This is it, then.*

31

I'm really doing this. My thoughts wandered to Kyle, where he always whispered late at night when we were sure our 'mother' was asleep and we couldn't see.

"*I saw a clan or gang in a dream once,*" he'd said, eyes distant. "*Not Mom's friends—different people. They had silver hair and these strange, glowing tattoos. They promised they'd come for us.*"

At the time, I'd dismissed it as another one of his dreams. But now, being this close to magic...

In the distance, I could narrowly make out what looked to be a pair of eyes behind branches, vanishing when I blinked. I stared where it vanished, and nothing moved. *Must be my imagination, though it wouldn't hurt to check.* After a minute of skimming my surroundings, I found nothing but a divet where I could hide temporarily. I lay awkwardly on the branches and leaves.

. . .

MIKE

The roaring wind awoke Mike. He sat up, eyes watering from the sunlight. Dew sparkled on the leaves, causing a nearby spiderweb to shimmer. It took him a moment to take in the sun's warm rays before he stood.

Is anyone else awake? Mike scratched his forehead, scanning his brothers. All of them were still asleep. And safe. His stomach growled, claiming his attention.

We need something to eat. No plants offered any berries or edible greenery around him. Birds chirped in the distance, but no sign of other wildlife. *There has to be something to hunt.*

"Did that girl remind you of anyone?" Luke softly

asked, startling Mike. His brother stood and picked up a pebble near his feet, tossing it and shifting uneasily.

"No, not really." Mike raised an eyebrow. "Why?"

"She, well, kind of reminded me of our younger sister—one of the twins, you know, her and our brother."

Mike's heart dropped, recalling the girl's long hair, tan skin, and oval face. It nagged at the edge of his memory like déjà vu. *That doesn't mean anything. A decade had passed since the twins were captured by our Mom, by Nemesis, and plenty of people looked like someone you used to know. In fact, we crossed a few just recently that led to dead ends.*

Probably a trick of the mind, since we haven't seen them in years. He decided to indulge his brother anyway.

"What makes you think that?"

Luke lowered his head. "The cloudy blue eyes, her brown hair, the independent personality. I know it's a long stretch, especially since we haven't seen the twins for over ten years now. Yet, if they're still alive, they'd be about her age, in high school."

Shaking his head, Mike blinked. The twins *would* be about her age. Has it been that long? They hadn't mentioned their little siblings or their search out loud in years, besides the false leads. Almost as if a veil tried to shield him from the thoughts. He absently rubbed his thumb against his palm, biting his inner lip.

After ten years, hope was a dangerous thing. He couldn't afford to let it cloud his judgment.

"They're still alive. They must be, but they wouldn't be out in the open," Mike replied firmly as Luke threw

33

another pebble. "And it's hard for me to admit it, but it's unlikely that girl was our sister. I can see why you thought so, but it's wishful thinking after not seeing them for a decade. That girl reminds me more of Nylan."

Luke's eyes faded dark, shining silver like water. "Still, I hope she's okay. There were old and new bruises with scars on her neck and arms." He clenched his hand. "You don't think that attack seriously hurt her, do you? It seems to happen with everyone we befriend."

Mike's heart leapt at the mention, memories flashing through his mind of previous Nemesis battles. *Whitney almost died when I got distracted attacking two Umbra Soldiers. Nylan and Alisha risked everything to save us from those hybrid creatures. Atticus got caught during a flood while infiltrating their base with us. So many others... so many unnecessary injuries and deaths.*

This time, we saved someone. But who knows who'd be next? He took a deep breath.

"She'll be okay," Mike reassured, placing a hand on Luke's arm.. "I know you've heard this, but Alisha and Nylan made their choice. If we didn't let them, they wouldn't have saved us. Their sacrifice would've been in vain." Sighing, he ran his fingers through his hair. "Not to mention yours and Zack's best friend Atticus... I'm so sorry. I should have—"

"As you said, it had been their choice or none at all. The past is the past, so don't blame that on yourself either." Luke clenched his teeth, reaching into his pocket and taking out a bag of beef jerky. He tossed it to Mike. "I just wish we could at least see the twins and our friends again."

"Me too. Yet every time I let myself believe we'll find them, it feels like losing them all over again. I don't want to

34

forget, but it's like holding onto ghosts." Mike rubbed his thumb against his palm again. *But not letting myself or my brothers hope? That's another kind of death.*

After a moment, he glanced at Ryan and Zack. "Should we wake them up?" A mischievous thought darted across Mike's mind. "Or… leave them to find out where we went? I think it's time we had some fun."

His brother grinned. There'd been a feud going between them and Zack and Ryan for a while. Six years, to be precise. Given the seriousness of things, the little gestures helped lighten the mood.

"Of course. Perhaps we can even pretend we're scary monsters about to kill them. OoOoOo!"

Laughing, Mike followed his younger brother out into the forest. This promised to be fun, and hopefully, Ryan and Zack wouldn't be *too* mad or frightened upon figuring out they were gone.

. . .

IZZIE

"Luke? Mike!? Where did you go!?" Zack shouted, climbing a boulder.

It had been an hour or so since I woke up to them shouting. I kept my distance, but my eyes were mostly on them.

Ryan scoffed, his voice betraying him as he spoke. "They're doing another prank on us, aren't they?"

Muffled voices echoed throughout the trees. Words I couldn't quite make out. Zack glanced back and forth. "Mike? Luke? Was that you?"

I crept to the noise, a stick cracked further up and to my right. I jerked sharply, barely able to make out something in the shadows. They concealed something or someone inside them. I focused more intently as a dark figure took shape, facing Zack and Ryan. *Luke.*

An eerie hush drifted over the area as Zack and Ryan went around the large foliage ahead. I hurriedly kept up, watching as they ran into Mike. Someone had tied him against a rock, and he strained against the ropes with wide eyes.

Zack knelt, untying his brother's wrists. "Where is Luke? Are you alright? What happened?"

A nearby shrieking vibrated in my ears. Ryan sharply twisted as Zack instantly made his way in front of him, taking a defensive position. *Please say that voice belonged to Luke.* Ryan backed up and proceeded to finish untying Mike.

Like lightning, Luke parted from the cover of the trees, tackling Zack to the ground. Ryan fell in response, snorting. Catching his breath, he rolled over and finished freeing Mike.

I grinned, recalling the times Kyle and I fought when 'Mom' blacked out. He claimed he would let me win, but I knew that wasn't true. I would let him win. A pang hit my chest at the thought.

To my right, leaves rustled. It went unheard by the brothers, as another form made its way through the early morning shadows, swiftly heading straight toward them.

They seriously cannot catch a break. I scrambled out from the trees, yelling, "Watch out!"

36

The shadow bowled over Zack, and his head struck the ground, knocking him out instantly. Around it, the trees twisted unnaturally, casting long, dark shadows that shifted as the creature's image emerged, bleeding into a morph of a giant pig. Its wings, too small and grotesque for its size, fluttered eerily, and its black eyes gleamed with something far more intelligent than a simple beast.

Luke darted at it with a blade in hand, slashing the air wildly in a blur of motion. It side-stepped, faster than him as he whizzed past, gliding straight into a tree.

I exited the cover of the foliage, with Mike and Ryan meeting my gaze. "What the hell are you doing here?" Ryan shouted.

Ignoring him, I squinted at the beast. *For having powers, they aren't the greatest against this creature.* It bellowed. Its eyes glinted with a green hue, its mouth black. The creature hunted, looking to kill. *Why does this animal look this way? What happened to it?*

"Ignore her! Focus on its legs first!" Mike barked, lifting his hand.

Facing him, the creature tossed its head back. He had little time to react as it plowed over him, crunching into the bushes as the wind picked up and died. It turned to me, glaring, wiggling its gnarly head back.

Reminds me of my 'mother.' I gave it a slight smile, noting the low-hanging branches on the tree less than one meter to my right. "Hello, there."

The odd-looking pig hesitated for a second before it charged. I took the extra second and hoisted myself up the tree. It barely missed my leg as I kicked it out of range. *Thank goodness for P.E.* Rough snorting rang out below me as the creature swung to the side, hitting the tree repeatedly.

Backing up, the creature squinted at me and switched its green-hued eyes on Ryan, its wings twitching like broken limbs struggling to move. He knelt at Zack's side, dark brown hair frayed over his frantic gray-brown, golden-rimmed eyes.

Seeing it lock onto him, he twisted and raised his fists, positioning himself between the pig hybrid and Zack. "Bring it, you ugly beast!"

I don't want this creature to get near him. I clenched the small dagger as the Morph thrashed below, gritting my teeth. *I protected Kyle before, shielded him from 'Mom,' this was close to no different.*

I let go of the tree, dagger poised, and landed awkwardly on its head. The odd pig shrieked, sounding like nails dragging down a chalkboard, and reared.

Struggling to keep a grip on its horns, I wrapped my legs around it as its wings extended and the creature spun violently. I slid myself up, stabbing the dagger into its head and then the eye. A sharp smell of cheesy bacon hit my nose, and my stomach growled, making me light-headed. Shrieking louder, it circled and bucked, going to a tree and slamming its back into it, crushing me into its bark, then taking off.

My body dropped to the earth, landing in a hard pile of dirt while dust billowed around me. "Are you stupid?" Ryan yelled. Darkness edged over my eyes as I tried to move, creeping over me as I blacked out.

>>>

38

"Look, I'll look at her when she wakes up. Right now I can only help you." I recognized Ryan's voice, but I couldn't be sure.

"A Morph knocked me out! A Morph!" Zack said disgustedly. "I have never met one like it, but it is hard to think they have gotten more powerful."

"You aren't hurt?" Ryan questioned.

"No, like I said, I smelled that cheesy bacon smell when it stomped over me. Knocked me out instantly."

Sensation came back to my legs and arms. I opened my eyes with a start, my cheek on rough dirt. The air was humid and warm, and the daylight almost fully pierced through the trees. After a few minutes, I dragged myself to the trunk of a nearby tree and stood. The scenery spun, slowing steadily.

"Sorry guys, I shouldn't have rushed it," Luke muttered, his voice distant.

Hazily, I stumbled forward. My mind began to clear as I moved. *Wait, the pig-creature. Did I scare it away?* Aches spread across my back and neck, annoying but not as bad as when that woman inflicted it. *I can ignore it.* I approached the brothers.

On a patch of dirt, Ryan knelt by a bush with Zack. Off to the side, Mike leaned against a tree, his arm discolored and swollen. Luke stood beside him, resting his arm on the trunk as they talked. He had a nasty puffy eye, a likely candidate from face-planting into that devil tree.

"Are you guys okay?" I asked, panting.

"Woah, you're awake." Zack arose, walking towards me. His eyes narrowed. "You have been through a lot, haven't you? Are you okay?"

"What were you thinking?" Luke interrupted from beside the tree, shaking his head, revealing another fresh, deep cut running along the side of his face. "Almost getting yourself killed like that!"

I waved Luke and Zack off, my tongue heavy like lead. "Sorry. Don't worry, I'm fine."

Ryan strode in front of me. "Yeah, okay. Sit down." I complied. "Anything hurt?"

"I'm okay."

"Not what I asked." He knelt in front of me. "That Morph slammed you against a tree."

"A what?"

Ryan raised an eyebrow. "A Morph, one of Nemesis's creations. In this instance, it was a pig with wings and horns, but a Morph can be any animal combined with another. You didn't know that?"

"No, of course I didn't." I refrained from rolling my eyes. "That seems kind of cruel for Nemesis to do that publicly."

"Well, it's in line for them," Mike cut in, standing. "The public is on Nemesis's side, so I believe you wouldn't know. Of course, they weren't always bad. They started with good intentions, but the power got to their heads."

Nemesis... isn't my 'mother' friends with them? I pinched the bridge of my nose, trying to remember. *They're that vigilante group aiming to 'protect people' from those with powers. Rumors had gone around that they were evil and inhumane, running experiments on people and creating hybrid animals. But those were rumors, and if they were true,*

40

it only had to be a small portion of them.

I looked back up. "Before it ran off, I stabbed its eye. I think that's what made it go away."

"You stabbed its eye?" Ryan tensed, his teeth clenching, though I could detect a hint of concern in his voice. "And you didn't get hurt?"

I scratched my head. "Like I said, I'm okay."

"That's not the question."

"Why do you even care?"

"I don't." His voice was clipped. "But you're a liability. Liabilities get people killed."

My muscles tensed. "I'll prove I'm not."

"Yeah right." He wiped his forehead with the back of his hand, scanning me over.

In the corner of my eye, Luke brushed his dirty blond hair from his face. Defeat hung dry in his dark gray gold-rimmed eyes and his curved posture. Blood streaked down his cheek, shiny and dark. I could make out the tattoo on his arm now, being a heart on fire with a lightning bolt piercing through it.

"Is he okay?" I asked, stiffly pointing to Luke.

Ryan glanced over his shoulder. "I checked on him. He'll be okay for now."

Mike came over with Zack, and Luke eventually followed. "How about we address the elephant in the room," Mike said, his expression guarded. "Why did you follow us?"

My heartbeat spiked. "I uh—found Ryan's dagger and was trying to give it back to you." I pointed behind me at the ground where it laid.

41

"You left it in the jacket?" Mike asked coldly, folding his arms.

"It's magic— I can summon it, so I didn't think it'd be a big deal." Ryan defended himself as he went to retrieve it. "And it's not my fault she thought trailing us into the middle of nowhere was a good idea."

"But you followed us," Zack repeated softly, straightening his jacket. I returned my attention to him. Under his shirt poked out a chain necklace. "You didn't just find us."

"I was waiting for the right time to give it back," I said weakly, staring at my feet. The brothers shared looks, expressions still neutral. *This isn't off to a great start.*

"She almost got us killed back there! Should we leave her?" Ryan suggested, rejoining the group. "Have her find her own way back?"

"That's an idea," Luke agreed hesitantly.

Shaking his head, Mike rubbed his eyes. "No, she'd either keep following us or get lost. It's better if she stuck with us to be safe until we can figure out the best course of action."

"Seriously?" His brother scoffed, tilting his head, eyes focused on Mike. "We've spent years avoiding Nemesis, and now we're taking a stranger into the fold? Can we even trust her?"

"Hey!" I raised my hands. "Look, I'm sorry for following you. I didn't know how to go about it and you never answered any of my questions. But I saved you from that pig—Morph thing!"

"And endangered yourself while doing it," Ryan

snapped. "You don't get it, do you? The media would have a field day with that story— 'Local teen girl almost killed by magic wielders.' You think that helps? We aren't some escape from your problems. We've been hunted for years. There's a reason we don't take in strays."

Zack held out his arms. "Whoa, Whoa. That's enough, Ryan. Let's keep it calm and think this through."

"Look, I understand more than you think." I matched his intensity. *They don't really want me here. I'm a burden to them, another problem they have to worry about. Honestly, what'd I expect?*

Luke shifted from where he sat, relaxing. "Look, we've all needed help at some point, right? Even if we didn't deserve it. Plus, from what I heard, she held her own."

"Guys," Mike said loudly, crossing his arms. "I understand the concern. Again, in this case, rather than having her trailing us and giving away our position, we can keep her close until we have time to bring her back home."

Home... with Kyle and that woman. I shivered. *No, I'm going to save him. They can help me save him.*

Luke chuckled softly, shaking his head. "I like her. I agree, we should let her stick around."

Nodding, Zack placed his chin on his hand while Ryan didn't respond and sharply turned his head. Silence fell over the group.

Eventually, Luke unevenly stepped forward. His eyes flicked between everyone. "So… what now?"

Letting out a heavy sigh, Mike looked at him and then at me. "We continue going for the flash drive Nemesis has, then take her home." He paused, then added more

43

gently, locking eyes with me, "And thank you for helping with the Morph. We will do better to ensure you won't have to endanger yourself again."

He held out his hand to me and I shook it.

Luke scratched his head. The blood on his cheek dried, but the life in his eyes dimmed. "So, kid, you never told us your name, with all the chaos and such."

I smiled. "Izzie. I'm Izzie Kilos."

"Nice to meet you, Izzie," Luke replied with a grin while Ryan sniffed, turning his back to the group.

"Do you mind if I talk with my brothers for a second?" Mike asked, side-eyeing Ryan.

Nodding my head, I walked away. The forest grew incredibly thick and dense, with willow and oak trees spread throughout. Green and brown moss, rocks, and ferns covered the floor, with a few bushes dotting around. I shivered as a breeze made its way through, and almost tripped over a tree root.

I leaned against a tree, out of earshot from the brothers, and released a sigh, tension easing from my muscles. *I didn't think they'd let me stay. I thought I'd help, they'd get mad and leave me behind again. But they didn't. Instead, Mike thanked me.*

Maybe this won't be as hard or hopeless as I thought.

I gazed at my arms, tracing the varying bruises, scrapes, and select scars. They didn't end there; they were all over, except my face and neck. Pain lingered in my leg, a remnant from earlier that morning.

"You're going to school?" The woman, 'Mom', *slammed the glass bottle on the counter, cracks spreading*

around its base. Strands of her long brown hair fell loose, and her gray eyes looked almost red. Wrinkles plastered her forehead, yet she still looked mid-forties.

Unusual behavior, she typically blacked out by the time we got up. That day, it caught me by surprise.

Shrinking back, I nodded. "It's my turn—"

"DON'T TALK BACK TO ME!" my 'mother' shouted, standing and stalking toward me. "You stupid, selfish child. I wish you were more like your brother!" She slapped me across the face.

Behind me, I could hear my brother's footsteps. The woman grabbed her bottle from earlier, along with another. She got back in my face, hers beet-red. "And you're wearing that? Are you trying to get pregnant?"

I raised my hand, seeing my long-sleeved shirt and down at the holey jeans, which reached below my knees.

"No! Stop it!" Kyle shouted as she smashed the cracked bottle against my leg and the second on my side. "Get away from her!"

"Make sure only you go, or else tonight will be hell." Stumbling back, Mom's face turned neutral as she returned to her chair, slouching and growing unconscious.

Stop it. I have to stop thinking about it.

I peeked around the tree to see if they were still talking. Mike held his arm against his side, eyes darting to me as he talked. With his other arm, he waved me over.

Rejoining the group, I waited as Ryan grabbed a short-length stick and cut a small root with his dagger. Using the root to bind Mike's arm, he huffed. "It's probably bruised, but I'm being cautious—you won't need it on for long." Finishing the knot, Ryan made sure it stayed secure. He frowned. "My powers would be much more useful if I could heal non-magic-inflicted wounds. Life would be so much easier."

"There are exceptions to your powers?" I probed.

He shifted to Luke, gently touching the cut down his cheek. "Yeah, I can only use it a certain amount per day, depending on what magic caused the injury. That kind of thing."

I nodded. A faint, blue glow emanated from Ryan's calloused palms, but it flickered like a dying flame.

"What's up?" Luke groaned. More blood crusted on the collar of his shirt and chest than I had noticed. "My insides are beginning to feel like they're on fire."

"You're being dramatic," Ryan said, annoyed, sweat beading on his forehead. Trying again, the light sputtered. He gritted his teeth. "It's not working. The Morph did this, yeah?"

Zack knelt beside Luke, tearing strips of fabric to create a makeshift bandage.

"What's happening?" I tried again, my brows pressing together. "Why can't you use your powers? I bet you've taken entire squads with a flick of your wrist, but you're holding back."

"Magic's tied to our energy," Mike explained, grasping Ryan's shoulder. "The more Ryan heals, the more it drains him. If he pushes too far, he'll collapse or worse."

Ryan smirked, shaking his head. "Don't worry, I'm fine. I just need a second."

Mike's hands stilled, his eyes narrowing. "The

46

Nemesis also tracks magic use with detectors they invented. Every time magic sends out a signal, like a beacon. We've learned to be careful, and we keep moving."

"A signal?" I blinked. "So every time you use magic…"

"They can find us. Careful, but not invincible," Zack muttered, his voice low. "There are limits, of course."

I drew back, eyes wide. *The rumors said that magic users tracked down Nemesis to kill them, not vice versa.* Being with them now, especially after saving me… I was more inclined to believe the brothers.

"What does the Nemesis want with you?"

Mike narrowed his eyes. "They think they're saving the world by taking us out. They've convinced everyone that XXS is a threat to humanity."

Yet you saved me. The sun melted off the ground as dark, stormy clouds clasped over. The humidity seemed to increase drastically. *And you can save my twin too.*

Another thought crossed my mind. "Shouldn't we go soon by chance then?" I widened my stance. *Especially if the Nemesis will be here soon?*

"I, for one, plan on it," announced Zack, running his fingers through his hair. "I do not want to get any wetter if it rains."

Standing, Mike hoisted Ryan up. "We've used enough magic for today. We have to move before Nemesis locks onto our location."

"It's not like we have anywhere to go," Luke said, energy suddenly back as he threw his hands to the sky.

Mike stared at him. "Has your sense of maturity vanished when you so gracefully face-planted into that tree?"

"What do you mean?" He gave an innocent smile, his stormy eyes rimmed with gold shimmering. The clouds broke and rain poured, soaking everyone within seconds. "Frick! Now I'm wet!"

I found myself staring at them and forced myself to look away. *If they do save him, Kyle could get along with these guys after warming up. Perhaps our family could've been like that.*

The brothers got up and we rummaged through the forest. A sense of urgency pursued their steps as they searched.

I pushed strands of my dark brown hair from my face. *The trees offered decent cover, but those bushes and ferns hugging the trunks would be better.* A hedge and bush covered the base of an oak, forming a small arch. *That could work.*

I went over and crouched, shifting some branches and weeds over. Almost no rain seeped through, and no animals hid inside. *Is it an abandoned den?* Enough room remained for the five of us, with some moss lining the ground.

"Here's an okay spot," I called. "It seems like it could work for a bit."

Mike walked over and examined it swiftly. He curtly nodded in approval, climbing in after Ryan. Luke and Zack went in after. And at last, I crawled in, soaked and freezing.

As I settled into the cold, damp space, the hairs on

the back of my neck prickled. A faint, unsettling sound came from outside, rustling beyond the wind. I jumped, my breath catching as I glanced toward the entrance, shrouded in darkness.

I can't believe I'm doing this. I recalled the attack on my school. Jane. *But if I return, I'm powerless to save him. To free us. And if I stay, they may be the only chance I have at saving Kyle. They look after each other.*

I glanced at the brothers as they settled in. *I have to convince them to let me stay. Then, when I figure out if I can trust them, we will rescue my twin. No matter what.* My mind drifted to Kyle on a night like this. Cold settled deep in my bones.

In the night, it had been raining then, too. Kyle sat next to me on the shredded couch, his fingers nervously tapping the edge of the cushion, his brow furrowed in thought.

I nudged him with my elbow. "You're overthinking again."

He shot me a look, half-amused, half-serious. "It's called planning. You should try it sometime."

I swatted his arm, noting the exhaustion pulling at the corners of his eyes. The nightmares had been bad lately—he rarely slept through the night without jolting awake, drenched in sweat.

"I'm serious, though," Kyle continued, rubbing his temples. "We can't keep dealing with this. One of these days, we're going to—"

I placed a hand on his shoulder, squeezing gently. "Hey, we'll figure it out. We always do."

He stared at the floor. When he finally replied, his voice was a whisper. "I don't want to disappear. Like Dad. Like our siblings."

"You won't. I promise."

Kyle looked at me, his eyes searching mine as if trying to believe me. "You don't know that."

"I do," I said firmly, pulling him into a quick hug. "You're stronger than you think, Kyle. I won't let anything happen to you."

Chapter 5

IZZIE

The storm outside should've been the main concern, but something else gnawed at my gut. At the edge of the abandoned den, Mike rested his arm on his leg. Luke and Ryan sat with their backs against the walls, heads tilted back and eyes closed.

"We slept an hour or two ago," I brought up, after replacing the branches over the gap. My voice echoed slightly in the still den, yet I couldn't shake the unease slipping up my spine.

"It was more than that," Zack yawned, rubbing his eyes.

"So why are they sleeping?"

"Like I said, we have to get a lot of rest depending on the day," Mike replied, a slight rasp in his voice. "Using magic can be draining. Plus, you never know what can happen or when's the next time you'll sleep peacefully."

Wiping off the water on my arm, I nodded. Zack stared at it in thought.

Leaning forward, he hesitantly gestured to them. "What happened? Where'd you get the scars?"

My body tensed, and I pressed myself back against the wall. "It's nothing. Just falling... a lot." I brushed the hair from my face, folding my arms.

He nodded, settling back to his spot.

He's... not going to press?

Lightning struck nearby, illuminating each of our faces, followed by a sharp crack of thunder. "What are the counters to your powers?" I asked, almost too quickly.

"Well," Mike said slowly, rubbing his thumb against his palm. "Of course there is. I'm not going to tell you, as a precaution, even though Nemesis has it figured out. But they utilize it to capture, torture, and kill us." He shuddered, his focus shifting to the entrance where the storm raged on. The wind grew intense, rain pelting the leaves.

Where do I know that motion with the thumb from? I bit my lip, trying to place it. *Never mind, probably making it up.* I shifted and played with the dirt, letting it fall between my fingers.

Is the Nemesis that malicious? Well, if the woman is with them, I can't see why not.

My stomach growled. "Don't you guys have anything to eat? It's been..." I cut myself off.

"I think I still got some trail mix from a week or two ago." Zack rummaged through his pocket and pulled out a small, crinkled bag. He held it for us to see. "Not sure if it is good anymore. Other than this, no, we ate what was left two days ago. And we have not gone hunting since the attack at your school."

I eyed it eagerly, a sharp pang twisting in my stomach. It had been so long since I'd had anything solid, let alone safe to eat.

"Unlikely it's gone bad," I said, forcing my hands to stay at my sides and not reach for it. The faint aroma teased me. "Can I see it?"

Zack held it out to me. I snatched it, analyzing it closer. No mold, strange smells, or chemicals in the bag. Just sealed and dry, with its usual ingredients of nuts and raisins. Nothing's wrong.

'Mom' taught us to figure that out the hard way.

I tore it open, pausing to inhale the scent of nuts and raisins. Zack tilted his head, eyeing me as I took a handful and ate it, the taste a rush of relief, even if it left a stale aftertaste. Both he and Mike held out their hands reluctantly, and I set the bag between us.

It wasn't much, but it took the edge off. Hopefully, by tomorrow, there will be more food.

"So." I swallowed. "These powers... Are they random? Is there someone with the power to grow food? Like plant powers?"

Chuckling, Zack scooped another handful. "Probably. But I bet it only lets its holder control or grow the plants and food, not summon them out of thin air."

"Ah man, you should try to find someone with it. It'd be a whole lot easier out in the wild."

Mike shook his head, smiling.

We continued talking for a while. Soon enough, I lay down. *I'm just going to wait out the rain, it's not that I'm tired. It's only resting.* The ache in my leg dulled, blending with the other pains across my body as I drifted off.

In a cloud, I floated, a blurry figure in front of me with sharp blue eyes, the iris rimmed with gold.

Then the nightmares came in waves. First barren wastelands, then extreme ways of death, such as drowning or falling. Sometimes a serial killer hunted me, his footsteps mere inches behind mine. But no matter where I went, *she* always found me. Her voice echoed in every word, every step I took. I could never get rid of it.

My 'mother' always watched. Her friends were always watching.

Large, oddly-sized decaying apartment buildings surrounded me. The windows were blackened— faces shadowy and indistinct appearing and vanishing in the cracks of the walls—eyes, many eyes, glowing in the dark— focused on me.

The woman, that *monster,* stepped out from behind a rusted car. In her hand dragged an ax, blood splattered on it and dripped from the blade. The metal scraping over concrete grated against my ears, the blood leaving a trail in her wake. Dark figures gathered behind her like loyal servants, silent and waiting.

I staggered back, tripping over a long object. My back hit a cold wall. No place offered safety. Nowhere to run.

"See what leaving did?" Her voice sounded distorted and rough, like listening through a broken speaker. She limped closer with her soulless eyes and her wild hair, which were just decipherable in the fuzz. "You sealed your fate. Your twin's fate."

I glanced below, pressed against the wall, my breath catching in my throat. My twin, Kyle, lay sliced at my feet, lifeless. I screamed, raw and desperate. The shadows swarmed in, and it switched to black.

Only a faint voice lingered in my mind, "You're in danger, child. Your mother and Nemesis aren't your only threats. Others know about you. About what you could become."

>>>

I woke to the day in a cold sweat, with flying monkey horses inciting chaos around me. Not loud, but enough to want to throw yourself out a window.

I'm getting irrefutable evidence that these men can't catch a break. Outside of the old den, these hybrid monkey horses trampled everywhere. Vegetation became trampled, and young trees were knocked down. Clearly, they had no idea what they were doing, with the majority of the chaos being the owners trying to contain them.

One in particular on his horse trotted in front of the crowd, commanding people on how to regain control. He strained to be heard, often going himself to bring the monkey horse back to its rider.

After they all calmed down, he rode in the center. "They were last seen here yesterday! Quiet and calm down! Spread out and search, those men couldn't have gone far."

Someone rode to his side, posture straight as a stick. "Sir! Where should we meet if— once we find them?"

"Right here, General." The leader nodded, galloping into the inner circle of his pathetic army. I estimated there to be about ten people in addition to the General and Leader. "Lucas!"

"YES SIR!?" Another man rode out of the cluster and

55

stopped a few feet short of the commander.

"You stay here in case they decide to come back." Lucas inclined his head, hands tightening on the reins.

A sense of residual energy, almost like static electricity, came from the clearing. I carefully shifted back from the opening. *They're looking for the brothers. What should I do? How can I keep them safe?* All of them still slept, undisturbed by the racket.

Moving toward Zack, who lay the closest, I nudged his arm. Prodding him again, I waited, silently pleading for him to be quiet.

He jerked up, and I fell back, startled, something catching in the back of my throat.

"What?" he whispered harshly, alarm in his eyes. I attempted to stop an oncoming cough, my throat flaring. Instead, a choking sound escaped from my mouth.

I pointed outside as a voice cut in, "What was that?"

The monkey horseman, Lucas, rode over to the hedge, a sword swinging at his side. Somehow, the coverage lay thick enough that he couldn't see us. "I know you're here! Show yourself or selves and we— I mean I won't hurt you!"

My breath caught as I stared at Zack. He squinted, tilting his head. Closing my eyes, I took a deep breath to steady myself before heading to slide out the back. Tension coiled within my muscles. As I moved, Zack snatched my arm.

"I'll deal with this!" I snapped quietly, shrugging it off. "They're after you, not me. I'm the one who alerted them, and I owe you."

56

Haze overtook my mind as I stumbled out, rounding the bush straight into Lucas's path. His lips curved in a faint smirk, body relaxed on top of the monkey horse. Lifting his chin, Lucas peered down at me with narrowed eyes.

"It's just me," I muttered through gritted teeth.

"Oh, really? You are?" he replied, eerily mimicking Luke's innocent tone from yesterday. "I guess, since you're alone, no one can hear your screams." He jumped off his horse and stalked closer, each step punctuated by the clanging of his armor. He knew. "You're that girl Jane mentioned. Where are your mates?"

"They're not my ma-friends! I don't even know them." I balled my hands into fists. "They left without me because I'm a kid and would put them at risk."

A kid that no one wants.

"Lies, all of it," he spat, only a few feet away. His posture shifted, his form portraying an entirely different person. A breeze ruffled his brown mullet as he sneered.

"Sorry, what?"

"Enough chatter, kid!"

The man lunged at me. I braced, flinching as a powerful gust of wind slammed into him, knocking him aside. The wind whipped at my clothes as I straightened, still rigid, eyes flicking toward the hedge.

Smiling, Lucas brushed off the dirt on his pants. "So I was right! You aren't alone." He scanned around, focusing on the tree branches. "Come on out! I know you boys are here!" He bit his lip, eyes growing wider. "Oh, wait for a second, I know how to get you guys out." He smirked, stood, and unsheathed his sword.

With a twist, he swung at me. I twisted sideways, the blade whistling past so close I felt the rush of air. The sword struck a rock, shooting sparks like a tiny firework. The screech of metal on stone pierced the air as Lucas dragged the blade back and jabbed again. This time, pain flared as the edge sliced shallowly across the palm of my hand, coming extremely close to slicing open my stomach.

Luke leapt out of the hedge. I shook my head at him, wiping my bleeding hand over my jeans. *No, why'd you—?*

Excitement danced in Lucas's sharp blue eyes. "Found you!"

One by one, the brothers emerged behind him, their faces painted like stone. I froze. *What are they doing? Are they crazy?* I got us into this mess. They shouldn't have to risk themselves to get us out.

Why do they even care?

Wind whisked through Mike's hair, and he brushed it aside. At his side, sparks flared from Zack's arms and hands. A vein shone on Ryan's forehead as he shifted back and forth. *Do they know him?*

"Lucas," Ryan spat, his voice low. His knuckles whitened as he gripped the dagger that appeared in his hand, the blade trembling slightly. His eyes burned with barely contained rage, his stance taut.

That's a yes.

Backing up, I hit a tree, and the blood running from my hand splattered onto my shirt. Lucas didn't react. He simply smiled, his gaze cold and unwavering.

"Hello Ryan," Lucas replied in a steady voice. "It's nice to meet you again. Shall we have a rematch?"

Chapter 6

MIKE

Why is he here? Mike thought, jaw clenched. He rubbed his thumb against his palm. *How did he find us?* The serial killer took another step toward Izzie. She dropped her hand to her side. *He can't— I won't let him kill another person. Not after everything he has done…*

"*Your twins are under our control now,*" Lucas had said, popping his neck. "*They really are playful. And annoying.*"

"*How do we know you actually have them?*" Mike asked. "*Why should we trust you?*"

"*There's a reason your mother took them to us. Her last name, or rather your last name is Hyphenx, isn't it?*"

"*I don't believe you.*"

Holding out his hand, Mike used the connection he felt with the air around him and forced the wind to bend, like pushing a boulder out of the way. Lucas flew off his feet, spinning upside down.

The *Orprious* charged at Mike, its furry hide glistening under the moonlight, screaming monkey gibberish. Mike grabbed the mane of the monkey horse and leapt, using the momentum of its charge to land squarely on its back. The *Orprious,* disoriented, let out a high-pitched whine, thrashing in an attempt to shake him off. Its long tail thrashed wildly.

"Calm down, it's alright," he murmured, brushing the creature's dark mane, keeping his other hand out to hold Lucas afloat. *The poor creatures. Another of Nemesis's cruel creations.*

Zack grabbed Lucas's wrist, blue electric bolts crackling around his arm, causing Lucas's skin to fade to a ghostly pale.

Ryan and Luke went to Izzie's side as Mike released Lucas from the wind's grip. Striking the ground, Lucas collapsed to his knees, gasping. He trembled uncontrollably, his body wracked with spasms, yet somehow, a twisted laugh escaped his lips. "You really think they'd leave me here after I heard you?"

Mike met Zack's gaze and widened his stance.

"It was a setup, and you idiots walked right into it!"

A stampede of *Orprious* thundered into the clearing, encircling them. Dust kicked up around their hooves. The leader dismounted his monkey horse, clapping slowly, a smug smile curling on his lips. "Bravo, Lucas. You've really outdone yourself this time."

The hell? Mike backed up.

The man pulled out and leveled a sleek, unfamiliar gun at Mike's head. "All of you! On your knees with your hands behind your backs!"

"No way!" Luke shot back, stepping in front of Izzie. "You think a gun will stop us? I'd rather die standing than let you take me. And I know my brothers feel the same."

The man chuckled, patting the barrel of his gun like a favored pet. "Oh, my baby ain't any gun. It's a little something my team whipped up. It neutralizes anyone with powers, like you lot. But if I shoot someone without them—" He shifted his aim, settling coldly over Luke's shoulder on Izzie, who remained silent. "—it's not so pretty. I'll shoot her and drag you away. Your choice."

No. Not again. Not if I can help it.

"Wait—!" Mike blurted out, surprised by his own voice. His chest tightened. "We'll do it. Please don't hurt her."

Dismounting slowly, Mike swung his leg over and dropped to his knees, placing his hands behind his head. *I don't know how he knows she doesn't have powers, but I won't let another person get hurt. Not because of me.* There had to be another way, but what else could he do?

"No!" Izzie rushed past Luke. Terror flickered in her wide eyes, though the rest of her body remained tense. Luke reached to pull her back, but she ripped her arm away. "You can't let them take you because I'm in danger. Don't just sacrifice yourselves and be stupid. Fight back!"

"Listen to me!" Ryan stepped in front of her, scowling, yet his eyes were soft. "You don't get it, do you? Even at the cost of our lives, no one is going to get hurt when they're with us."

Mike's heart swelled. His lips twitched. Ryan was always stubborn and harsh to newcomers, but like Mike

61

and his brothers, he always protected anyone, even a stranger.

Ryan faced the leader and knelt, placing his hands behind his head. Zack tilted his head, eyes wide in disbelief. He glanced at Mike, and he nodded. Slowly, Zack followed suit, with Luke reluctantly doing the same.

"I'm shocked you believed me," the leader sneered, replacing the gun in a holster. With a swift flick of his hand, he commanded, "Cuff them. Reiner will be pleased."

More soldiers dismounted. They swarmed in, closing the circle and securing their prisoners with a mix of metal and black wooden cuffs. Mike, Ryan, Zack, and Luke were roughly hauled to spare mounts and seated.

Mike glanced back at Izzie, wisps of her hair flowing in the wind. She held her bleeding hand against her chest, her eyebrows pressed together.

Go home. Don't let this be a waste.

. . .

IZZIE

I locked eyes with Mike as he and his brothers mounted the monkey horse. The soldiers ignored me and mounted up, departing rather quickly.

The leader dismissed me without a second thought. Despite Lucas's warnings, he saw me as insignificant. Extra baggage. A mere kid with nothing to offer, and that he had no order for.

Once again, they put their lives before mine. I blinked. *And I stood there, letting it happen. How useless can a person be?* I punched the tree beside me, wincing as pain

62

shot through my knuckles, already raw and streaked with blood from the earlier cut. *They're going to die— Kyle's going to die, because of me.*

Tears built as I pressed my hand against my face.

It's not your fault, I told myself. The words felt hollow. Deep down, I know I should have done more. For them. For Kyle. *All I did was make it worse.*

Should I return? My throat clenched, recalling Mom's swift hand, the sharp glass... her cold, calculating gaze. If I went back, she'd kill me. Worse— she'd hurt Kyle worse than she already had. We'd never escape. We'd never see daylight again. Not unless we ran.

I took a shuddering breath. *Then what do I do? Where do I go?* I glanced at the sky where the brothers had been taken, its weight sinking upon me. They'd risked their lives to protect me, and now they were the ones who needed saving. I couldn't abandon them— not like I'd left Kyle.

Helping my twin or not, I had to make this right.

Retracing where they left, I followed the tracks of the *Orprious,* including trampled greenery, until they faded at the forest's edge, bleeding into the vast moorlands. I tilted my head toward the empty sky. *That's where they must have gone.*

I picked my way forward, watching the sun sink lower, painting the sky with streaks of orange and pink. The darkness spread like ink blotting out the day. Maybe this turned out for the best. I couldn't afford to stop and rest until the last rays vanished completely.

Where could they have gone? A knot tightened in my

stomach. A small chance of escape existed, yet the possibility that they wouldn't search for me after…

I paused. I should give up. This whole thing was a gamble. I was so stupid to think that—

A whisper brushed against my ear, as if carried by the wind, like a recording laced with the breath of the night. *"Not much farther, make haste, for an Irie holds their place. Don't be afraid, because you only, have the chance to see their escape."*

My muscles tightened. My gut screamed at me to obey. But my mind resisted, buzzing with questions. I shivered and entered the grassy moorlands.

An hour drifted by, and the sun finally slipped beneath the horizon. Taking its place, a full moon rises, blazing watery light onto the grass.

It felt strange being alone. The emptiness around me felt foreign. I guess I'm not used to it anymore. The thought of Kyle's presence, the brothers' presence, felt like a distant memory, a comfort I took for granted.

Trekking through tall weeds, weariness tugged at my eyelids. A heavy urge to sleep pressed down on me, almost overwhelming, like a thick blanket ready to suffocate me.

"No," the voice snapped, jolting me awake. *"It's happening soon, and if you sleep, you won't be able to stop it."*

"Stop what?" I asked aloud, rubbing my eyes, adrenaline beginning to pump through my body. No answer.

With heavy steps, I climbed another hill, reaching the summit. A massive building slowly rose into view, its silhouette etched against the night sky. Its edges were brimmed with cameras, barbed wires, and wired guns. This place stretched nearly to the size of my destroyed school. The Nemesis had to be holding them here, but I had no idea where to start.

I stepped forward, flinching as a flash momentarily blinded me. I reopened my eyes, *floating* barely off the tile in a completely new place. *What? Where am I? How did I get here?*

"Calm down and look," the voice insisted.

My eyes flitted, searching the room until I saw them. Mike, Ryan, Zack, and Luke stood unconscious, restrained in human-sized cylindrical containers, like those tanning machines at salons. Their expressions got obscured from the glass, but the cold, clinical environment was unmistakable. Wires spidered from behind it, connecting to computer monitors mounted on the walls.

Two vents lay in opposite corners of the room, and the metal door had a small window. Outside hung a small blue picture frame of an ocean.

Voices seared into my thoughts, resembling static through a radio. "The Iries are working on them. We're containing their power and harnessing it. It won't be long until Reiner sees their true value and potential."

Iries? Is that what those containers are?

A brief pause followed. They had to have seen me, wherever they were, right?

"Anything else?" Another voice inquired, bored.

I drifted around, jumping when two scientists in lab

coats walked through me, focused entirely on my friends. A man, twiddling a pen between his fingers. The other, a woman, with full attention on the Iries in front of her. They didn't acknowledge me. *What's going on?*

"Yes," the woman hesitated, her tone dropping. "We preferably need a blood relative, someone connected to them to complete the process."

"But they don't have one alive!" The guy slammed his hand on a table, sending the glass vials rattling.

I inwardly flinched, recalling the smashed bottle against my leg.

"Well, there are three that we are aware of," the woman countered, "but we don't know who or where they are. But we can fix it."

I leaned closer. *Three family members? Who are they? Why aren't the brothers with them?*

He grinned, almost giddy. Wrinkles deepened on his face. "How exactly?"

"Well, that girl Jane found, or someone from XXS, if we take—" The woman's voice abruptly cut off as I stumbled backward, ending on my back in the soft grass. Long blades waved over my face, tickling my arms and legs.

"Get up!" The voice pierced inside my head. *"It's not too late yet!"*

Too late for what? What was that? I pressed my hand to my head. *Can you explain what happened? How did I see them?*

Silence.

I took a second to steady myself before standing.

I have-have to keep going. Whatever happened, whatever that woman talked about, had to wait. I'd ask the boys later, because dwelling on it now wouldn't help me save them.

If that was a vision—I at least have some idea of their base. If I can slip past and reach that room... I might barely have a chance.

Ahead, the building or lab still loomed, rising from the hills. I crouched, sticking behind a cluster of overgrown bushes. The cameras panned lazily side to side, and guards patrolled along the barbed-wire fence.

I crept toward the building, timing them. The two pairs of security vanished around opposite corners of the border in unison. An unguarded side entrance sat just inside the border, likely a service door next to a vent. The guards reappeared, crossing the opened front entrance, overlapping, then vanished again.

With a hard swallow, I darted, reaching and hugging the fence as I moved. Entering through the gate, I dashed for the door. My breath caught in my throat as I reached it, fumbling with the handle. Locked.

Of course.

I crouched, trying the vent. Also secured. Heart thundering, I scanned around. Midway up the wall were a few windows, one slightly cracked open next to a set of pipes. It was just wide enough to squeeze through. Getting in, especially unnoticed, would be hard, but I didn't have a choice. I climbed the pipes, gripping tight as the slick metal threatened to slip from my fingers.

Voices echoed around the corner, accompanied by

the flicker of a flashlight. Shouts erupted as I reached the window. I wedged myself through, scraping my arm on the sill, and tumbled inside, landing hard in a narrow, cluttered hallway.

Ducking behind a nearby cart, I caught my breath and braced myself. The shouts outside died down.

When nothing happened, I peeked around the corner. No reaction. Forcing myself up, I hesitated before moving. No one gave me a second glance, being too focused on their work. *That's odd.*

I strode into the first room in the hallway, weaving around the scientists. Inside, screens and computers lined the walls, vacant chairs at their stations. *Wow. This is incredible. The technology here—there's so much of it. How did they manage this?*

I glanced at a nearby computer screen. *Holly has been reported captured after three other scientists were killed. Our plan is proceeding as expected. Soon enough, we will be safe.*

A sneeze in the hall caused me to jump. I ducked behind one of the desks and waited. My heart pounded. No one came in.

Reluctantly, I exited, careful not to draw attention. The walls were lined with a variety of paintings, but it wasn't until I was down the hall that I spotted the ocean painting from dream-like vision.

Sirens blared to life from the overhead speakers. Cold rushed through my body as I stepped against the wall. *What do I do? Can I fight?*

"Overheating in the generator. All advanced

members are required to assist."

I let out a breath of relief, relaxing my posture. Floods of people swarmed past, jostling me to stay against the wall. Soon enough, the hallways emptied. I crept towards the door and peeked through the window. There they were, trapped in the same sort of glass containment. Iries, I believe, from what the scientist said earlier. *What are they capable of? I've never seen anything like it.*

The scientists weren't inside. Only the men.

I turned the doorknob, battling the urge to flee or burst in and free them frantically. The knob abruptly jerked and I yanked it. *Dang it.* Twisting the lock once more, I dropped my hand. It isn't going to do any good to keep trying. I touched the keyhole, looking over my shoulder. *Where are the keys?*

If I were lucky, I should be able to find them without much trouble. *Unless they're on someone.* I searched around the door and spotted a code pad instead. The same voice from earlier returned. *"Three, eight, one, seven, four, one, one."* I punched in the code.

The scanner beeped and a robot's voice replied, *"Authorized."*

The voice knew the passcode?

I stepped inside. Squeezing past a corner of a metal table, my already scabbed hand reopened against the sharp edge, leaving a streak of blood. My body trembled as I reached them, desperately searching for a release mechanism.

I flicked the lever, and Mike's head jerked up. He winced, masking it with a strained expression. "You shouldn't have come," he said tightly before going limp. I reached out and caught him, readjusting my stance and grip to keep him up. His muscles twitched under my grip. "You got to stop putting yourself in danger. Did they see you?"

"No, don't worry," I responded and eased him to the floor. "Are you okay?"

"Yeah." He placed a hand against the floor and wall, rising back to his feet, only to heavily lean against it. "On second thought, I'm not so sure."

I pulled down another lever, and Ryan's head snapped up. He scanned the room frantically, his breath ragged and shallow. "What happened? Did they get you to? Why are—"

He breathed in as his legs buckled. I scrambled, managing to catch him as well.

After a second, he sighed. "Thank you, Izzie."

Setting him down, I pulled down the levers for Luke and Zack. They reacted similarly, panicking and collapsing. Though, at least their reactions were muffled. My head ached. Then I heard voices approaching.

Chapter 7

IZZIE

"Follow me!" I whispered rashly, spotting one of the vents. I took a scalpel from the metal table and used it to unscrew the already loose vent cover. Pulling it off, I signaled them to move quickly.

Ryan went in first, taking the scalpel, Zack right behind him. Luke and Mike followed, their movements stiff but determined. I'm the last to slide in as the door swung open. I replaced the wall vent, securing its weight on a hinge.

"If we can somehow—" The female voice cut off, "Where'd they go!?"

The male scientist picked up a glass vial from the metal table and threw it against a wall. I recoiled, breath catching. "They're gone! I'm not sure how—"

"Wait," the woman interrupted, picking up another vial. "Look, there's blood on this table and vial."

"C'mon!" Mike hissed. I squeezed to the side and twisted. They were already ahead, ready to turn the corner.

"I'm coming," I replied, clenching my teeth. *You're an idiot, Izzie. Why are you even risking your life to save*

71

them? You couldn't even stop yourself from making a mistake.

It's like 'mother' always said.

A memory of ten-year-old me arose as I crawled towards them. It was after Kyle and I had been in the sterile room, with beeping and blue lights. When we got home, inside her room, I found a file next to a dagger. For some reason, the woman hid it under her mattress and forgot about it, and that day, she demanded I make her bed.

When she saw me with it... I...

I shuddered and glanced back at the vent. *Stop it, Izzie. You're here now. You know why you came after them.*

We continued, navigating multiple turns and tight spaces. At last, Ryan spotted the exit.

"It looks clear," he noted, waiting for Mike's signal.

I took a measured breath, and Mike nodded. After a few quiet seconds, Ryan took down the vent and climbed out. Reluctantly, Zack slid to the edge.

"Come on, Zack!" Ryan urged. "We oughta hurry, and you won't die here. I promise you that much."

Zack's arm vanished as he exited. "Finally. How long?"

Luke jumped out after him, with Mike seconds behind. The slice on my hand threatened to reopen further as I squeezed through; the air hitting my face like a cold splash of water. I land on the grass, scanning the area.

"You guys okay?" I checked while Luke stretched.

"I'm good," Luke yawned. "That machine felt awful."

Mike, Zack, and Luke left to scout around the corner

while Ryan's gaze fell on the blood painting my hand. It trailed toward the tips of my fingers. "Were you cut again?"

"My palm?" I held it up, taking in the fresh blood. "Yes, in the doorway where you were kept."

"What on?" His jaw clenched as he forced a neutral expression, but the tightness in his shoulders gave him away. He ran a hand slowly through his hair.

"Uh— the table. The lady I overheard mentioned a vial. Why?"

Shaking his head, Ryan took a deep breath. "They now have your blood to do some testing. It's what they wanted in the first place, and now they have it."

"How bad is it? Very?"

"Yes. And it explains why they hadn't turned on the alarms. That, and they're dealing with the generator overheating. So we have to keep moving."

Mike returned from scouting around the corner with Zack and Luke, scratching the back of his neck. "What happened? Is something wrong?"

Ignoring him, Ryan brushed his dark brown hair away from his face. "Hold out your hand for me, please."

I extended it, feeling the blood trickle to my fingertips before dropping to the grass.

Luke squinted, his dark gray eyes curious and stance wide. Straightening, he gestured to the wall. "It's clear right now, better go while we still can."

"It's not too bad, you bleed a lot though." Ryan looked at me. "We'll deal with it later. Just try not to leave a trail."

I followed them up a small hill, ending at the towering rock wall. This specific spot had no camera focused on it, and it made sense. The wall loomed over us, vast in height, taunting. There's no way we could climb it directly, and Mike couldn't use his wind on us after being in the Irie.

There has to be another way. I scanned the top. A tree branch drooped over its edge to my right, long enough that if you rebounded off the wall, you could grab it and use it as a rope to lift yourself over. That was, assuming it didn't break and the barbed wire was easy enough to crawl through.

I approached it, ignoring the bickering about "where to go now" behind me. I sprinted and leaped, rebounding off the wall to snag the branch. Taking hold of it, my hand slipped and I fell. I bit my tongue, refraining from crying out. *Dang it, stupid bloody hand.* Rising back to my feet, I went again, this time ensuring a solid hold by quickly wrapping the vine around my hand. One hand in front of the other, legs on the wall, I hoisted myself up. At the top, I checked for guards and then let go. I rolled under the barbed wire, landing on a small cement edging at the other side.

"I got it!" I called, regaining my footing.

"How'd— what?" Ryan shouted back. "What'd you do?"

"Rebound off the wall and use the tree limb to climb the rest of the way out. You can roll under the barbed wire."

I waited, eyes fixed on the top of the wall. As the guys made their way over swiftly, I smiled as a memory floated to mind of my brother and me climbing over tiny walls and fences when we were kids.

Before she kidnapped us.

"One day, if we keep training, we'll be superheroes!" Kyle said joyfully.

My brother… My fists clenched so hard my nails dug into my palms, but the pain barely registered. *I'll free him…*

"Izzie! You will never be anything. You are nothing but a fool! Quit trying to protect your brother!" The woman screamed.

For the past week, I've been out here, free… while he's trapped there. With her. My fingers numbed. *I left him. With her and her friends.* *What kind of person does that?* My stomach churned. The air grew harder to breathe. *She must've hurt him. Hurt him because of me. Because I ran.* The world turned fuzzy, and I swallowed the lump rising in my throat.

"Hey, are you okay?" Mike asked, landing beside me. The color had returned to his skin, yet concern shadowed his gray, golden-rimmed eyes. "You seem—"

"I'm fine," I interrupted, my voice tighter than I meant it to be. The words tasted bitter and heavy. My chest felt like it was collapsing as I recalled Kyle's tired smile. *My twin will hate me.* And he should. I *left* him. Chose myself.

I forced my face to remain neutral. "Thinking of my twin brother. That's all."

"You have a brother?" Luke prompted, being the last to land. He twisted the black leather bands on his wrists. "How old is he?"

I nodded, but the lump in my throat grew harder to ignore. I bit the inside of my cheek and breathed out deeply.

We moved deeper into the forest, the silence filled with the crunch of leaves underfoot.

"When we were younger," Luke began, glancing at his brothers. Zack and Mike nodded slowly. "We have two others in our family. Twins, younger than me, but—" He paused, his dark gray eyes rimmed with gold misting over. "Our Mom kidnapped them. The day she was supposed to leave our family for good."

"Oh my gosh," I murmured. *What do you even say to that?* "I'm sorry. That's awful."

Zack let out a long sigh, fiddling with the chain on his neck. "It's our fault. We weren't watching them closely enough. One slip-up and they were gone. And now, they probably don't even remember us. Not after all this time." He shut his golden-rimmed gray eyes tightly, stifling a breath.

"What about your father?"

"He died of cancer," Ryan answered instead, softer than I'd ever heard him speak. Regret laced his words, like a wound he couldn't heal. He jumped over a log, his brown hair bouncing. "If only I knew of my powers back then... I should have saved him."

I shook my head, instinctively reaching out but stopping short of actually touching his arm. "I get why you feel that way. But Ryan, you can't blame yourself. From what I've pieced together, none of you are responsible for the twins or your father's cancer."

I glanced at them, moving a tree branch aside,

76

searching for the right words. "The past... is behind us. You can't undo it, but you can use what you've learned to move forward."

Luke nodded slightly, though his gray eyes remained fixed on the ground, picking through the varying undergrowth. Mike gave me a small, grateful smile, adjusting his dark brown hair. Zack took a deep, long breath, his jaw clenched. And Ryan stayed silent, but the way he exhaled made me think that my words had gotten through.

Ahead grew another hill, the forest bleeding to only blue and green pine trees.

"We should hurry," Mike said firmly, all traces of emotion from the conversation gone.

The others nodded in silent agreement, and with a burst of energy, they took off, racing up the hill with ease and vanishing into the pines. I jogged close behind, my mind a whirlwind, replaying our conversation over and over.

Their father... their lost siblings... my own brother. They'll understand. Maybe they will help me if I tell them.

Please, be okay. I silently pleaded, pushing myself to keep pace. *I'm going to tell them about you, Kyle. I have to trust them just like they're starting to trust me. Stay strong a little longer.*

As we wove through the trees, past skids of charred plants and dirt, I wondered about those machines. Iries. The brothers seemed unaffected now, with no signs of fatigue they'd shown earlier. *Did the machines do anything to them? Or is this pure adrenaline?*

I tried to shake off the questions. *They'll explain, eventually.* I reasoned. They were holding things back like I was.

Adrenaline coursed through my veins, helping me stay on their heels. It's going to be okay.

Then why doesn't it feel like it will be?

Chapter 8

IZZIE

A day later, I placed sticks onto a makeshift campfire. Off to the side, Ryan wiped his dagger with the edge of his shirt. His brows furrowed.

"You good?" Zack softly asked him.

I turned, busying myself with more sticks. Luke and Mike had gone off to hunt real quick, leaving us to set up camp. While we walked, Ryan insisted on bandaging the cut on my hand, wrapping it tightly with a strip of cloth.

"It just bugs me," he began and folded his arms.

"What does?"

"Having to patch everyone up like we're invincible."

"I don't think anyone thinks we're invincible."

"You don't get it—every time I heal, it's a risk. Someday, I might just... not get back up."

I shifted farther away, arms full of sticks. *Every day is a risk, healing or not.*

"I can understand that," Zack replied. "What matters is that we get through it."

Ryan tensed. "I don't need reassurance. I just need you guys to understand we can't keep using magic like it's endless. It's draining."

"I know," Zack said, his voice soft.

I stood, tossing the sticks in a pile beside the fire.

>>>

"It's time we talked more in-depth with you," Mike said, looking at his brothers. Luke smiled, tilting his head while Ryan frowned, his brows furrowing.

Zack nodded after scanning the area. "Yeah, that is a good idea."

I raised an eyebrow. It had been a few days since I rescued them. The days had blurred together— cloudy skies, long walks, breaks to hunt for food and water. Nothing too eventful, only quiet moments of recovery. Mike's makeshift cast came off, too, his arm had healed impressively well.

"We joined our Clan not long after our father passed away," Mike began, his voice steady and calm. "With nowhere else to go, it was the only place that offered us a real shot at finding our brother and sister."

"The Clan's called XXS," Zack added, picking up where Mike left off. "It is a place for people with powers or none at all. They took us in, helped us discover our unique abilities, and sent us on missions to spy and retrieve data on Nemesis. We have been with them for about a decade now, with many... sacrifices." A shadow crossed over Zack's face, and he faced Luke.

"And then, recently, we ran into you," Mike added.

"You were reckless, I'll admit, but brave too. That's not what most people would've done after things had gone sideways."

"Thanks..?" I replied, unsure whether the remark counted as a compliment.

So XXS took them in, and Nemesis was trying to hurt them. I've always thought Nemesis as good, believing their noble goal aimed to protect those without powers from those with. Yet, I was wrong, as was the media.

Zack continued, "As Mike said, one of our main reasons for joining XXS was the hope of finding our younger siblings captured by our Mom and Nemesis. That is what kept us going. It filled the void…"

His words hung in the air. Their bond reminded me of mine and Kyle's. I swallowed. "Your family sounds important to you," I said, a sudden surge of confidence rising within me. *They're beginning to trust me with their past, so I should try to trust them with mine.* "Like mine is to me. My brother—" I hesitated, the words stuck. I met Luke's gaze. "My brother— Kyle, I left him with my 'mother.' I— I need to go back and get him."

Luke's smile faded. "It's too soon after the attack on your school, and you seemed very insistent on not going back. Are you suggesting bringing him?"

I dipped my head.

"Look, you already followed us when we didn't want you to," Mike said firmly, but kindly. "It's obvious you miss your brother and family a lot. I think it would be best if we brought you back home and decided what to do when we got there."

"Not to mention we risked a lot for you," Ryan spat,

81

folding his arms. He turned to me, eyes narrowing. "We barely survived last week. You better not have expected us to take in another kid to protect. This isn't some daycare service!"

"Shut up, Ryan." Zack shot, his voice sharp. It eased back to his regular tone. "Mike said we will figure it out when we get there. We did not agree to bring her brother along yet, and he might not even want to come. Let us make sure she gets home safe first."

"I don't want to be an inconvenience," I interjected, my voice trembling. *It'll be like before if they leave me with her. Or worse.* "You've already done so much for me, and he's super important to me, but if you have other priorities, I understand."

What are you doing? An idea popped into my head. My voice grew louder, desperate to stop them from arguing. "Earlier, you mentioned you usually have a mission to complete. Do you have one now?"

Mike adjusted his dark brown hair away from his eyes. "Actually, before your school was attacked, we were heading to get a flash drive from someone at the Nemesis base, then to check in and regroup. And now." He hesitated. "If we head back for your brother— I don't know. I'm beginning to think you should stay with him, Izzie."

Memories hit like a punch to the gut. *Kyle stubbornly pushed me out of the way, shards of glass everywhere. "No, stop!" I cried. My 'mother's' twisted smile as she attacked him. He held up his arms, taking the hits.* I'll never forget the sound of her laugh, sharp and cruel.

"You want some too?" The monster snarled, lurking

toward me.

"No!" Kyle pleaded, "Take it out on me!"

She'd never let us take it for each other. She'd hurt both of us, worse than before, even past cutting—

"Whoa!" Luke's voice snapped me to the present. I hugged myself, kneeling on the ground. "Are you okay?"

"Please," I whispered. "You don't understand. I *need* to save my brother."

Mike's and Zack's expressions soften. Mike's partially curious, but guarded. Zack's gaze dropped to my arms, where faded bruises and scars were still painted. They didn't say anything.

"Your brother can wait, can't he? We have to go back and report," Ryan muttered, folding his arms. "We've got bigger things to handle right now."

"No, you don't get it—" I began, but he cut me off with an irritated wave.

"You worry too much, kid, jeez."

My nails embedded into my palms. Heat flushed through my chest, but I forced myself to swallow it back down. *He won't understand, yet I can't blame him.* He focused and worried only about his own family, like I focused on mine.

"You never fully know someone's story," Mike interjected, shooting Ryan a warning look. "We shared ours with her. It's only fair she gets to share hers." All of them shifted their focus to me.

"He's going to get killed," I confessed steadily, refusing to let tears break. I tightened my grip on the hem of

83

my shirt. "Because I left, he will get hurt badly. We tried to protect each other, but it didn't matter— she'd hurt both of us. Leaving was a mistake." I swallowed. "If I don't go back, she'll kill him."

"She hurt you?" Zack's face darkened, a vein appearing alongside his cheek.

"Every day. That's nothing compared to what she'll do to him now." I clenched my fists until my knuckles turned white.

They stood there in silence for a second, sharing eye contact. Zack glanced at my arms again, posture stiff.

"We should get your brother then," Mike said eventually, clenching and unclenching his hand.

"What about the Clan report?" Ryan asked, clearly frustrated. "We might as well be dead if we don't check in."

Lifting his head, Luke avoided my gaze, his shoulders sagging. "Ryan's right, we need to go back to XXS first. After that, we can focus on getting your brother out."

I can't expect them to want to help me. After all, I followed them. So if they must go, I'll go back to protect him. Even if that means I'll never be free. I clenched my hands. Relying on others had never gotten me far. *All of this was pointless.*

"Why can't we do both?" Straightening, Mike bit his lip. He rubbed his thumb against his palm. "While we can't ignore our responsibilities to XXS, her brother is in real danger." Light flashed across his eyes, a misty hint in them.

Zack chimed in softly, "Mike is right. We can not leave your brother to suffer."

Luke rubbed his chin and nodded in agreement. For the first time in years, my chest felt lighter. *They're going to help me.*

I don't want to put them at risk, but I can't save him by myself.

Ryan groaned but gave in. "We have a duty to XXS. We can't just drop everything because she's got a personal crisis. But... fine. We'll deal with him on our terms."

I crossed my arms, the twinge of hope growing. "I didn't mean to drag you all into this, but Kyle is all I have left. The sooner we get him out, the better."

Mike faced Luke and Zack. "You two will go back to report to XXS. Hopefully, Luke's speed will make it a shorter trip. Please, be safe." Turning to Ryan, he offered a hand and helped his brother up. "I need you with me," he said softly, along with other words I couldn't hear.

Clenching his jaw, Ryan gave Mike a sharp look but nodded. Despite his posture still tense, I noticed a glint in his eye that made me believe he wasn't as annoyed as he pretended to be.

Saying goodbye to Zack and Luke, I took off in the direction Mike had shown me. Leaves and twigs snagged on my clothes, yet I didn't slow down. Footsteps stayed close behind me, meaning Ryan and Mike were on my tail.

A sharp, metallic taste of blood filled my mouth as I pushed myself harder. I jumped over a log and around a large divot. *Please don't be hurt. Does he hate me?* I couldn't blame him if he did...

We ran until the sky darkened, shadows creeping into the woods. Mike forced me to stop. My legs ached, and

85

my breath shallowed. Borrowing Ryan's dagger, Mike went out to hunt while Ryan and I set up camp in silence, dry leaves crackling underfoot.

After Mike returned and we ate, Ryan went out. My eyelids weighed on me, but I couldn't fall asleep. Adrenaline fought my body. I was so close, so close to Kyle. I almost felt it, but my body was at war with itself. I knew if I drifted off, those nightmares would return. And I spent the night restless, thinking. Remembering.

'Mother' strode ahead of us, her head covered inside a hoodie. At my side walked Kyle, his head down and hands in his pockets. His scuffed, falling-apart shoes hit the sidewalk. Behind us were two of her friends, laughing quietly while the sun rose. Both had swords swinging at their sides.

We were ten years old.

"Ew," a girl yelled, standing next to a boy on the other side of the sidewalk. "Are they homeless?"

I turned to look at her, but Kyle nudged me.

"Ignore her," he hissed.

A few more blocks later, we rounded the corner and down a vacant alley, which ended at a run-down storage space. One of Mom's friends unlocked the door and stepped inside.

"Get in." The woman, 'Mom', commanded, gesturing to Kyle and me.

"What's inside?" I asked hesitantly.

She straightened immediately, narrowing her eyes with a fierceness that could cut a diamond.

Taking my hand, Kyle led me inside the almost

86

pitch-black container. The only light filtered through the cracks at the edges, the air stale. Her friend inside exited with the door, a lock clicking and echoing.

"Wait!" I let go of Kyle and slammed against the door. "We don't have food or water."

"Not my problem," the woman, 'Mom', replied, the same time as her friend answered.

"It'll only be a few days."

"Mom, please!" I called out as their footsteps faded away. I fell against the door to my knees, fighting back tears.

A hand found my shoulder. "Izzie, hey."

I turned. His outline was barely decipherable, and he hugged me despite shaking too.

No one heard our cries and screams. Eventually, we gave up. All I had was Kyle. All he had was me.

We were stuck in there for such a long time...

The next day became the same— jog, stop, jog again. By the time the faint outline of buildings loomed in the distance, dusk settled. Legs like lead, my thoughts lagged. I slowed, squinting at the shapes ahead.

Ryan caught up beside me, panting heavily. He shook his head, nearly tripping.

"Damn it!" he hissed and touched my shoulder. "Izzie, wait up. Mike and I need to be careful around here. People don't like those with magic."

Nodding, I took in a deep breath but pressed forward. "Where is it?" I muttered, scanning the street. We're close. I squinted, forcing the fading shadows cast by the streetlights to take shape. "Three more houses on the left."

"Why are we slowing down?" Mike joined us. His hair clung to his damp forehead, his golden-rimmed gray eyes glinted in the moonlight, reflecting a hint of brown.

"Because I don't want her or her friends hearing us." I stopped at the bottom of our driveway. Tonight was unusually warm. Crickets chirped in the distance.

A figure emerged from the shadows near Mom's car, barely visible under the flickering streetlight. His blond hair reflected the light for a moment.

Kyle. What is he doing outside?

Dried blood ran down the side of his face from a gash on his forehead and a split lip. His arms were covered in dirt and bruises, as well as more blood mixing with the grime. Another faded bruise surrounded his right eye, and he looked thinner. A whole lot thinner.

I froze, my chest tight. *I should've been there.* My breaths shallowed, the world around me fading. *I won't let anything happen to him again.* I clenched my fist, every bruise and cut on his body burning into me. *She will pay for this.*

Before I knew it, I rushed to him as he rushed to me. We collided and I wrapped my arms around him, feeling the tremor in his shoulders. The sharp scent of dirt mixed with blood struck my nose. My hands trembled as I gently touched his rough, bruised face. The tears I fought back burned my eyes. I wanted so badly to take all the pain away from him.

"Izzie," Kyle said, his voice raw. "I thought you were

dead… after the school bombing. I—" His voice broke, and he pulled back, wiping his eyes with the back of his hand. "I hoped you were alive. Or… that I could join you."

My throat tightened. "I'm here now. It's okay."

His gaze shifted over my shoulder, narrowing as they fell onto Mike and Ryan. He stiffened, taking a step back. "Who… who are they?"

I glanced over. Mike's expression was unreadable, though his eyes flickered between us and the house. His hand poised by his side.

On the other hand, Ryan grimaced, mouth pressed into a thin line. His gaze locked onto Kyle, assessing every bruise and cut.

"They're Mike and Ryan," I explained. "Our school wasn't bombed. They saved me."

Kyle blinked, his golden-rimmed brown eyes pinned on them. "Why? Why would they help you? No one has done that for us before."

Before I could explain, the garage door groaned. I stepped between Kyle and it as it slowly rolled up. First came the busted-up shoes with the slightly stained leggings, followed by the nice but over-loose blouse. Lastly, her face.

She stood there, the dim light catching the edge of a hammer gripped in one hand. A sickly sweet smile spread across her lips, not reaching her eyes. Her bleached hair stringy and short, her skin full but pale, and faint smudges under her eyes spoke stories of restless nights. Nights I used to know too well.

"Well, well, if it isn't my daughter," she cooed. "You

decided to come back!"

Chapter 9

IZZIE

I braced myself, shielding Kyle as 'Mom' smiled widely, the kind of smile that never reached her eyes. She extended her arms as she strolled toward us. For a brief moment, her attention fell on Mike and Ryan, and her expression faltered. Something unreadable crossed her face.

"And who are these fine gentlemen?" she asked, her gaze lingering on them longer than it should've. "Who brought you home?"

Her tone was thick, sweet, and deliberate. The thick stench of weed, smoke, and alcohol clung to her and rolled over me, yanking me back to every night she'd screamed and broken things, blaming us for her misery. A familiar instinct to shrink and make myself invisible kicked in, but I shoved it away. *Not this time.*

I shot Mike and Ryan a look, warning them. Ryan shifted back and forth on his feet.

"I'm not coming back," I said, lifting my head. *Leave, run, escape.* My instincts pleaded, every fiber of my being screamed to flee, but I held my ground.

Ignoring my implication, Mike tilted his head, unfazed. "Your acting is good, but it reminds me too much of someone I once knew. Someone who took my siblings away. They never got to know us or their father— never will because of her."

Mom's smile didn't falter, but the light in her eyes shifted. Calculating. "Oh? Has Izzie been spinning her wild stories again? My, she has such a wild imagination," she slurred. I cringed hearing my name on her lips. "Such a wild imagination, my dear. You always did have a flair for storytelling."

Her words echoed, mingling with years of her accusations. Of the times I cried, begging her to stop, she'd twist our words into something imaginary. A story she could dismiss.

You liar. That's what you do!

She sighed theatrically, stepping toward me. I flinched. "I'm nothing like that. My only children are here with me, safe. And their father, bless his soul... passed when they were infants."

Mike shook his head. "I don't believe you."

She shrugged casually. "Believe what you will, but I've done nothing but protect my children. I've kept them alive after all. Ask them."

Ryan straightened, his dagger suddenly appearing in his hand. "Explain the black eye and the cut lip, then," he said calmly, pointing to Kyle.

Bewilderment leaked into her eyes as she turned her attention to me. "What'd you—" I shrank away as she cut herself off. 'Mom' shut her eyes. "Izzie always had a way of twisting things, like her father." Lifting the hammer, she tilted her head unnaturally. "Are you two going to take my kids from me like he tried to? I was under the impression you two boys were better than that humiliation to society!"

Kyle scowled, his eyes blazing, feeling like it could ignite the very air around him. "Shut up! Just shut up!"

Her smile vanished, her voice dropping, "Don't you dare speak to me that way, boy! I'm just getting started, you ungrateful piece of—"

"We're leaving," Mike announced behind me and firmly grabbed my arm. "And don't try to stop us. These kids are with us."

"Hold up!" Mom's voice rang out, a forced calm returning. "It's Ryan and Mike, right? Come inside our house so we can have a nice, civilized talk. I promise I can explain—"

She knew their names. How does she know their names? Did she hear me tell Kyle? My blood ran cold.

"She's trying to work her magic on them. Manipulate them." A familiar yet strange thought entered my mind. *"If we wait any longer, her magic will get to them. She'll twist everything until they trust her,"* Kyle's voice said, but his lips hadn't moved.

Kyle?

He peered quizzically at me. *"Wait, you heard me?"*

I nodded as Mike's and Ryan's stances slackened, their eyes glazing over. Even Ryan's grip on his dagger loosened.

He's right, but we're too late to stop her. It's over. My

93

breath shook. *She's won.* Cold sweat broke down my back. *We'll never escape. I thought maybe I would have a chance with them, but...*

My twin let go of my hand and shoved Ryan, shouting, "She's going to trick you! You've seen what she's done! Run, dude!"

No. I won't let her win.

I grabbed Mike and pushed him. It took a second, but they shook their heads, eyes wide. Automatically, Mike raised his hand and placed himself between the woman and me, the wind swirling leaves at our feet. It strengthened, pushing my 'mother' back while Ryan raised his dagger, advancing.

A shiver slithered down my spine. *She's trying to make them leave us.* Like a wave, a compelling urge to run kicked in. The brothers turned on their heels and sprinted. I ran after them, believing Kyle kept close up beside me.

"Izzie! Keep going!" Kyle's voice cut through the night.

I slid to a halt, my breath hitching as I saw Mom's hand clutch Kyle's arm. Without thinking, I raced back as Kyle screamed, a sound so raw it cut into my soul. He thrashed, yet slowly, he stopped to an eerie stillness.

Sleep, the monster's voice insisted. I visualized the invisible dark tentacles of her magic wrapping around his mind, tightening its grip.

"Let him go!" I cried, almost within reach.

My twin stirred. In a burst of strength, he violently punched her in the face. "*NO!*"

The woman's arms got yanked apart as he broke free. A single tear streaked down his cheek as he took off down the street and passed me. I sprinted after him, my lungs burning as I pushed harder, desperate to keep up.

Labored breathing arose behind me, growing louder each second. I forced my legs to move faster, my breath dropping to a rasp. Then the heavy breaths vanished, and only our footsteps and breaths could be heard. We kept running, past the blackened trees and into the heart of the forest.

When we reached where Mike, Ryan, and I camped the night before, we slowed, gasping for air. Mike borrowed Ryan's dagger, swiftly leaving to check if we were in the clear. Minutes later, he returned, confirming there were no signs we were pursued. We collapsed. *I did it. We did it. We finally escaped her.*

It feels almost too easy... Did she let us go? Is she planning something? Working with someone? How long before she found us again?

Eventually, Mike stiffly left again to hunt with a vein showing on his temple, leaving Ryan to examine Kyle's cuts. "They're not infected, but I'd keep an eye on them," he said. "Let me know if any of them become hot or red."

"Thank you," Kyle replied, rubbing his arm.

"Hold on. When Mike gets back, you need to moderate the amount of food you eat," Ryan added, leaning back. "Presuming you haven't eaten consistently for a while, you're going to need to get your body used to it again."

Kyle nodded. The damp earth overtook the tang of blood in my throat. I touched my right arm, where a sharp, persistent pinch ran through it as if a needle pierced it. I examined it, seeing nothing.

Mike quietly returned with a small, stringy deer. He and Ryan left to prepare it to cook, leaving my twin and me alone. Kyle sat with his knees pulled to his chest, staring at the flickering shadows of the campfire. His lip was still swollen.

I wanted to say something, but the words tangled in my throat. Instead, I sat beside him, scanning for any other injuries and letting the silence stretch between us.

"Do you think we'll be free of her for long?" Kyle eventually whispered, playing with a hole in his jeans.

"I don't know," I admitted, my arm brushing his, "but I swear I'll do everything I can to keep you safe."

"I know. I'm sorry I couldn't stop her. I should've done more." He glanced at me. "But thank you. For coming back. Even if she'll come back."

I narrowed my eyes on him and reached out, grabbing his shoulder. "Okay, first off, of course I came back. Secondly, it's not your fault. We survived, and that's what matters."

He nodded, wiping his eyes. I pulled him into a hug.

"And because we did, we're finally free," Kyle whispered over my shoulder, hugging me back.

I squeezed. "We are. It's okay now, and I'll make sure it stays that way."

After a moment, we pulled back. I watched the firelight dance across his face, softening the bruises that woman left behind. The woods around us were quiet, but the silence didn't feel suffocating anymore. It felt like breathing after holding it too long.

Maybe the scars would never fully fade. Maybe we'd still flinch at slammed doors or certain smells. Maybe I'd still wake up thinking I was there. But right here, with the fire crackling and no doors, I could finally believe it. We were safe from her.

It almost made me want to say something profound, something that would make him feel better. But all I could think was what now? What were we supposed to do? Follow the brothers? Did we have another choice?

I nudged his shoulder. "If this is what being free feels like, it's kind of weird. I thought it'd be more like those television shows."

Kyle gave me a half-smile, rubbing my arm.

When the brothers returned, they roasted the deer, and we ate. Ryan said he'd keep the first watch, yet I slept fitfully that night, as if I hadn't processed the fact I was free.

The next morning, we finished off the remnants of the deer. As we packed up, I filled Kyle in a little about the men I traveled with. Eventually, we set out to the meeting place with Zack and Luke, which was a much longer journey walking.

We arrived when the moon swashed high in the sky. My brother settled on a log between two trees. Mike propped himself against one of the trees, and Ryan flopped flat onto the ground next to a rock. I sank beside them, my hand drawing to my right arm. The ache was still there.

Thanks to them, we're safe. At last.

>>>

Branches snapped, the quiet abruptly broken as leaves cascaded down. I glanced over to see Zack emerging from the underbrush, Luke close behind.

"Oh, hey guys," Luke said casually, sending Kyle a nod. "Is that him?"

I stifled a yawn. "Yeah."

"I am glad you found him." Zack smiled. "Was there any trouble?"

"Sort of, but we figured it out," Mike answered, his eyes closed and arms resting behind his head.

"I'm sure Mike or Ryan would love to explain," I suggested helpfully.

Groaning, Ryan sat up, to my surprise, and recounted the journey. Luke and Zack nodded as he spoke. My twin shifted closer to me as they talked, hugging his knees. When Ryan finished, Luke informed us they hadn't encountered any trouble themselves.

As the conversation waned, light snowflakes began to descend, odd given the season. The sun hid behind a blanket of clouds as a cold breeze settled through. I shook Kyle's arm gently, scanning our surroundings for a decent shelter. The area was barren except for the trees, logs, and a few bushes. No old den or refuge in sight.

I stood. "There's no shelter around here. We'll need to find a place to hide until the storm passes."

Zack stretched, then his shoulder slumped as he scrubbed a hand over his face. "You are right. And of course, it has to snow when I am exhausted."

Studying the sky, Luke brushed off the snowflakes piling on his cheeks. "I think we may have passed a thicker canopy when we came here."

"We did?" Zack raised an eyebrow. "Lead the way."

Luke retraced a narrow path, swerving around rocks and holes. I allowed my arms to hang loosely at my sides, the right one twitching, but I ignored it.

My brother's safe.

Luke halted a few feet from two large trees, whose large roots had tangled, breaking up the ground, creating a space underneath their branches and leaves. A bug zipped past my face, almost hitting my eye, and I blinked, groggily taking in the place he suggested.

Mike's muffled words came from behind me, "This should be alright until the snow stops. Hopefully, it'll be warm too."

Shrugging off the snow, Luke climbed in. I dragged myself after him and shuffled to the side. It was a tight fit, especially for six of us, but it would do for now.

Right after me, Kyle stepped through. It struck me odd that his gaze was unfocused, almost glazed, as if he were somewhere else entirely. He squeezed next to me, and I nudged his arm. "Are you okay?"

He hesitated before answering, "Yeah, I'm okay. You tired?"

I nodded, rubbing my eyes.

"You should get some sleep while we wait out the snow," Kyle whispered, sitting straight. "I'll catch up with them while you do."

I leaned against him. *I don't want to go to sleep. The nightmares...* But the comfort of my twin beside me for the first time in a week was enough to convince me.

"You should get to know them. I don't know them very well yet, but they're good people. I guess."

He chuckled, swatting my arm as I smirked back. Closing my eyes, I drifted off to sleep. And the nightmares came once more.

. . .

MIKE

Mike grinned. Izzie's twin Kyle was fun. Despite only knowing them for a short time, he already felt connected with them. He noticed Izzie had fallen fast asleep against the edge, but didn't comment on it.

Outside, sleet replaced the snow, making the already glum weather even more miserable. With the storm showing no signs of letting up, there was nothing they could do but wait.

I guess it's for the best. I barely know anything about these kids, or what they've been through. Mike thought, rubbing his thumb against his palm. *And with the upcoming battle against Nemesis to finish the war...* Everything had felt so rushed; he hadn't had time to process much of it.

"So, Kyle is it?" Luke asked, tapping his chin thoughtfully. "You said you're not sure if Kyle is actually your name? How does that work? What did your parents call you before?"

"My 'caretaker' always called me trash names. As for Dad..." Kyle picked at the grass. "I don't recall much about him. Namewise, for as long as I can remember, my sister called me Kyle and I've called her Izzie." He glanced at her, gently tucking a

100

strand of her hair behind her ear. "Say, she told me that your younger siblings were taken. How old were they? What were their names?"

All eyes drew to Mike. "I don't remember," he said ashamedly, rubbing his thumb against his palm. *How often do you forget your siblings' names?* The memory felt blocked, like it's behind glass. "Dad would mention them from time to time, but I kept silent to avoid bringing up the pain. It's terrible, but due to the circumstances, I guess I forgot while focusing on taking care of him and my younger brothers. I didn't want to cause more worry than we already had."

Zack bowed his head, the pink tips in his hair more apparent. He sighed. "I do not remember much either. It is strange, like it is barely out of reach. What I do recall are some fond memories and stories about a younger brother and sister before they were taken. Shared memories, I guess, like games."

"They were too young to remember any of it," Ryan added bitterly, carving a stick with his dagger. "To remember us."

Luke remained silent, staring at his hands.

Guilt pressed in Mike's chest like a heavy weight as he watched Izzie roll over, her dark hair falling. His fingers fidgeted with the edge of his shirt, twisting the fabric.

Fuzzy memories of his father's strained mentions and requests of the kidnapped twins flew through his mind, blending with the countless days he'd spent trying to shield his younger brothers. And himself. He almost heard the echoes of his own silence, the times he'd kept his own struggles buried to avoid adding to the pain. Because that's what he did.

Mike's shoulders hunched inward as he swallowed, the realization of his lapse stung. They've been looking for a decade, yet they forgot the twins', his siblings', *names.*

Kyle shook his head. "I guess it was worth a shot. What was he like? What happened after he died?"

Mike leaned back, tracking the canopy of roots, branches, and leaves above them. "He was a wonderful dad. Always cared for others, always did things for us despite his illness. I began to work to help cover expenses. We barely made enough to live, let alone pay for medical bills. Ryan was in medical camps too, at the time. Only about a few months later, he passed away." With a deep breath, he rubbed his hand down his face and continued, "So we joined XXS, and they helped us discover our magic and gave us hope— hope that we might find our siblings again."

"Your dad sounds like a great person… Do you think it's possible that we—?" Kyle cut himself off, but Mike pieced together his half-question. *If we were related? If we were your lost siblings?* "Never mind, what does XXS stand for?"

In the corner, Luke leaned forward, dropping something. Zack rolled his eyes.

Mike scratched his chin. "Good question, it's not an acronym, but otherwise I'm not sure."

He glanced at his brothers one by one, then back at Kyle. "And about your half-question, as much as I wish it were true, it's highly unlikely. You and Izzie could pass off as being related to us, but that's only because we share a few physical traits. And, well, that means nothing. Our siblings were captured by our mother, who looked a lot different than yours, and Nemesis." He looked down. "You heard your mom. She said she only had you two."

The wind howled, making the hedges tremble. Mike leaned forward, watching the sleet switch back to snow. "One more question," Kyle said, shivering. "Since you guys have magic, is there a chance Izzie and I might have it too? I mean, it has to come from somewhere."

Zack raised a hand briefly, then lowered it. "We don't know where it comes from, but I think it's possible. Especially if your mother had it."

"Uh—" Ryan interjected, shifting. "That's quite a bit of snow."

A pile of snow collected on the roots, deepening further from the tree. Mike estimated as the snow settled into a lighter flurry. "A few inches, maybe?"

"Yeah, it is." Luke nudged Ryan, the edges of his mouth twitching up. "Glad we got here after you did, huh? Did you have fun with all the running?"

Rolling his eyes, Ryan leaned away from him. "Oh yeah. Just a normal few days."

Mike raised an eyebrow, turning to Zack. "Did XXS have any other assignments for us?"

"Nope, only the flashdrive," he said, stretching his arms.

The sun peeked out from beyond the clouds as the snow continued drifting, and a nearby tree shed an avalanche of snow, showering the hedge. Clouds of air formed in front of their faces as they shifted away from the entrance.

Mike rubbed his eyes. The shelter was a tight fit for all of them. The snow swirled in as they settled, gradually fading along with their conversation. *If it wasn't for XXS.* Mike leaned back. *I wouldn't want to think where I'd be now. I wonder if they'll let us bring the twins in.* He drifted off, dreams invading his rest.

Chapter 10

IZZIE

Birds chirped, a light melody with the early chill. Bright sunlight filtered through the branches, dancing on my face. I groaned, not ready to wake up. Rolling over, I spotted my brother sound asleep, his arm draped over his eyes. The others were also out cold. Outside, the snow from last night had settled to about an inch.

Well, that's not so bad.

I let out a short breath, a headache surfacing. Stretching, I tried to shake it off, but the frostbitten air made my teeth chatter. I wrapped my arms around myself and rubbed them, squinting around. The glare of the sun hurt my eyes as it reflected off the snow, creating a crystal-like shimmer.

Facing Kyle, I grinned and shook him. His eyes snapped open. "Why—why are your hands so cold?" he hissed gruffly.

Warmth seeped into my hands as I pressed them against his arm. "Not fair!" I teased. "You're warmer than me!"

Sitting up, he wiped his nose with the back of his

hand and then dragged me into a hug. I froze for a moment, then relaxed in his arms, wrapping mine back around him.

"I missed you," he sighed, letting go and scooting back. "I can't get myself to stay mad at you for disappearing. I knew you were either dead or had to leave. I just wish I were able to do the same."

"A giant cat seal creature attacked our school," I explained. "These guys showed up and fought it while I froze there like an idiot. I probably would've died if it wasn't for Mike and Luke."

"That's insane." Kyle ran a hand through his blond hair, his gray-blue eyes sparkling. A gust of wind circled through the den, shaking some old leaves. Kyle flinched, seeing the leaves, then relaxed again.

I told him the rest of the story, finishing at the building where I rescued the brothers from the Iries. "I convinced them to come with me to save you. But I'm so sorry for leaving." My voice caught, and I allowed a single tear to run down my cheek. "You didn't deserve it."

Kyle gave me a small smile and wiped the single tear with his thumb. "It's okay, Izzie. At least you were safe. That's all I could've asked for." The smile drew attention to his partially healed lip. His black eye had started healing, too. "I'm just glad we were able to get out of the hellhole."

Gesturing to the guys, he breathed shakily, "I think it's time to wake them up."

"I don't know, I think we should let them sleep," I said, a mischievous grin spreading across my face. "When I followed them, I saw they had a fun little feud going on. Maybe we should join in?"

"I don't know Iz. How would we get around them without waking someone up?" He met me dead in the eye. "And are you suggesting we prank them?"

"Oh, they're heavy sleepers. Talented fighters, but heavy sleepers. As for the prank." I smiled, both of us getting into a squat. "You're correct. Have any ideas?"

"I suppose—" He led off. "There's a few that won't go overboard, but they're pretty bad…"

. . .

MIKE

Mike watched Zack jump as a stick scraped his knee. Luke stood next to him, flushed from running around. "Found them yet?" he shouted, his voice tight. None of his brothers confirmed.

An additional half-hour dragged by. Still nothing. The silence in the forest grew thick. Suffocating even. *What if the Nemesis got ahold of them?* His breath hitched, growing uneven. Mike closed his eyes and steadied it, rubbing his thumb against his palm. *They wouldn't leave in the middle of nowhere. Something's wrong. What if they got hurt? Worse…*

I can't protect them. The thought twisted in his gut. Nemesis would use Izzie and Kyle against them, against all of XXS. Especially now with the upcoming battle. *One that will decide everything. A battle Ikris should've prevented or fought. But now that the Ikris are gone, it's XXS's problem now. Our problem.*

"Over here!" a distant voice called out.

Mike's eyes flew open. He ran to the sound, weaving

106

through sparse undergrowth until he reached a small cliffside. Izzie stood below it, barely visible against the towering pines. A strong scent of sap and dust hit his nose.

Kyle was nowhere in sight.

She faced the opposite direction they were coming from. Luke blurred next to her. Ryan, catching up, climbed down and asked where her brother was. Izzie gestured in the direction she looked but didn't respond.

What have you gotten yourselves into?

A large thud of crashing rocks echoed. The sky stretched above them, clear and indifferent, but an unnatural heavy shadow blocked the sun's warmth. It casted a cold, creeping dread through the forest. *Great, exactly what we needed.* Mike slid down the rocks to Izzie's side, Zack joining.

"What were you doing by yourself?" Zack asked, going closer to her.

"I wanted to stretch my legs. Kyle went with me, but he vanished."

Something struck Mike heavily in the back. He dropped to his knees, a scream caught in his throat. The attacker moved quickly in front of him. He froze as Kyle appeared, raising his hands. The wind whipped Mike's face as cold slush seeped into his clothes. With a wide smile, Kyle placed a finger over his mouth.

Are they seriously—?

Sunlight illuminated Izzie's twin as he lunged at Ryan, striking him with enough force for Zack and Luke to hear. They turned, their stiff stances immediately relaxing.

107

Izzie bursted out laughing and Kyle joined in. "Did you see your faces?" Kyle managed in between giggles, eyes alight.

Luke twisted his leather bracelets as Ryan stood, brushing the snow off his clothes and muttering incoherently under his breath.

Was it that easy to surprise us? Mike wondered, pushing to his knees. He scratched his head. *They're lucky we didn't immediately use our powers on them.*

"Yeah, you got us," Luke admitted with a grin.

"At least it was not as bad as Mike's and Luke's prank," Zack coughed, receiving a playful shove from Luke.

Ryan folded his arms, shaking his head. "You really do act your age. Be more careful next time, you guys could've been in real danger." He smiled slightly, light dancing in his eyes.

Rising to his feet, Mike smiled, his heart lighter than it had been for years. That missing piece returned, a feeling that he never wanted to let go of. Yeah, icy fingers clung to the trees and through his clothes. The weather wasn't the best, probably because this pine forest wasn't as close to where they once were, but they found a moment of joy. A piece of normalcy he never wanted to lose. For himself or his brothers. His brothers were happy.

Ryan nudged him with the side of his hiking shoe. "Stop thinking so much, Mike," he said with a smirk. "You'll strain something."

Shaking his head, Mike laughed. "You can lighten up more than once in a while, too, you know."

Ryan half-smiled, his eyes catching the light in the snow as Zack, Luke, and the twins played. "Eh, I'll think about it."

. . .

IZZIE

A few more days slipped by since we rescued my brother. Mike seemed to be bothered by our little prank for an hour, but Luke got him to let it go. Ryan double-checked Kyle's injuries, and thankfully, they were healing well.

Our time with 'Mother' will always be evident. And the thought of her endlessly following us kept me close to the brothers.

We spent more time catching up. Zack and Luke informed Kyle and me that they needed to collect more information at Nemesis's base. Nemesis's leader was believed to be hiding there.

"We need you guys to stay safe, and we can't ensure that if you come in with us," Mike explained. *"Not to mention you've had no training or discovered powers."*

Mike had a point. I agreed with him, though my thoughts felt sluggish as if they were grinding the inside of my skull. Perhaps it was from all the recent exercise I've been getting, or that weird pinch in my arm from a few nights ago.

I massaged it absent-mindedly. The small Nemesis base rose, placed snugly between two hills, stretching over a decent chunk of land. It was an older building, built with bricks, and had no fence. No obvious guards surrounded the perimeter, which I guessed kept a low profile.

How does XXS know where a majority of Nemesis's bases are? That information would take ages to get. Has it been that long since they've been fighting?

"We're almost there," Mike said over his shoulder. "It's about time for you two to wait for us."

Luke fell into step with me and winked. "Don't get into trouble without me. I've already reserved the privilege to die first."

I smiled, shaking my head. On the other hand, Ryan groaned, dragging his fingers down his face.

"We will go collect the data Whitney and Olli wanted and come back." Zack placed his hand on Kyle's shoulder as we stopped. "Please, do not get caught."

They turned to leave, but my twin's voice stopped them. "Hang on. We don't have anything to defend ourselves with. How do we know no one will attack us?"

"Here." Ryan retraced his steps, carefully holding his dagger out to Kyle. My eyes widened as Kyle took it slowly. "Be safe and protect your sister."

I stiffened, straightening as they departed, disappearing beyond the hill. My jaw set into a tight line as I squared my shoulders.

If anything, I'd be the one protecting him.

Moments later, their distant figures could be seen carefully moving along the building's side and entering through a low vent.

"Are you sure we can trust them?" Kyle asked, holding up the dagger. "I still don't know why they helped us out."

I closed my eyes. "I think we can. And we needed it."

"They're nice, I guess..." Kyle paused, fiddling with the dagger. "But it's like I have to repay it somehow, or we'll be left behind. Because people are nice before they leave. Or they have to want something."

"They don't. And if they did, what else were we supposed to do?" I asked quickly yet sharply, reopening my eyes. "What would they even want from us?" I adjusted my hair. "I can't think of anything and I don't care, because anything is better than *her*."

Crunch.

To my left, leaves crunched. An outline in my peripheral vision shifted. I twisted sharply, catching my brother absently examining the dagger. A figure through the branches moved closer to him.

I leapt forward, ripping the dagger from Kyle's hand, cutting between him and the shadow as it stepped out into the light.

A woman fell back, almost colliding with another woman inches behind her, but managing to catch herself. Both eyed me and the dagger, bodies rigid.

"What are you doing here? Explain yourselves," the first woman demanded, her black hair cascading over her brown face. She held herself straight, with her shoulders back. Even in her loose-fitted hoodie, black scrubs, and boots, she was strikingly beautiful.

Kyle's relaxed posture straightened, like a string pulled too fast, adopting a defensive stance. He blinked rapidly. "Who are we? You were stalking us! What are you doing here?"

Woman two pushed her friend forward. Her red hair pulled back in a loose ponytail, a few curls brushing the freckles on her cheeks. She wore a plain tank top and shorts, which accentuated her appearance. Her sunset eyes were intense. "Does it matter? We asked you first."

I scanned her briefly. *No noticeable weapons or symbols.* "It's not your concern as to why we are here," I replied coldly, lifting the dagger.

"Then it's none of your business either," The redhead huffed, crossing her arms.

Kyle waved at me, the movement jerky. I turned enough to see both the intruders and my brother. His ears wiggled, a warning to be careful. Like back at the stairs with that woman. Or in that sterile room with the beeping and blue lights. He rubbed his forehead, narrowing his eyes.

"Do.. Do you work for Nemesis?" he asked, sounding distant.

"Uh—" The first woman stammered, backing away. "We weren't leaving, that's for sure. We're going back, actually."

Her friend elbowed her, and she closed her mouth.

Did they escape? I bit my bottom lip, rescanning their bodies. The first one had bruises over her arms, but the second had none. *I thought this place was important to Nemesis. Shouldn't they have guarded it better?*

That is unless it's a decoy building... If that were the case, either way, why did they have prisoners?

"Don't worry, we don't work for them. We're waiting to meet up with someone." I lowered the dagger.

Their eyes flicked between us, but they relaxed slightly. The second woman's eye twitched, lifting her head.

I shifted closer to my twin, but froze. His breathing had become shallow. I faced him as he swayed. "Kyle?"

No answer. Instead, he rubbed at his temple like something was drilling into his skull. His gaze unfocused, then flicked away. His hands trembled.

"Kyle, hey—look at me. Are you okay?"

My brother roughly lifted his hand to his face, and his whole body began trembling.

His knees buckled. I dove, catching his head before it struck the ground. My twin shook violently. His face scrunched, and his skin felt hot to my touch. I stared at him.

What's happening? What do I do?

The second woman with red hair whispered to the first, then approached us. I shielded him as much as I could with my body from her. *Stop shaking, please.*

"Look, he's having a seizure. I know we're total strangers near a Nemesis base, but please let me help."

Slowly, I straightened and shifted away. She dropped to her knees, lightly running her hands over Kyle's chest. "Can you hear me?" she asked, then shook her head. "No, that was stupid. He can't respond. Alright—" She looked at me, her red hair flowing over her shoulder. "Does one of the people you're waiting for know medicine or magic?" I nodded, tightening my grip on his shirt.

The redhead came closer. "If you know where they are, you need to go get them now. If this is his first seizure, there's a chance he might get injured or encounter worse

113

complications if not treated properly." I hesitantly moved aside as she took my place, unintentionally leaving the dagger resting in the grass.

"You have to trust us, at least for a little bit." The brown-haired woman moved to freckle's side. "We'll watch him while you get help. Then you'll never have to see us again."

I clenched and unclenched my fist, teeth pressed together. *I can't trust it. But I can't let Kyle die. They have no visible weapons and didn't attack us on sight.* Kyle shook on the ground, face pale. *I have to risk it. If I'm fast enough, they won't have time to hurt him. If they do...* My stomach dropped. *They will be sorry.*

I bolted. Trees wisped past me; the grass whipping my legs as I approached the building. Anything suspicious I avoided, sliding past the walls and ending at the vent I saw them climb into.

Tearing off the cover, I got in and replaced it. Hushed, indecipherable voices reverberated through the metal shafts. The dusty vent split yards from the entrance, one slightly illuminated while the other was dark and musky.

Zack's voice filled me with relief. "Hurry up, they're going to catch us."

Metal groaned, then cut off. *They know I am here,* my mind reeled. I opened my mouth and a familiar weight pressed down on my chest. My throat tightened, and the air around me felt thick like smoke. I tried to speak, but nothing came out except a squeak. I coughed into my elbow.

Dark halls. The woman. Yelling. Too much to bear. No,

not now, please not now. I covered my eyes with the palms of my hands.

"Who's there? Kyle? Izzie?" Mike's firm voice echoed.

I blinked hard and tried to speak again, but only a sharp sting in my chest responded, like a cold hand wrapping around my lungs. I clenched my fists. *Just say it.* The more I pushed, the tighter the silence wrapped around me. My breath quickened. It wasn't new, but it's never felt this suffocating.

I nodded, knowing it was useless in the dark. I punched the vent, and Luke came into my line of vision, holding a small flashlight.

"Izzie? What are you doing here? Where's Kyle? Did something happen?"

I slid back as Zack peeked around Luke. I mouthed, *I can't talk.* Luke's face scrunched. He opened his mouth to say something, then hesitated.

"Can you not speak?" Zack raised an eyebrow. His light blond hair with pink tips fell inches from his eyes.

I nodded and rubbed my head, an idea arising. I signed: Don't know, but K-y-l-e had (a) s-e-i-z-u-r-e.

"Kyle had a seizure? Where is he now?" Zack asked.

Thank goodness someone knows Sign Language.

I signed: He's where you left us. We need to go, or he might die.

"Lead the way."

Dust billowed around me as I backed out, kicking

off the cover. Luke and Zack came out after, and I saw Ryan sliding out with Mike as I sprinted. Sweat ran across my jawline as we climbed the hill. The familiar tang of metallic blood ran in my mouth. *Please be okay, please be okay.* Those women I met appeared in view. Kyle was unharmed, and the trembling was dying down.

My voice refused to work as we reached them, dropping to a brisk walk. The women backed away as Ryan ran past me and dropped next to Kyle.

"Who are they?" Mike gasped, hands on his knees.

The women looked at me with wide eyes. I faced Zack and signed: They came behind us. I believe they e-s-c-a-p-e-d the base.

The redhead picked up my sentence. "The Nemesis captured us, and we barely got out. We ran into these two when this boy had a seizure."

Ryan mumbled under his breath as he propped my twin's head on his legs. I clenched the edge of my shirt and knelt beside him. Kyle's eyes were closed, and his blond hair stuck to his sweaty face. I shot Ryan a questioning glance, and he avoided my gaze, his expression carefully controlled, yet his lips pressed into a thin line.

My fingers ripped at the grass. I wanted to talk to him, but my voice wouldn't work.

Did that woman do this? The idea spread like wildfire. I skimmed over every strike, kick, burn, and slice that I had to hide under long sleeves and high collars. It was always strategic, placed where no one would see. Unless it was a holiday, those were the worst. Then nothing was safe. And her control, how she managed to make everything feel

116

like my fault—or Kyle's...

"Another one may start soon, depending on what caused the first. If it does, usually we shouldn't try to restrict his movements, but right now we're too close to the Nemesis," Glancing at Mike, Ryan wiped his head. "Could you try and carry him until we're farther from here?"

"Yeah, I got him," Mike replied, picking his way over and carefully lifting Kyle. Throwing his head over his shoulder, he said, "Luke, Zack, watch our flank."

Zack inclined his head while Luke gave a thumbs-up.

I stepped towards Kyle, glancing at the women. *What about them?*

I can't help my twin further, but I still can protect us. Or thank them.

I reluctantly lingered behind as the brothers moved out, a stick cracking under Zack's foot. Mike vanished beyond the tree with my twin in his arms, Ryan next to him. *I have to keep up with them.* I bounced on my toes. *But I can't do anything to help Kyle. He has Ryan... And these women are still a concern. I'll deal with them quickly.*

"Hey." The first woman with long brown hair scratched her head, shifting uneasily. "Can we follow y'all for a bit? For safety measures or whatnot?"

I attempted to talk. Giving up, I signed: Thank you for helping us. You may come briefly, but if you follow, the others may not be okay with it.

"Okay, thank you." The redhead sighed, her freckled nose scrunching. She explained what I signed to the other.

"I'm Rose, by the way. This is Iris."

I didn't sign a response, letting my hands fall limply to my sides. We set off after Kyle and my friends, passing through a denser part of the woods.

Birds sang but got cut off when sirens wailed in the distance. We immediately took off running. It slowly faded, replaced by our footsteps. We didn't stop until Iris staggered, catching her breath with her hands on her knees.

You good? I signed while gasping. She smiled, a little too wide for someone who had been struggling to breathe. She pointed ahead to where Luke's arm disappeared behind a bush. Next to her, Rose's eyes flashed. The scent of pine mingled in with the oak, and the returned chirping of the birds grew increasingly irritating, grating against my nerves like an itch I couldn't scratch.

Sticks cracked as Luke reappeared, relief washing over his face when he spotted me. The tension in my shoulders drained in return.

"There you are! I must've run past you." His eyes landed on the women behind me. "You two came?"

"She said we can come with you for a bit," Iris explained, folding her arms.

Luke squinted at me. "Okay… we outta talk with my brothers about it first if they want to stay longer."

A strong gust of wind swept around us, tugging at my clothes. The trees nearly bowed under its force. *Mike? What's he doing? Can't Nemesis track recent magic use?*

Rose and Iris shared a look, and Rose shrugged.

"Is one of you causing this?" Luke asked, his

118

green-blue eyes rimmed with gold, switching between them.

"I am," Rose admitted. "The weather around me occasionally acts based on the way I'm feeling. It'll pass soon."

"So the wind is—"

"Me being anxious," she said, twisting her foot around. The wind picked up more in response.

"Alright, come to where everyone else is." Luke shook his head. "It's a decent place to rest for a minute. Then we gotta get moving."

Without another word, he headed off. Hesitantly, I followed, breaking through the dense undergrowth. Ryan knelt on the opposite side of Kyle, who lay under a hedge. Mike leaned next to Zack, a few feet away against a small blue pine. The women trailed me, a leaf drifting and brushing Iris's scarred cheek.

Upon seeing us, Mike stood. Luke walked over and spoke to him in a hushed tone. Straightening, Zack tilted his head and rubbed his chin, nodding as they talked. It went on for a few minutes, but at last, Mike addressed us.

"They want to come?" he asked. I slowly nodded. His smile faltered. "I'm not sure... we don't know them, and Luke said they have powers that may be dangerous. And even if they supposedly escaped the Nemesis, we can't trust them. Our group is at risk already at our size."

"It's okay," Iris piped up. "We'll leave if that's what you prefer. I don't want to cause you any trouble. We've got other places to be, other adventures to chase. We appreciate and are grateful for you letting us tag along for a bit. C'mon, Rose."

I pressed my brows together and signed: I thought you wanted to stay longer.

Grinning, Iris's golden eyes seemingly lit up her brown skin. "I guess, but it's good y'all. We should go. It was nice for a little while, thanks again."

Without another word, they left. I rubbed my eyes, watching the mint-colored leaves and branches danced in their wake. A small ladybug landed on the leaves, crawling around it as if to follow them.

Coughing snapped my attention back to the group. My twin sat up, hacking into his elbow. Ryan had one hand on my twin's back. He scooted away as I approached, and the coughing eased. Eyes drifting to mine, Kyle offered a faint, confused smile.

"You okay?" I asked, my eyes widening. Ryan got up and back around me as Kyle nodded.

"Here." Ryan handed him a leaf he plucked from a tree. "Eat this and rest. It's a herb that helps with seizures called Ginkgo biloba. If things go well, you should be better within a few hours."

Chapter 11

IZZIE

One sunrise faded into another as clouds lazily drifted across the sky. Thankfully, Kyle didn't have any more seizures. He was pretty confused for the first hour, but Ryan said that was normal.

The mystery of why my voice left stumped me. Mike and Ryan gave some suggestions, such as shock or fear, which I guess make sense. Or there's more to it.

I kept my focus on the ground as we walked, the rhythm of our footsteps filling the silence. There had been a moment Kyle and I sat while the brothers went off to talk. Where he tucked his knees to his chest and didn't say anything for a while.

Eventually, he admitted, "I thought I was going to die in there.

And I laced my pinky through his, like we used to do as kids in that woman's house. Whether he was talking about her or the seizure, it didn't matter.

"You didn't. If you did, I would be super mad." I assured, making him chuckle.

Now Kyle's safe. That woman can no longer reach us. At least I think so. Does she have something planned? Agh, quit being paranoid, Izzie. What next? Where do we go? The brothers seem fine with us being with them now, but won't we become a burden?

Running my hand over my face, I glanced at Kyle. His hands were in his pockets, eyes distant. *Could we last a day by ourselves out here? We don't know how to fight or hunt. We don't have magic.*

My gaze shifted to the brothers. *Am I relying on them too much?* I clenched my hand. *No, I will prove we can be useful. That we belong with them until we can survive on our own.*

Luke suggested we head back to their Clan and provide XXS with the data they retrieved. My brother and I were surprised we would meet them after all this time.

Trekking along the self-made path, the forest cut off, bleeding away into the moorlands. The moors weren't very big. The mountains poked out from the edge of the horizon, stretching into the sky. Zack estimated it would take a few days to reach it.

Luke offered to take the drive himself and run there. His brothers quickly disagreed with the idea. It would wear him out too fast, and besides, Kyle and I were eager to meet their Clan in person.

"Do you know if they'll let them in?" Ryan whispered loudly to Zack, half-serious.

If we're with them, why wouldn't they?

Kyle gave me a side glance. "Exactly."

"Yeah, they will," Zack said curtly, rolling his eyes.

Two days passed, and at the end of the third day, we sat around a warm fire, with a couple of squirrels and birds roasting on a stick. Ryan and Kyle found a few plants and berries to eat too. The flames flickered in the darkening forest, crackling and sending embers rising into the night.

Ryan handed me a few berries, which I ate. He went to sit by Zack, chuckling to himself quietly.

"What?" I asked, crossed-legged next to Kyle. "Did I do something?"

"Oh, you wouldn't know." He shook his head. "Years ago, Zack couldn't even start a fire. We'd be out here shivering because he insisted he could light it with magic."

Zack's eyes didn't leave the fire, but he smirked.

Luke joined in, "Oh yeah. Our friends would be laughing at us if they saw us now."

"Especially… you know, Atticus. He was always prepared." Zack leaned forward, clasping his hands together. The chain necklace on his neck swung forward.

I exchanged glances with Kyle.

"Yeah, well, Atticus could build a temporary stick shelter in his sleep." Mike ran his fingers through his hair. "He'd probably say we're doing alright, considering everything. If I'd known… that… would've killed him… I would've told him to be more careful."

"You know." Luke tapped his chin, his black wristbands sliding down his arm. "Remember that time Atticus tried to fix up that broken car we found? He was so sure he could get it working again."

123

With a chuckle, Zack touched his chain necklace. "Yeah, and it exploded oil all over him. He was furious but tried to play it cool. 'It's just a setback,' he said. But we could not stop laughing."

"Or when Atticus tried showing Luke how to throw a knife?" Mike added, sitting opposite from Zack. "He was so serious about it, even though Luke nearly took his hand off every time."

Ryan leaned back, placing his hands behind his head. "You mean every time he had to dodge for his life?"

"He never gave up on teaching him." Mike ate some berries. "Kept saying Luke would get it right one day."

Luke grinned, the scar on his lip pulling upward, yet something about his face threw me off. "I don't think I ever thanked him. Or, you know… told him I appreciated it. He probably thought I didn't care."

With a small nod, Zack nudged him. "I think he knew, Luke. Atticus was good at reading people."

It's clear they've lost many who've been important to them. I yawned. My twin rubbed his arms, an angry scar standing out on his wrist. *I'm grateful that Kyle's with me. That he's not dead, especially as we go to their clan's base.*

Ryan took off two of the roasting birds, taking out his dagger. *XXS is in a war with Nemesis. After helping us escape and survive, they deserve our help in return. If we can give any.*

"Yeah, well, we gave him hell." Ryan handed the birds to Mike and Luke. "Remember the time we convinced him that tree sap was good for you?"

Luke snorted. "You mean when he downed half a jar before he realized it was practically glue? He didn't talk to us for a week."

Tree sap? Kyle brushed my hand and squeezed it. I shot him a questioning look, and he nodded.

Mike took a deep breath, looking at each of his brothers, and his mouth wavered. "You know, I think about him and the others every time we get close to another fight," he admitted, his voice rough. "Wonder if they'd have done things differently"

"Atticus sounds important to all of you," I observed. "More than just… a teammate."

"He was family," Zack said simply. "We all are, even if it is hard to remember sometimes." He shifted his attention over to Kyle and me. "Family is a choice, blood or not. We chose to stick together."

Kyle shifted. "Exactly. Izzie and I—we've had to rely on each other. I don't know what I'd do if…" He trailed off and gave me a small smile. "Anyway, we've had each other's backs for a long time. Feels strange to think about letting anyone else in."

After another pause, Ryan took the roasting squirrels off. "The thing about family is… You don't let them in halfway. You're either in or you're out. And when you're in, you take on the risk. No matter what."

The brothers exchanged a look. I shifted closer to Kyle, glancing at the fading bruises and cuts on his arms.

Mike looked across the fire at my twin and me, his gaze softened. "You're here with us now, for better or worse. Whatever happens… you're part of our team."

Luke reached over and clapped Kyle on the back. "Welcome to the family. Don't make us regret it," he said, grinning. Kyle rolled his eyes but gave a short nod.

>>>

An unearthly deep, guttural groan rose from the basement. The woman secured five blurry locks on the door, revealing the modified gun in her pocket. To my left, Kyle hugged himself, yet shifted to be more in front of me as I held my arm. We pressed against the wall, watching her work.

I flinched when the woman turned, tapping a finger on her arm. She tilted her fuzzy head and frowned.

"Love is a weakness," the woman said mechanically, eyeing Kyle. "I gave you trash something better. It keeps you alive, and follows you no matter how far you go."

My brother began to fade. I reached out, my hand passing through him. A cold sweat broke across my skin.

"Where'd he go?" I demanded, voice breaking.

The woman's figure began to blur more. She shook her head. "Does it matter? You'll never keep him safe. You're not strong enough. You'll never stop me from getting him."

I sat up abruptly, dark leaves and sticks hitting my face. My breath came rough. *We're still there. We never left. We aren't free.* I pressed my hands to my face, forcing myself to take measured breaths. My heart pounded, and cold sweat clung to my skin.

It took a second for me to look around. To take in my twin next to me and the brothers. That I was not there anymore. But the image of her wouldn't go away.

>>>

In the morning, we arrived at the base of a mountain, no buildings in sight. Mike led us up a steep incline to an indent in the mountain, where small bracken and dark green moss blanketed the rock in a lush layer. It looked soft to the touch, and the air damp, filled with an earthy smell of vegetation.

"Watch your step. The moss can make it quite slippery," Zack warned us.

A second later, I slid and shot my hands out. Kyle caught my arm, keeping me up. After making sure I was okay, I saw his lips twitch upward. Ryan let out a quick exhale, covering his mouth with his hand. Ahead, Luke moved smoothly along the terrain. He glanced back, his brows raised, and he laughed out loud.

Mike went to a wall of the mountain and brushed aside some moss in the far corner. The illusion vanished, and where his hand hovered, an entrance unfolded. Two glass doors, at the end of a tunnel, lead to a larger clearing. Awed, Kyle stepped in front of me, blocking my view.

Chuckling, Ryan made his way to the side and whispered into a rock. Something clicked, and the rocks shifted out like a door, revealing a massive clearing. In the back rested a building that seemed to stretch the height of the mountain itself.

"Be careful. These guys are exceptionally good with security and defense," Ryan smirked, stepping inside with Zack, who fidgeted with his chain necklace.

"Don't worry, you're with us," Mike interjected, shaking his head. "But if you'd like to note, the mountains in front and around here are cast with illusions. They act real until you know how to take them down."

Kyle and I head in after Ryan and Zack, with Mike and Luke on our heels. Before we made it halfway to the center, a woman with a captivating smile intercepted us. She had long brown hair, brown skin, and a confident stance that drew you in. I felt a strange pull toward her like she could ask me to do anything and I'd comply. Yet another part of me resisted.

My brother ignored the gut warning and walked closer, smiling like an idiot. I trailed after him, suppressing a sigh. Grass swept across my knees as I neared her.

Kyle? What's wrong with you? Don't tell me—

"Her name is Whitney." Ryan laughed, watching Kyle grin at her and adjust his blond hair.

Mike greeted her with a wave, and she hugged him. They broke apart and faced us. The woman folded her arms.

"Hello! Are these newcomers?" She questioned enthusiastically, sweeping her gaze over us.

"Yeah, they are," Zack answered, pulling a flash drive from his pocket. "Here is the drive you have asked us to retrieve, holding all the updates, plans, plus some whereabouts on the Nemesis."

She snatched it out of his hands, stuffing it into her pocket. Her eyes glided over mine and she winked. A bee whizzed by as the silence dragged out. In thought, Whitney held my gaze, her sparkling eyes bursting from the light.

To my right, Luke stepped back, triggering cameras that retreated after recognizing him. Whitney lifted her chin. "These are interesting friends you've made. Let's see if they have powers like you. Come." She waved her hand from us to her and turned, striding to the building.

Just like that? What? Reluctantly, I trailed my twin, who went after her in an almost robotic trance. I kept my hands close to my body and caught up with Kyle, elbowing him hard in the side.

"*Dude, that hurt!*" Kyle winced, holding his ribs. "*But thank you.*" He stared after Whitney, who talked closely with Mike. "*Why do I find her so attractive? Like I want to be close to her all the time.*"

"*I don't know,*" I replied, deciding between a logical and a teasing answer. "*Maybe it's because you liiiike her..?*"

My brother swatted my arm, defiantly pulling back in front of me. I tilted my head back, grinning as we walked. The skyscraper cemented building was now within reach. With detailed architecture and depth, its structure looked spectacular yet modern. Its doors clicked open as we ventured into the lobby.

Inside, it was far less interesting than the exterior, with plain white concrete walls and a nice marble desk in the center. Dozens of people milled about, their voices echoing down the hallways. Some carried supplies, others in heated discussions.

Two doors and hallways branched off from the main room, one each in the far corners. One open doorway led to a set of spiral stairs going up. Two of the hallways extended straight ahead, and the last doorway led to descending stairs. Groups of people climbed the stairs and entered either of the two hallways, not once glancing at us.

Whitney paused at the desk, taking a pencil and

scribbling something down on a piece of paper.

"I'll be there in a minute." She waved us off. "Go take those two to the testing range. I can get to know them later."

I scratched my forehead. Mike gently nodded and walked to the left doorway. Kyle trailed after him with Ryan and Zack.

I watched Whitney, tucking a piece of hair behind my ear. *What if we don't have powers? Would they kick us out? Erase our memories like in those sci-fi shows? What are they capable of?*

Luke nudged my arm. Distracted as I was, my legs started walking. Darkness devoured all traces of light as I descended the stairs. I ended up bumping into Kyle at the bottom, who hissed, "Watch where you're going, Iz!"

"Sorry," I mumbled, stepping back. "Hey, can you guys turn on the lights?"

Kyle's silent for a moment before responding. "What do you mean? The lights are on."

"Are you serious? I can't even see your outline." I bit my lip. "You're messing with me."

"I'm not," he replied flatly.

"No, it isn't lit," Zack added. "The lights must have switched off due to a malfunction or something."

"If you can see," Luke said behind me, "You could have developed night vision."

"How does that work? I could never see in the dark before," Kyle responded with a slight strain in his tone.

"It's where we are," Mike explained. "Only select

people have it, but with the right circumstances, magic tends to reveal itself to those aware of it. Being around magic long enough can trigger abilities, so this area is uncanny for those types of discoveries."

The door squeaked open, followed by the footsteps of someone descending the stairs. The lights switched on as Whitney entered, ending up beside Mike. Her hand rested on his shoulder as she surveyed us, focusing on Kyle. "So this boy has night vision? Fascinating."

Kyle closed his mouth, his head drawing back. "That was too quick. I didn't even know you were testing me!"

Laughing, she twirled. "It will be full of unexpected twists and turns! I love discovering new people with powers. This place is perfect to awaken it."

Off to the side, Ryan, Zack, and Luke began talking quietly. I folded my arms, biting my bottom lip. I don't like the way her smile curled so perfectly. Not that she's bad, but my gut twisted. Yet, a part of me couldn't help but be drawn to her. I wanted to find out if I had any powers. Kyle was already eager to learn more, talking to her and Mike.

What would be the harm?

>>>

"Let's go, one more time," Whitney said, clicking her tongue. Hours passed in the notably warm room. Parts of my hair clung to my forehead, and my muscles ached. The training room was spacious, with stone walls and tile flooring. A few doors lined the walls where we've done obstacle courses, practiced combat, and taken numerous tests.

Luckily, Kyle had made progress. He discovered he

131

had another power: teleportation, during the obstacle course. It was only short distances for right now, but he grinned like a kid each time he blinked out of sight and reappeared somewhere else. One of the first times he did it, he ended up behind Ryan and Luke, jumpscaring them.

I wasn't as fortunate. I haven't found a single power of my own. My nails bit harder into my palms with each failure as I tried to focus. *I need to try harder. I can't be the only one without powers.*

At least the day wasn't a complete waste. I'd learned something useful: the basics of combat. But even then, I wasn't great. I could punch and attack with weapons, just not dodge, or I would leave myself unguarded.

"Alright," I said curtly, dropping my arms. "Nothing's worked so far. The four main elements, ice, weather, flying, anything with plants, speech, teleportation, night vision, speed, lightning—"

"We get it!" Ryan shouted, exasperated. "Keep trying, Izzie."

"At least you learned combat." Kyle chimed in helpfully, tying his shoe.

Mike, Zack, and Luke all added in their own encouraging responses. The brothers, during this time practiced, left, and returned to watch us.

Sighing, I faced Whitney. She wanted us to try healing now. Before me lay a small animal. A brown lizard with a broken leg, the limb dangling at its side. Quietly, Kyle walked to the tiny creature and crouched.

"What do I do?" he asked, tilting his head.

Shrugging, Whitney looked at me expectantly. "I don't know either," I admitted, holding my hands up. "Bandage it?"

The little lizard darted off awkwardly to Ryan, who scooped it up and left the room. Tapping her chin, Whitney narrowed her eyes on me. "I think you boys need to go. This room's too crowded and I want to talk with Izzie alone."

Zack exited without a word, a black and red spiked sword strapped securely on his back. When they left earlier, each of the brothers, except Ryan, got a new weapon. I guessed this was normal since their weapons were stolen frequently.

Kyle didn't move. He frowned and scratched the back of his head, but Mike nudged him, giving a look. The door shut, and we were the only people left in the room.

"Is it possible I just don't have powers?" I kicked at the floor. My scuffed Converse had holes in the toe.

"Umm." Whitney played with her hair. "Unlikely since your twin has them. But it's possible, I suppose."

Lights blinded me, quickly fading as I observed, floating from my body, Whitney in slow motion. She ran and struck me. I watched myself fall awkwardly onto my arm and stifle a cry of pain. The vision vanished as fast as it came, and my normal perspective of the room switched back. I spun around to find Whitney hadn't moved yet.

"Hmm," she mumbled, brows furrowing. "Perhaps something happened earlier, and we're just not catching. There are a few scarcer... I wonder..."

Is she going to hurt me? I narrowed my eyes. Her eyes flicked around wildly, jaw tensed. Eventually, her gaze rested on me. *Is Kyle right to not trust them?*

Without warning, Whitney charged. She raised her fist, exactly as I saw before. The angle of her strike, the sharp twist of her wrist. My instincts kicked in from years of surviving Mom's violent outbursts. It trained me to move before thinking. To shield. Ducking out of the way, I stuck out my foot and tripped her. She sprawled onto the floor hard before lifting herself swiftly.

"What was that for?" I snapped, my body trembling. Flashes of that woman replaced Whitney.

Never again. That woman always went for a different tactic to hurt me or Kyle. Kept me on my toes.

Never again.

I knew I couldn't trust her, yet why did the brothers? I balled my fists, panting.

"Incredible! The whole idea was a gamble, but it worked! How'd you know what I was going to do!?" she exclaimed, her eyes gleaming with triumph.

"I don't know!" I blinked, forcing myself to breathe in deeply. *Is she insane? I can't tell if she's trying to help or hurt me.* "I saw you coming at me. I had a vision of you replicating it. But what the heck is wrong with you?"

Her brows curved up. "Wait, how could you have foreseen me?" She tapped her lip with a finger, looking at the ground. "You had no prior information and little time to react, especially to defend yourself. Could you have foresight? Is that a power you can even have?"

I backed away. "I don't think that's what it was, and you didn't answer my question. Can Kyle or someone come back—?"

"Then what was it?" she pressed, leaning closer, eyes searching mine. "How'd you know what I was going to do?"

"I saw you! And I didn't foresee the morph or my school getting attacked!"

She ran her hand through her hair. "Okay, I'm not positive. It's safe to say it either began today like Kyle's or within these last few weeks. Obviously, you had no control over it, so I doubt it'll happen often. Probably only when you're the exact person in danger or the sort. That is interesting, though. No one has had this power, even with all the variations."

Before I had a chance to react, she lunged again, sweeping my legs out from under me. I struck the tiles hard at an awkward angle, a jarring pain slicing through my arm. Gasping, I struggled to sit up, my left arm throbbing.

You're crazy! The heck was that?

Whitney dropped beside me, her face pale and mouth agape. "I'm incredibly sorry! I thought you would have seen that! Oh my gosh, this is bad. This is all my fault, I'm so sorry!"

Lifting my arm, there already was swelling around my wrist. A door creaked open, and Mike tentatively stepped in. "I heard some noise and wanted to see if—" His eyes widened as he saw me and Whitney on the floor. "What the— what happened?"

Kyle followed Mike in as he rushed to my side. "Whitney," Mike breathed, exasperated. "What'd you do?"

"Is this why my arm's hurting?" Kyle said tightly and went to my other side. "Are you okay?"

I closed my eyes without answering. The shock over me retreated, and pain replaced it, coming over in flashes, sharp and unrelenting. Not touching it—moving it—hurt. I wanted it to stop. *Ignore it, you aren't weak. You can't be left behind.*

"Is there anything we can do to stop the pain?" Kyle flinched as he saw my arm again.

"No, it's okay," I said, hugging my arm close to my body. Her voice lingered in my head. *You won't get rid of me that easily.*

"Luke!" Mike yelled, brushing Whitney's arm. "Grab Ryan, please!"

. . .

MIKE

One week went by since Izzie sprained her arm. Whitney explained everything, in detail, about the incident. Luckily, her arm only needed a cast. And hopefully, it would heal quicker with Ryan and medical assistants treating it.

At least she had powers.

Soon, they'd have to leave to fulfill their next mission. *Should we bring the twins when one was hurt and neither had close to enough training? They've been with us so far...*

Mike rubbed his thumb against his palm. He had mentioned it days ago during breakfast to his brothers. After some back and forth, Zack and Luke convinced him it would be fine to take them, as long as everyone learned to fight with both hands. Ryan didn't like it, but he relented.

"Something about her magic feels... wrong, not like ours. It's unstable, something unlike ours," Ryan said softly, ensuring they were the only ones in the room.

"What are you talking about?" Luke asked. "Just Izzie? Not Kyles? Are you sure it isn't that you still don't like her?"

"I can't explain it." He glanced at Mike. "Do you feel it too?"

"No." Mike played with the edge of his shirt. "But we'll keep that in mind. For now, she's-they've done nothing wrong, and like Zack and Luke pointed out, we'll keep them by our side for now."

"Okay, but don't say I didn't warn you."

It's been decided that two days from now, after breakfast, they will leave.

. . .

IZZIE

Far from being a small, secluded hideout, XXS felt alive. People passed by constantly, their voices echoing faintly through the hallways and open areas. Most headed out toward the forest or moorlands that surrounded the base, likely for patrols or training. Others worked in groups, discussing strategies or supplies.

After the initial test and wrapping my hand, I counted at least two dozen people in the first ten minutes. "How many live here?" I asked Mike while exploring the building.

"Hard to say. It's always changing," he replied. "Officially, there's about fifty or so, but most are out on missions or training in the forest."

The activity was strange yet comforting. It wasn't just the brothers anymore. An entire Clan interacted here, people with purpose and power, working toward something bigger.

Kyle and I had been here for a week. At first, I didn't like it—Whitney in particular. Everyone seemed to gravitate toward her like moths to a flame, including my brother. But after seeing her quick thinking and how she guided others so effortlessly, I realized her confidence wasn't arrogance. It was genuine care. And she made a point to encourage me. Little things like nodding when I landed a move correctly or offering advice on how to read opponents' movements.

Despite it, I couldn't shake a lingering wariness. Maybe it was that uncanny pull she had on people, or my gut telling me to stay cautious.

"See ya!" I waved awkwardly with my right hand. The wind welcomed me warmly as I walked out the entrance.

At long last, after days of training, we finally left. It took some convincing, but the brothers agreed to let us join for now on. Whitney had Kyle and me practice with our non-dominant hands— something Mike insisted on before we left. It proved tough, but we had to be ready for anything.

Learning to defend myself was hard. But we had to learn how to use both arms. Anything could happen, and now I knew exactly who I fought for—and what I was willing to become to protect them.

Chapter 12

IZZIE

Exiting the tunnel, I realized how much I'd grown to like that strange, hidden place. It's home for the brothers and anyone part of XXS, and perhaps, it'll become home for Kyle and me too.

We re-entered the woods. I breathed in the plain oak smell and smiled, trailing behind everyone.

I think I misjudged Whitney. She tried to help, but I remained skeptical of her. Not everyone deserves mistrust, especially not her.

The trees steadily changed, bleeding into more purplish colors, and the grass became a strong dark green. To my right, a small pond glimmered, with frogs ribbiting and bugs swarming around us.

Zack slowed, touching a leaf. "I think we have just crossed into it," he said, getting Mike to stop.

"Into what?" Kyle swatted a bug flying in front of his face.

"The place," Zack informed, "is referred to where some legends say you can find a unicorn."

"A unicorn? You're kidding," my brother scoffed. "They aren't real."

"Well," Mike remarked, "they can be. We've seen magic mutate animals before. This is also where the Rhopalocera's territory begins, so avoid anything with metallic blue wings."

"Rho-pal-ocerea?" my twin pronounced, giving him a puzzled look.

"They're butterflies," Luke clarified, picking up a rock, tossing it in his hand, then chucking it over the trees.

"We're scared of butterflies now?" I repeated, raising an eyebrow. "That... encouraging"

"I'm serious," Mike said. "They might look harmless, but they can be deadly."

"What do they do?" Kyle asked.

"Uhm," Mike continued forward. We trailed after him, the pond fading from view. "No confirmed reports on what they do, so don't let your guard down."

"And the unicorns grant you a wish if you can convince one," Ryan picked up, then focused on me. His eyes dropped to my arm while we walked. "How's your arm doing?"

I glanced at the dark green cast, barely noticing a throb. "Good."

He nodded. "Give it a day or so, and we can test if it's ready for the cast to come off."

On my right, the bushes shook violently as a flock of butterflies erupted into the air. Their wings swirled with blue, green, and black. An eerie purple shin shimmered

140

with each flap.

"A kaleidoscope," Luke observed, breathless. "They're so pretty."

"A—" I stopped myself. "You know, I'm not going to bother."

None of the butterflies acknowledged us, their wings glinting like stained glass. They kept flying on their merry way until they were out of sight. *Great, at least the powerful butterflies do not care about us.*

While we walked, I caught Ryan flinching at a tree branch poking his arm. His shoulders were stiff, eyes darting to every rustle. *He seems paranoid.* The edges of my lips twitched upward. *I could try to help him lighten up...* I stalked over to him, careful to stay out of his line of sight. I lightly touched his back.

He twisted, stumbling and barely snagging a tree limb to stop himself from face-planting.

"Hey!" Ryan barked, scowling. His face flushed. "Why'd you do that?! Are you trying to give me a heart attack?"

I stepped away, holding my hands up. My twin passed me, shaking his head. Luke chuckled, covering his mouth with his hand while Zack raised an eyebrow but kept walking.

"You were being so jumpy, you got to relax, man! Izzie's doing you a favor." Luke called over his shoulder. I managed to catch a glimpse of his heart tattoo with a lightning bolt through it.

I smiled.

MIKE

The butterflies flew over the trees, wings glinting like bits of colored glass. For a second, Mike wished he could be like them— drifting along. *It starts like a weight you can bear, but over time, it turns into part of you, until you aren't sure where it ended and you began.*

He glanced over at the others. Ryan tensed as a coiled spring, every noise setting him off. Behind him crept Izzie, fighting herself from giving her position away.

"Boo!" she exclaimed, tapping him on the back.

Ryan's startled yell echoed through the trees, followed by his indignant scowl. Mike barely held back a laugh as Luke defended her.

Heaven knows they don't get many chances to laugh. But as much as he wanted them to have these moments, his mind kept circling back to what came next. The danger wasn't over, not by a long shot. And he couldn't shake this nagging feeling that they weren't ready. *It's exhausting to keep holding it together, but if I don't, who would?*

If one of them got hurt because he wasn't watching, because he let himself get distracted by a joke or a pretty scene, he'd never forgive himself. He'd failed them before—Atticus's death was proof of that. And that wouldn't happen again.

Mike brushed his sword's hilt as they moved through the forest, keeping an eye on the path ahead. *Even if they don't realize it, they need someone to look out for them. To stay focused, so they could have these moments of normalcy.*

Kyle, who pulled ahead, waved over Zack and Mike to peer through a bush. They huddled, and Mike squinted around the leaves. In the clearing beyond stood a shimmering horse with a red horn. His mouth hung open.

. . .

IZZIE

My brother was way ahead of us, joined by Mike and Zack, peeking through a bush.

"Guys, come look at this!" Zack called, waving us over.

I went behind him and peered through the branch he lifted. Two boys, probably teenagers or older, stood with their backs to us. They looked like they were guarding something, but I couldn't decipher what.

The hedges shook as a horse trotted through. Its gleaming white coat contrasted sharply against the brown pine trees and purple hue. Then I saw the crimson horn.

It's a unicorn, for real.

The boys strutted next to it. Their eyes glazed, actions unnatural and rigged.

"A unicorn?" Kyle asked, eyebrows furrowing. "You said they granted wishes?"

"Yes," Zack gawked. "We should go meet it."

"Great idea," Mike said, patting Zack's back.

"Wait, what if it's—" I began. The brothers and Kyle rushed past me before I could mention how terrible an idea that was.

If they've never met one before, then how do they know

143

it's safe to approach it? Granting wishes always had a catch! They halted a few feet out from the hedge, their movements eerily synchronized.

"Kyle? Luke?" I called out, breaking out of the foliage after them. "Are you guys alright?"

As one, they turned toward me with vacant eyes. Expressionless. None of them blinked or twitched. It was like puppets being pulled by the same invisible strings. A cold knot twisted in my gut. The two boys I've seen before approached, with the Unicorn trotting behind them. Its crimson tail swung side to side lazily, muscles rippling underneath its white coat.

It neighed, a voice ringing cold in my mind. *"Leave. Leave us and we will spare your life, child."*

A cold sweat broke across my skin. I evened out my weight, rolling to the balls of my feet. *Spare my life? What is this creature doing to them?*

"What?" My voice cracked.

The air in the clearing grew thick. Mike's jaw twitched, his voice deadpan. "Leave, or we'll have to kill you.

"Kill me?" I repeated, tilting my head. *They'll kill me? What?* "I don't—"

"You heard him," Luke growled, throwing his arm at me, the leather bracelets shifting. "Leave."

"You should listen," Ryan added, twirling his dagger in his hand.

Backing away, I clenched my teeth and collided with Kyle. His hand gripped my shoulder. *How'd he arrive? Did he teleport?* His eyes glowed, void of their usual emotion. "Why aren't you leaving?" he asked coldly.

I whipped towards the Unicorn. "Wait, wait, wait. I'm confused. What are you doing? How do you have control over them? We didn't want to kill you or take anything—"

"Kill? You wanted to kill her?" Zack's voice turned dark, followed by laughter. His mouth curled into a chilling grin, with sparks crackling at his fingertips. "You're going to regret even thinking about it."

Off to the side, Mike made a slicing motion with his hand. Air ripped from my lungs. My chest seized, and I gasped. Nothing came. I doubled over, clutching my throat, barely managing to keep the darkness creeping at the edges of my vision at bay.

"Please—" I choked out. *Mike's that powerful?*

Wind swirled around me, taking me into the air. Mike's eyes blazed, both hands raised. Zack's arm extended. The world spun, increasing at incredible speed. I knew what would come next.

I lifted my arms in a cross, blocking an electric bolt aimed directly at my chest. The cast from my arm ended up on the ground, melted in half, and smoke rose from the charred fiber. The smell of burnt plastic filled the air. The sky darkened, menacing clouds rolling in.

Or was that me hallucinating?

Ryan moved under me, his fingertips glowing. Luke blurred to the other side, his katana drawn.

Mike clenched his hand, and I felt my lungs start closing in, the little air left escaping and coming close off. A rustling came out from my right or—left—which caught his

145

attention, and he dropped his arm, releasing me.

I struck the ground, gasping and coughing. Cradling my neck, air swept back into my lungs so fast it burned. I lifted my head. My vision blurred. *Where— My arm kills, my eyes can't focus…*

Luke, I think, went back to watching me, bouncing on the balls of his feet. The unicorn was closer, its white coat fairly visible against the blur.

If I could reach it.

I drew my arms underneath me, slowly pushing up. Bending my knees, I lunged and landed at its side, barely managing to snag a hair off the Unicorn's shimmering mane. The unicorn reared, a piercing shriek filling the air as I yanked out a strand of its crimson hair. My friends and brother hissed, eyes locked on me, but frozen in place.

The unicorn whined, circling and snarling as I lay on the ground. It eyed the hair I held, pinched between my fingers. *You get one wish.* A harsh puff of air exhaled from its nose.

A hair gets you a wish? I swallowed. *I can free them. But one wrong word and they'd be lost forever.* I opened my dry mouth.

"I-I wish that-that any enchantment." I hacked, with the metallic taste of blood on my tongue. A sharp pain tore through my chest. "Charm, or any spell cast by any unicorn or person, is re-removed from these people. And… they'll never be-be harmed or controlled by any unicorn again."

You'll regret that wish. You've tampered with forces you cannot begin to understand. The Unicorn hissed through my mind like a cold wind. That hair in my hand

146

disintegrated, and it bolted.

An eerie stillness fell over the clearing.

I clutched my throat, trying to suppress another cough. A pounding ache radiated through my arm and skull. Every breath sent a sharp reminder of how close my lungs had gotten to collapsing, aching as the air went in and out. Where my arm had been hit left faint lines from the electricity, wrapping around like vines.

You're fine. I shifted my attention toward my friends. The unicorn vanished.

Ryan looked back and forth, rubbing his temples. He groaned, "What happened?"

They're okay. The brothers, Kyle, are themselves again...

My breath caught, forcing me to gulp. I punched my chest and hacked, the cough racking my entire body. But it worked, and my breath went back to a loud rasping sound. *It's becoming—difficult—to breathe.*

"Izzie?" Kyle called out, staring at me. "Hey!" He ran and slid on his knees, ending at my side.

I'm fine, don't worry. Just give me a second.

"Are you okay? No, no, no, please."

Luke trailed not far behind him. "What happened? Why's your cast off and smoldering?"

No, it's good. And don't worry, Kyle. It isn't your fault.

The other men who had been with the Unicorn prior were talking between Mike and Zack. They seemed lost, yet relieved.

147

Blinking, the two boys' figures were bubbles, yet I felt them watching. I recalled their futuristic, unique style of hair and clothing. It made me curious about who they were and where they had come from.

A stifled groan escaped from my lips as I sat up. Light swirled in circles. I collapsed onto Kyle, who caught me, looking at who might have been Ryan.

I guessed Mike or Zack approached next. To be honest, I focused more on my breathing. Another hand brushed my neck, peeling off my hand and then feeling around gently. I again guessed Ryan, who must've been checking for damage.

"Izzie," Kyle said softly in my ear. "You're okay. Please tell me you're okay."

Ryan touched something sensitive. I jerked, pulling away. Kyle tightened his arms around me, and my breath hitched. *Agh, no, you're right. I'm okay.*

"Does anyone remember what happened?" Ryan's voice asked gently, his touch dropping to my arm.

No response. I clenched my teeth, shutting my eyes. *Prove you're okay.*

"U—unicorn."

"Unicorn? What about it?" Mike prompted.

Attacked us, you were under a spell. I opened my mouth but shook my head when nothing came out.

Kyle tucked a piece of my hair that fell in front of my face behind my ear. His blurry eyes narrowed, flicking between me and everyone around. "Maybe you guys should go talk to those boys. They might know something."

The air shifted, signaling a few people parting. I believe Ryan still sat there with Kyle and me. His hands softly moved my arm.

I know it wasn't their fault. They could not control it, the unicorn made them. If anything, I should've been able to free them without getting hurt. And now, I might get left behind if I...

You don't deserve... You don't... Agh, that voice is becoming too close to my 'mother's'.

"Can't you use your magic to heal her?" Kyle pleaded. "Could I do something?"

"I have to know what happened for it to be effective. What magic, if it was magic at all..." Ryan went back to my neck. He brushed the sensitive area. "Izzie? Are you able to tell me what happened? I mean, I can guess by the cast being burnt, though I'd rather hear it from you."

"N-no," I whispered, my throat raw and scraping. "It's— I'm f-fine."

"No, you're not," Kyle said sharply, lifting me from his lap to sit straight. "Listen to yourself!"

Lifting my head to him, I smiled as he let go, taking a second to catch my breath. "See? I'm fine."

"Yeah, right." Ryan stood. "You can barely breathe or talk, let alone sit up. If you were, you'd be able to stand." He stuck out his fuzzy hand. "If you really are fine, then prove it. Stand, Izzie."

I took it. Kyle shifted away as Ryan helped me to my feet. The forest swayed again. I stumbled into Ryan. He caught me and kept me up. My vision darkened.

149

No, why can't I stand? I'm so stupid. I wanted to scream at my body for being so weak. Or facepalm. *I should've stopped it sooner. What did Mike or Zack do to cause this?* Ryan and Kyle were quiet as multiple footsteps approached.

Sleep is good— my mind lured me. *Come on. Just a minute.* Giving in, I let the darkness claim me.

<div align="center">~~~ ~~~ ~~~ ~~~</div>

OTHER

Nyke observed his sister strike, her movements fluid and exact, her long hair flowing over her shoulder. His brother, Steven, wiped his mouth and sat up. Wow.

"You did it again, Jade."

She sheathed the sword, landing next to Steven with her teeth clenched, "I can't seem to get it right. My weakness isn't making me stronger."

Nyke sat up in his seat. His eyes met Jade, and he was about to call out when her tense expression vanished.

It was replaced with fear.

"Nyke, watch—"

The explosion hit behind him. Heat licked Nyke's skin as he stumbled, covering his head from the blast. His brother and sister were already at his side, shielding their bodies with their wings from the debris.

Here is when the war began. The one that killed most, if not all, Ikris.

Chapter 13

IZZIE

Dreams. Night terrors. Usually, they never changed each night back at home. With that woman always finding me. Yet, this time, there were new ones.

A blurry figure, its thumb rubbing against its palm while that woman yelled at a male figure in the background. It changed where I was locked inside a cage, nothing surrounded me but blurred gray fog. There was no way out of it. The world appeared fuzzy, messing with my already clouded head. Panic coursed through me. Alarms ticked off and I fell through the gray haze. I dissolved into a different place. Mike, Ryan, Zack, Luke, and Kyle lie before me, faces torn apart, flesh and blood everywhere. Lifeless.

I searched for Kyle's pulse. *Nothing.* Tears filled my eyes, *they are dead. But how? Is it because of me?*

The scene switched. A giant chased me, massive and made out of stone. It cornered me at a dead-end, stalking towards me with hungry eyes. It leaped and I screamed.

My eyes snapped open to the dark sky, stars scattered like diamonds. I clenched the bottom of my shirt into a ball. Crickets chirped in the background. *A nightmare... It was only a nightmare.* Sweat brimmed my forehead as I sat up. *Where are we again? How is it night already?*

I pressed the back of my hand against my head, then lightly to my throat. *Right. The unicorn. I can breathe better now...* My breaths still came short and sometimes hurt, but I could handle it. *Did Ryan heal me?*

The brothers and Kyle were asleep. Mike and Zack lay the furthest, swords in their hands, next to each other.

Their powers... The brothers are dangerous. I couldn't even prevent them from hurting me, let alone kill me. I know I could not hurt them, would not hurt them. *Should Kyle and I stay with them if this happens again? Can I even trust them?* They weren't in control, but against them or without them, I don't stand a chance.

My breath grew ragged, hot flashes crossed my body. The woman... her hand... I flinched, dragging my knees to my chest.

I don't like that. I need to train more. I can't rely on others all the time. They'll leave me behind.

Should I run? Find a place where no one knows me?

I gazed at the sky, finding the waning moon. Stars twinkled faintly beside it. *What did the Nemesis want so badly? To control and harvest power? What made the boys I traveled with so special? What made XXS so special? Is it their magic? How did no one know where magic came from?*

One thought spiraled after another. *Maybe I should leave before they do. I'm becoming a burden. First the arm, and now this. I'm someone they need to protect. I've become a thorn in their side. They'd be better off without me.*

But what about Kyle? What if he needs me? I can't leave him. I would never forgive myself.

And the brothers... they've risked so much for me. For each other. Maybe it's time I stop running. My ragged breaths claimed me, dragging me back to sleep.

This time, it brought me to a park with Kyle. We played around a tree, with bugs, when a man spotted us. His own children ran around him and a cooler, but he didn't hesitate. Very slowly, he walked towards us. Kyle immediately stepped in front of me with his arm extended.

There was a kind sparkle in his eye as he offered ice cream. But we backed away, and so did he after saying he'll leave the cooler if we changed our minds.

After about ten minutes, I eyed the cooler, but Kyle handed me a dandelion with the white fuzz.

"Wish for something," Kyle said, "but don't tell me what."

I blew, the seeds scattered into the breeze. One floated past Kyle's nose and he sneezed.

We laughed and ran over to the cooler. I looked around but didn't see the man, so we opened it. Inside were popsicles and ice cream bars. Of course, Kyle took a red and blue popsicle. I took an ice cream bar and we ran back to the tree.

Kyle nudged me, his lips and chin blue. "Whatever you wished for, I hope it finds you."

I nodded slowly, finishing mine off. "I hope I find it! Because—"

"No! Don't tell me!" he cried, covering his ears and

darting across the park. I chased after him.

...

MIKE

After the Unicorn attack, which is what Mike assumed happened from seeing the Unicorn before everything turned blurry, Izzie went limp in Ryan's arms. She got injured badly, but couldn't or wouldn't say how. Ryan was going to have a very difficult time healing her with the little they knew.

"Izzie didn't say anything," Ryan said while setting her gently next to a tree. "I assume she couldn't speak much, but it must've been... well... you know."

Mike ran his hand through his brown hair. His brother's words hung in the air, reminding Mike of the distance in his relationship with the twins. Despite that, he loved them almost as his own siblings. They were people who risked their lives for others. For them.

He'll have to work on it.

Before turning in for the night, the group decided to talk with the men found entrapped with the unicorn— Nyke and Steven. The conversation yielded nothing. The men barely even spoke to them. Yet they were grateful to be freed.

The next morning dragged on. Mike woke up to find the two men gone. They must have slipped away after the conversation last night... He scratched his head but decided to let it go.

Checking if his other brothers were up, Mike walked around. Zack and Kyle talked at the edge, too far to hear, while Izzie, Ryan, and Luke slept. He hoped Izzie would be okay and heal in time to be ready for the upcoming battle.

They hadn't discussed the looming war, the final battle against Nemesis in a while, especially not with the twins. Earlier that year, Mike and his brothers had discovered the plans for it on a mission. A prepared full-out execution on XXS in an attempt to wipe out all magic users in the name of protecting humans. He rubbed his thumb against his palm.

The battle's expected to be a month away. Too soon for Kyle or Izzie to be prepared. The twins wouldn't be able to last in a battle this deadly. If they fought, Mike knew he and his brothers would risk their lives to protect them. He'd do anything, yet it put many others in unnecessary danger. The thought of losing anyone, like Alisha or Atticus, again...

Mike shivered. *No, I can't think about that. My brothers and the twins need me to be strong. But I can't put us at risk. We'll have to go back and drop off the twins at XXS.*

He headed to Ryan, who snored underneath a hedge. "Ryan, wake up."

He groaned, draping his arm over his eyes. "What is it, Mike?"

"It's time to wake up. We have to talk about the battle with Izzie and Kyle." He paused, "and also check if she's okay. You know this battle will happen. They need to know about it to decide what to do and prepare. Not to mention, we can't let them be manipulated or captured..."

Ryan snapped open his eyes. "Right now? Is Izzie awake? How is she?"

"Not yet," Mike helped him up. "We can't wait."

"With the battle? Where are you planning to start? Training? Go more in-depth about the Nemesis?" Ryan yawned. "Wouldn't it be better to have them hide and stay out of the way?"

. . .

IZZIE

I woke to my friends' voices, my breath short. During the night, after I woke up and went back to sleep, I had more nightmares after that… memory. It wasn't surprising, yet they felt so vivid. So real.

Is it my power foretelling of betrayal and war? Or a dream… No… I can't tell.

And with the little I remembered from the day before, the pain barely stayed. In my arm and neck. It won't change that I refuse to tell them what happened. *They'll hate themselves for something they had no control over. I should've prevented it.*

I sat up and waited for a second, dizzy. The grass felt prickly and a bit damp. I slowly crawled next to my brother, noticing that the two boys were gone.

"Where'd they go?" I asked, my voice hoarse.

"The boys?" Kyle said, smiling when he saw me. His ear twitched. "They left when we were asleep."

What's up? I tilted my head. *Are you okay?*

He shook his head. *"Fine, but listen to Mike and his brothers. They'll explain. And I should be asking you after yesterday. How are you feeling?"*

I'm fine.

Kyle brushed my arm with his hand. I focused on Mike as he sighed, "Nemesis has been preparing for a full-blown battle for years now. We've seen evidence of it multiple times, the most recent being earlier this year. XXS must prepare for war, where we have to succeed or die trying. But we're worried you two will not be ready in time and will be harmed."

A battle? So soon? Great.

My gut twisted. *What if the outcome would be worse if we weren't there. If I wasn't there?* "Kyle and I have learned to fight and defend ourselves. We'll be fine, don't worry."

"We know the risks," Kyle interjected.

Zack frowned. "It is more than that. We do not want you guys hurt or killed because one of us was not there to protect you. These guys are *powerful,* and you just discovered your powers. The Nemesis knows how to capture, torture, and use us against each other. To manipulate."

"Sounds like they would've gotten along well with our mother," Kyle said dryly. "And we still made it. My sister and I will fight whether or not we're ready. We already made that choice in joining you."

"Thousands of people and hybrids aren't like the fights you've survived before," Luke pointed out, his arm draped over one knee, his other leg extended. His blonde hair swooped to his gray eyes. "In a battle like this, it will be extremely easy for you to get overwhelmed or disappear, and no one will be the wiser unless our side wins."

A dreamish vision flashed, bringing me soaring

across a battlefield. *What?* Nemesis raided XXS's base, slaying and tying everyone. A third party in purple cloaks entered the sides.

Mike, Ryan, Zack, Luke, and Whitney... lifeless, tangled with mangled bodies on the muddy grass. The sight almost made me throw up. *Where's Kyle?* So many people were dying, dead, or chained in cages.

"If you want to stop it," the voice echoed, *"you must be there. This isn't set in stone. Change it. You and Kyle may save the land— only if one of you will take the stand."*

I shook my head as the vision faded. My twin sat with his hands clasped together, his gray golden-rimmed eyes squinting at the brothers. *Kyle or I will take the stand?* The voice said we had to be there, but I didn't want my brother to get hurt. I gave myself a small nod.

"Do you guys trust me?" I asked, squaring my shoulders.

My twin nodded while Luke shifted uneasily, running a hand through his blond hair. Ryan looked at his hands, mumbling under his breath.

"Yeah," Zack answered.

Mike scratched his arm. "Why?"

"We'll fight. You gotta let us be with you," I stated. Kyle shot me his look. He knew I was planning- that I knew something. "If you trust me, you have to believe that if we don't come, you'll all die and XXS will lose."

Ryan opened his mouth to speak, but Mike raised a hand. Everyone's focus shifted to Mike. "I trust you, but I'm not sold," he admitted. "The danger— I'll have to think about it. Though, Izzie? Do you mind if we talk for a minute?"

"Sure."

I shrugged, trailing after him. We continued for a few minutes before he stopped in a secluded spot. His gray, golden-rimmed eyes darted around, his fist clenched. I couldn't exactly place it. I was probably the same way. A sigh escaped his lips as he leaned against the tree.

"Did you have a vision about this?" he finally questioned, placing his hands behind his head.

"Yeah." *Why am I reluctant to tell him?* "Well, I have common sense too. You can't expect us to stay back and watch you guys fight. We owe you."

"Damn it, Izzie." Mike facepalmed. "You can't keep these things to yourself. You got to tell me, tell us. It's vital for trust. Not to mention, XXS can depend on it."

"I'm sorry. I know—"

"If you know, then why didn't you tell us?" he snapped. "Or why else did we bring you two?"

I flinched, raising my hands. My voice dropped, "I'm sorry. I was going to. It happened so quickly…"

Birds chirped, filling the tense silence. His eyes softened, meeting mine, and he sat, tilting his head against the trunk. "I'm sorry I yelled. I didn't mean to."

"It's okay. I'm sorry." I chewed my lower lip, lowering my arms. "I should've told you sooner. I didn't know it'd be—"

"Yeah, well." He cleared his throat, gesturing to where we came from. "It's hard. Every time I close my eyes,

159

I see you all gone. I can't let it happen again. I am responsible for keeping you all safe and leading us. Then we found you two, the pressure just added. Sorry, I don't know why I'm telling you this…

"Imagine what it'd be like with our missing siblings. It's already so hard trying to keep you all safe, and then someone argues with me or doesn't communicate... It adds to the pressure and puts us all in more danger. I've managed to keep it together, but lately… I don't know how much longer I can." He pinched the bridge of his nose.

I knelt beside him. "Hey, look. We're trying to help you too. You don't have to do everything yourself, ya know. Your brothers are grown. You don't need to protect them as much anymore. Kyle and I learned how to protect ourselves, and while it's a good idea to keep an eye out for one another, you can trust it will be okay."

Lifting his head, he let out a long breath, shoulders relaxing. I put my arm on his shoulder and pulled him into a hug.

"But it hasn't been in the past," Mike whispered. "I've failed to find the twins, protect my friends, and can't hold it together anymore."

"Everyone has a breaking point, Mike. It's okay."

"Yeah, you're right. You remind me a lot of my father." He pulled away, wiping his eyes with his arm. With a deep breath, Mike stood. "That's settled then. We should return to my brothers and hope they didn't hear anything. But please, if it happens again, tell me."

He drew in a last sniffle and headed off. My hands felt clammy as I followed him, my heart striking in my

160

chest. The faint smell of pollen lingered, tickling my nose like a feather.

Luke's laughing lit up the clearing, lifting my spirits instantly.

"Come on, Ryan! A potato could do better than that!" Zack teased. Kyle held a ball of moss, tossing it to Luke.

Off to the side, Mike fidgeted with a leaf, looking more interested in it than in his brother's antics.

A butterfly fluttered down, its delicate wings glinting green and blue. It landed on the back of Luke's shoulder. He immediately dropped his hands, now holding the moss ball, and stared off, not particularly at anything.

What did those creatures do again? Didn't they say they were powerful? I spotted Kyle, who now idly picked at thick, green grass. "I'm sure it's nothing," I mumbled to myself and headed off to him.

"Hey." I squatted next to him, earning a wave and a smile.

"When are we going to leave?" Luke asked, touching the scar on his lip.

Mike glanced up from his leaf, scanning the group. "I don't know, tomorrow? Make sure Izzie and everyone else are okay first. Have some food, while we're at it."

"Yeah," Zack agreed, rubbing his stomach. "I am famished. Does anyone know where the food Olli packed for us went?"

My stomach growled in response. Around us, small blueberries hung off the bushes about a hundred feet from the center. Above them, a tree was in full bloom, colorful with flowers and hidden. The pollen tickled again, triggering a sneeze.

The agony in my lungs returned. *No, no, why now? I thought Ryan healed it.* I gasped, but the air refused to fully enter. The world tilted. I tried to breathe, each inhale scraping like sandpaper. A jagged rattle echoed in my chest. Each one was like a knife tearing through me.

I clawed at my chest and neck, the lump in my throat that I'd apparently ignored for a while flared, crashing into me at once. *Ryan.* I tried to call out, but only a choked gurgle escaped my lips.

Kyle's voice sounded distant. *Wait, I messed up. How could Ryan fix it if he didn't know what was wrong?* I yanked open my eyes and collapsed fully onto the wet grass. The pain in my left arm spiked. Blurry images of Ryan and Zack, or Kyle form in front of me. They were talking. I couldn't comprehend the words. Flames crept in my lungs, each breath like acid. I couldn't smell anything.

My vision cleared for a second. I saw Ryan's face, tense, lines on his forehead showing. *He'd know what to do if you told him what happened.*

"Ry—" My voice caught. I coughed violently, splatters of blood painting the grass. "Wind... Elec—" I hacked harder, then I tried to breathe in, and my throat wouldn't let me.

A choking noise bubbled from my mouth. The words swirled in a chaotic blur of colors. A warm hand tapped my neck and removed my own.

Through the haze, a blurry butterfly landed on

162

Ryan's shoulder. He stiffened, pulling away. Tears stung my eyes. I spit, trying to clear my throat. *What is wrong with him?*

"Get it off him!" Luke cried.

. . .

MIKE

When Izzie collapsed, Mike tried to jump in, but Ryan told him to give her space.

Now Mike's stance went rigid as the Rhopalocera landed on Ryan. Straightening, his brother's expression slackened except for his lips, which were pressed in a firm line. Mike froze as Luke ran up, breathing heavily. "That thing controls your body. Get it off him!"

Kyle quickly swatted at it. The black butterfly with an iridescent blue-green hue on its wings fluttered, lifting its legs, then resettled on Ryan. Facing them, Ryan tilted his head, his grayish-brown golden-rimmed eyes blank.

In turn, Zack lunged, flinging it off him. In awe, Mike tracked it as it flapped away.

Ryan shook his head, rubbing his eyes. "What happened?"

"A Rhopalocera. Now help Izzie!" Luke panted.

. . .

IZZIE

Ryan's warm calloused hands returned, glowing on my neck. The pain stilled as memories slipped into my mind. A young set of twins playing in their room, an image of a grown man crying by Mike, then dying the next year at

163

the hospital. Stage four lung cancer.

The younger versions of the brothers, getting lost in the wilderness. Later joining a Clan, experiencing their powers, and finding themselves again. Then, befriending new people and—The visions abruptly cut off, the hands fell away from me.

Pain remained faintly in my left arm, but my neck was insanely better. Air flowed into my lungs, greeting it like cold water on a scorching day. I lay there for a moment, breathing.

What happened before Ryan healed me? He stopped right when I thought I was about to die.

Opening my eyes, Kyle extended his hand for me. His grip was firm as he pulled me to my feet. After making sure I could stand, he handed me a bottle of water, which I drank. "Are you okay?" he asked, then silently added, *"What was that? The light was so vibrant... and white."*

"You alright now?" Ryan interrupted, brushing the dirt off his arms. Blood dripped from his nose.

I nodded, offering him a slight smile. The only pain resided in my arm; a steady, manageable throb.

"Thank you... Are you okay, Ryan?" I asked, remembering what happened when he had healed Zack. "Healing me didn't hurt you, did it?"

"Yeah, I'm good." He stretched, sweat glistening on his forehead. He wiped the blood from his nose. "Just scratched. I should probably lay off my magic for a while, though."

"Do you need anything?" Zack called from his spot.

"No, thank you, though." I rubbed my neck. Ryan waved him off.

Picking up a bag, Luke brought it over and took out a granola bar. He handed it to me and I thanked him.

Ryan's expression darkened as he got back to his feet. "Izzie, can you please tell me what happened back there with the Unicorn? I recalled the three words you coughed out, but it will help if I need to heal you more. All I remember is Zack pointing the Unicorn out."

"Well," I led off.

"You heard him," Luke growled. "Leave!"

"You should listen," Ryan said.

I backed into Kyle, his eyes cold. "Why aren't you leaving?" he asked coldly.

I whipped towards the Unicorn. "We didn't want to kill you or take anything—"

"Kill? You wanted to kill her?" Zack laughed, with sparks at his fingertips. "You're going to regret even thinking about it, coward."

Mike held out his hands, lifting me in the air and taking away my ability to breathe. Zack struck me with lightning. The rest of them were ready to finish me off...

"I—, the unicorn controlled you." I stammered, backing up. "It— convinced you to protect it or to be its slave. Since I wasn't under its spell, it wanted me gone."

"How did you get hurt?" Zack interjected.

I swallowed, moving my raven hair to my shoulder. "I tried... reasoning with the Unicorn. Tried telling it we didn't want any trouble, and if it lets you go, we'd leave. It didn't believe me and threatened me to go or else I would die. When I refused— you all—" I cut myself off, glancing at Mike, who shut his eyes.

Don't piece it together, please.

"Who tried to kill you?" Kyle whispered. "Was it all of us?"

My eyes locked with Ryan's, who seemed to connect the pieces. I shook my head. "I can't," I whispered. "You'd hate yourselves for something you had no control over. Something I should've prevented."

I couldn't look at them. My chest tightened. I would do almost anything for anyone I cared about. Not in a million years could I live with myself if they hated me, or themselves, for what they couldn't control.

I spun away. "I need a second, okay?" I choked out. A hand grazed my shoulder, but I shrugged it off. "I'll be back in a little bit."

I dug my nails into my palm, jogging away. *You're being stupid and over-emotional.* The danger, keeping everyone safe, worrying, protecting them, not getting killed, stopping the Nemesis. I'm starting to understand the pressure Mike was under. That we're all under. *How does he do it?*

I shoved past more branches, approaching the edge of the forest. The ground became wetter and muddy. More swampish, seeping into my shoes. Veering to my left, I slowed, ending up surrounded by thick roots and branches.

"Where are you going?" A voice slithered into my head. I whipped my head side to side. *"It would be easier if*

166

you joined us, you know." I tripped, narrowly catching myself on a tree.

"Hello?" My voice echoed. *I swear if another—*

"The Nemesis," it replied soothingly. *"We only want what is best for everyone. You only listen to what those boys tell you. How about you hear what happened? Our side of the story."*

I facepalmed. *Nemesis? Yeah right, why would they be trying to convince me to join them? You are wrong. They wanted to hurt us. People with powers. You helped my mother...*

"Why do you think we are evil?" The voice purred. *"We have only wanted what is best for our world. You only listened to those boys. No matter, we will make it better, and not hurt your brother. I promise."*

I twisted in a circle, my nails biting my palms. "If you want me to join, then show yourself."

Across the clearing, bushes broke apart. A girl around my age stepped out. She held a clear vial with gray liquid in her hand, her hair draping over her face. Her skin was a light tan, with blue-black speckled sparkling eyes. I didn't recognize her, nor the vial.

"Hello, Izzie." She smiled slightly. "I'm Dravia. Do you remember me?"

Chapter 14

MIKE

Kyle tried to go after her, but Ryan pulled him back. Mike knew Kyle was right to worry, but she needed time alone.

"What if something happens to her? She was just hurt," Kyle pleaded. "Can we go look for her in a few minutes, at least?"

Thinking about it, Ryan eventually relented. To pass the time, Zack and Luke began joking and throwing rocks at each other.

Bugs flew past Mike's face. He shifted, glancing at the woods where Izzie vanished. "This running off-alone thing," he muttered. "I hope it's not an ongoing thing. She could get hurt."

Zack cut his conversation with Luke, catching eye contact with Mike. "It seems she has to handle things herself. She is carrying something she will not let us see."

Kyle slowed his bouncing on his toes, his blond hair messy. "Iz has been that way for a while. I even feel locked out sometimes. But it's normal."

"She's not the only one doing it, though, is she?" Ryan shrugged, leaning against a tree.

With a sigh, Mike paced. *No, no, she is not.*

"Is everyone else okay?" Zack eventually asked, rubbing his arm.

Luke nodded, checking the heart tattoo by his shoulder, and Mike paused, examining his brothers. He himself got a few scrapes, but nothing major.

"I'll take that as a yes," he sighed. After another pause, Zack hesitantly continued, "It sort of worries me. Each fight seems to bring us closer and closer to losing each other or being permanently separated."

Like the twins.

Going to his side, Luke wrapped an arm around Zack's back. "I see where you're coming from, man. I sometimes worry about that too."

He lowered his head, pinching the bridge of his nose. The pink tips of his blond hair swayed.

Mike rubbed his thumb against his palm, his brown hair almost reaching his eyes. "I get that, too. I'll do anything in my power so that it'll never happen."

Zack lifted his head.

Kyle bit his lip, eyes flicking to the trees. "Can we go now?"

"I guess—" Mike began.

The twin darted, already making it past the foliage. Mike shared a glance with his brothers.

Ryan cursed under his breath and rubbed his eyes.

"Wait for us!"

"Dude, slow down," Luke said, blurring past where Kyle vanished. "You rushing in head first isn't going to help her."

"Why?" Kyle's muffled voice asked, only his arm visible past the trees. "She's out here by herself, so why can't I?"

"You know why," Zack cut in, jogging to catch up with them. "We have been out here longer. We know what to expect. And Izzie saved us from the Nemesis by herself. She will be fine."

"Yeah, but after everything that happened…" His voice dropped. "What if this time she's not?"

Zack placed a hand on Kyle's shoulder. "It will be okay, she is strong. She can handle it."

Wind zipped around Mike. They walked at a brisk pace. Luke suggested yelling for her, but Kyle disagreed. The ground became uneven, growing mushy and soft, soaking the edges of Mike's pants. Mud clung to their shoes as they searched.

"Izzie? You around here?!" Zack said slowly.

No response. Mike stepped around a deep puddle, his shoes squishing. *We're going further and further from our destination…*

"This forest is too quiet," Luke murmured, his voice barely above a whisper. He twisted his leather bracelets.

Shrugging, Ryan ducked under a branch. "Probably the usual, but this is exactly how things go south when we're not careful."

Luke shot him a look. "Thanks, man. Real comforting."

"Just saying," Ryan replied flatly, the edge of his lips twitching.

"Izzie?" Kyle called again.

"I'm over here."

Kyle exhaled, and then his face went pale. He stuck out his hand, halting Mike and his brothers.

"We're coming! It's Zack and I!" Kyle yelled, giving Mike, Ryan, and Luke a look to go with it. He went forward, vanishing beyond the trees.

Reluctantly, Zack followed. Mike noticed that the trail narrowed. The swamp trees closed in, their twisted branches knitted tightly together like a canopy of bones. Rough rocks lined the edges, intertwining between the trees. Together, they provided a natural barrier that blocked any path but the one before them.

They had to be ready for anything.

. . .

IZZIE

Dehuman? *What the heck is that?* The hairs on the back of my neck stood. Dravia cautiously approached me, hand in hand. Bushes on my left rustled as Kyle and Zack emerged, stopping a few feet away from us.

"You think your leaders are any better? That they care about you? At least Nemesis, Reiner that is, is honest about who we are. Ask yourself, Izzie— are they?"

Dravia appeared as any regular human, except for

her red skin. She had dark purple-tinted hair cut in a short bob. I held up my hands.

"Why are you so afraid? You've heard what I've said. We only want the best." She hesitated, her eyes darting between me and Kyle, and Zack. *"Say, will you join if I promise not to hurt your friend and brother?"*

"Whoa, wait, what?" My fake smile wavered. "Hurt them? How do you know one's my brother?"

"Come on. You know you're curious about us. Save them in exchange for yourself. It is a good deal." Dravia tsked.

The only way out of this place was where Kyle and Zack entered. If there really was no choice out of this, deep down, I knew what I'd do.

"Hey, Izzie," Kyle called fondly, walking beside me. He gave me a side hug, mouthing, "You alright?"

Zack scratched his head as he followed my twin, eyeing the Dehuman. The sword strapped at his side swayed with each step.

"Yes," I said. "She said she's Dehuman."

"A De-what?" Zack questioned, raising an eyebrow. "What kind of nonsense is that?"

"Dehuman. Do not ask me what the heck that is. I only know what she said."

Dravia tapped one foot, arms crossed. *Ya done yet? The most exciting part of our meeting was about to commence.*

Grass crunched behind me, followed by a loud inhale. Mike's shrill voice cut in, "Look out!"

A gust of wind knocked me to the ground as a needle whizzed over my head. A figure stumbled, scrambling and thrusting his hand out to Kyle, desperate to correct his aim. With my leg, I knocked Kyle's legs out from under him. He yelped in surprise as he dropped. The needle hissed through the air over his head. The owner backed next to his partner with a growl.

Wait, I recognize him. It's one of the guys from the unicorn. He's with Nemesis?

"You missed," Dravia mused, *"after I did all the work, you had one job and missed."*

The boy glared, muttering under his breath, *"Whatever."*

"My turn now," she announced. Lightning struck her in the chest. She staggered into her partner, yet recovered as if uninjured, brushing off her shirt. "What the heck was that?"

Zack's hand extended, eyes glowing. Sparks flickered off him as he smiled, taking in a deep breath. "Really? I heard your last words before we came in, and you think we were going to buy that? You tried to kill them!"

Mike strode into the clearing, unsheathing his sword. "Don't get too close, Zack. I don't know what she can do." He ended up next to his brother.

I shook off the dirt and got up, holding my hand out for Kyle. Dravia coughed, a large black mark appeared on her red neck.

Mike straightened, his voice cold. "Six against two, not great odds."

The Dehumans exchanged glances. "There are only four of you," the man pointed out.

Ryan and Luke stepped out of the foliage with their weapons out. "Six against two," Luke repeated, a smirk tugging at his lips. "Scram."

The boy scrambled to his feet and sprinted, slipping by Luke and Ryan.

"It's not over! Izzie, think about what I said." Dravia followed him, disappearing beyond the leaves. "The truth is rarely what it seems."

My arms went limp to my sides as the leaves slowly stopped shaking. Her words replayed in my mind. *Could Dravia be right? Could Nemesis actually be on the good side? She seemed to really believe it. What if everything I'd been fighting for was a lie?* I recalled the brothers, who saved me. Who saved Kyle. *They weren't evil either, though.*

I think both sides have their reasons. It's like that saying, all villains are heroes in their own story. Is miscommunication and mistrust why XXS and Nemesis are at war with each other? According to her, XXS was as bad as Nemesis had been. Something wasn't right... Could we all be in the wrong?

"Let's go, Izzie," Kyle said. "We're not done yet. Not by a long shot."

>>>>>>

Miles and hours later, we gathered around a small fire. Mike and Luke had caught a few small game with their powers, three rabbits and three squirrels, that cooked over the fire Zack started. The smell of roasting meat made my stomach growl.

"Whitney sent word through one of the scouts while we were out hunting," Mike informed. "The Nemesis is moving faster than expected."

"Not faster than me." Luke jumped in, jabbing the meat with a stick. "Well, we don't have time to waste."

Nodding, Mike took Ryan's dagger and pulled off a piece. "It should happen where it all started, wherever that was. But it's no longer an option. Apparently, all the people in XXS Clan have to be there, no exceptions."

"Seriously? It's expected to happen in about a month, or sooner." Zack took a bit of meat. "Is that enough time for all of us to show up?"

"Wait, how'd you get word about that again?" Kyle interjected next to me, frowning. "We have less than a month to stop them? Why not longer?"

"Spies are relaying the info. Timewise, I don't know," he admitted, shrugging. The chain on his neck poked through his shirt. "We were thinking of recruiting more help."

Final battle… Nemesis… "You think your leaders are any better?" Dravia said. "That they care about you? At least Nemesis is honest about who we are. Ask yourself, Izzie. Are they?"

Are we any better than them? They're trying to do what they think is best. Both sides are. That doesn't mean one is explicitly correct, right?

"What if—" I began softly, but clear enough to catch everyone's attention. "What if they aren't who we thought they were? I mean, people with magic… we're terrifying to humans. Nemesis wants to keep humankind safe, right?

Even if they've messed up stuff to do that."

"That's ridiculous," Ryan immediately snapped, straightening. "You definitely don't know half of it. How they do it is *wrong*. Nemesis experiments whenever given the chance, creating weapons designed to kill or control us. They treat us like monsters, freaks. Worse, they torture animals in order to create hybrids to fight us. They're cowards. If they were good, they'd find another way."

I swallowed. "What if they didn't have any other option? No, what if they *think* they have no other option?"

Fire burned in his eyes. A stick snapped in Luke's hand. Mike and Zack exchanged glances, yet Kyle placed a hand on my arm.

"The Nemesis," Luke cut in, his body tense. "Don't care if we have families or loved ones. They'll tear it all down. They'll fight us until we are under control or dead. They're the ones who want to hurt people, not us. All under the guise of 'saving' humans from those with powers."

"They have done terrible stuff, yes, but so has XXS." I shifted. "What have you seen—?"

"Seen?" Luke leaned forward, his hands clenched tightly. "My and Zack's best friends, Atticus and Alisha… they murdered them! With many others! You're questioning us now? After everything? How could you even think that?"

"Yes," Zack added softly, touching his chain necklace. "XXS has done terrible things, too. But not on the same scale as Nemesis. What we have done has almost *always* been in response to them."

I took a deep breath, twisting the fabric of my shirt. *I shouldn't have brought that up.* "Never mind, I'm sorry," I

176

muttered, tracking the scars on my arms. "Are we going back to where Whitney and XXS are?"

Ryan and Luke exchanged a glance.

Mike reluctantly nodded. "That would probably be the best start, though we still need to reach Nemesis's base. We could return to leave you guys at XXS than—"

Kyle slammed his hand on his leg. "Are you kidding? Leave us? Stop it, man. We are coming with you. How many times must we go through this?"

"We've survived until now. We're stronger than you think," I added carefully.

The brothers exchanged looks, and Zack rested his chin on his hand. "Look, if you stay with Whitney, you could get all of your powers figured out, heal, and practice fighting while we handle this mission. XXS is not a prison. Also, we won't have to worry about you, so it'll be easier for us to retrieve and free our members in addition to getting more intel on Nemesis."

Vision or not, they're trying to protect us. Kyle doesn't want to leave, I don't either, even though to them we're still kids. A kid who brought up scars on the Nemesis. And after the Unicorn... Arguing further might make things worse.

"You know what." I rubbed my forehead, glancing over my shoulder at Kyle. "Fine. We'll go back."

"Seriously?" Kyle questioned, wide-eyed, before catching himself. He looked at me. "I mean, if that's what you want."

"Yes." I locked eyes with him, giving him a small nod. "It won't be for long."

He swallowed hard. "Yeah, okay."

The brothers mumbled in agreement, and I suggested we head to bed.

Eventually, dreams claimed me. No, not dreams, nightmares. The blurred figure returned, fiddling with something on its neck. I backed up, the scene shifting. Terrifying screeches and noises of anger chased me as I slid down a rocky hill. At the bottom stood a shadow operating a control panel. There was nowhere to go.

The dream shifted, putting me with Kyle in my arms. Mom's face flashed to my sides, visible only in my peripheral vision. I have no idea why, but it was my fault. It was all my fault he's hurt or dead. Chills spread over my arms. I couldn't do anything to save him.

I was in a new place. Purple fog everywhere. I couldn't see anything, but I ran again. I ran so hard that I felt like collapsing. The same man, Lucas's leader, aimed his gun, shot, and I fell.

I woke up in a cold sweat. Shooting up, I almost hit my head on a low-hanging branch. Kyle slept beside me. Everyone else was sound asleep, too. *It was not real.*

The sky began to lighten, a faint glow creeping over the horizon. A leaf landed on my head, sending a shiver down my spine as my heart leapt. *You're just a little paranoid.* I knew I was not. But it's the only lie I can cling to.

Pollen drifted from the gold flowers nearby and settled on me as I stood. My stomach whined. I rummaged through Mike's bag, where he stored the rest of the meat, and found some leftovers to eat.

The nightmares. I squeezed my eyes tightly, trying

178

to steady my heavy breathing. *What if they're visions? What if the Nemesis was on the good side and we have been tricked? Why does everything have to be so complicated?*

I nudged my brother awake, the warmth of his body seeping into my hands as the morning air clung to us. His eyes fluttered open, and he groaned. "Get up," I whispered. Kyle squinted, rubbing his face and stretching.

I moved to the others, crouching beside Mike and Zack, and woke them simultaneously. Zack's sleeveless jacket felt smooth. Mike stirred first, blinking wearily.

"Ugh, already? Why?" Zack complained, rolling onto his back.

I didn't answer. After confirming Luke and Ryan, who grunted, awoke, they ate the remnants of last night's hunt, then packed up and set out.

I pulled in front, with my brother beside me, the others trailing. The scent of earth and damp leaves filled the air. New mountains loomed in the distance, faint and hazy against the early morning sky. I knew the general direction, but Mike or one of his brothers would have to take the lead later.

Twigs snapped and crunched underfoot while we walked. The sun blazed down, not yet fully risen, but already hot enough to fry an egg. Its rays cast long shadows across the forest floor. To my right, I see my brother grinning, his attention towards the distance. *I wonder what he's thinking about.* Before long, Mike took the lead. The conversations in the group kept fairly quiet as we stayed alert.

Our journey stretched across two days. The

landscape shifted around us from the mushy wetlands, back to the moorlands, and eventually to the forest. During the day, we practiced our powers and fought, sometimes playfully, against each other. It was almost muscle memory at this point.

At night, we huddled around fires, talking and laughing in quiet voices. Kyle and Luke took turns telling stories, some based on real life, others not so much. For those few hours under the stars, it almost felt normal.

What if we fail? What if mom comes back?

On the second morning, the trees grew thinner again, the path steepened as we neared the base of the mountains. Kyle's usual smile had faded to a neutral expression. He didn't want to leave the brothers. I didn't either, but the Unicorn and Dravia changed their minds.

We only wanted what was best. I recalled Dravia's voice, almost as freshly as if she were next to me.

"I can still communicate with you, Izzie."

What? I almost collided with Luke as he stumbled down a slope. I paused, rubbing my eyes as Zack pulled ahead of me. *Am I hallucinating?*

"Don't fret, you're fine," she cooed. *"Now, remember our conversation? What do you say about the Nemesis? About our goal to protect humans from people like you?"*

Where are you? I looked around. Silence. *I'm sorry, Nemesis is wrong. Killing and capturing people who've done nothing is terrible, no matter the reason.*

"XXS is no better! You do the same," Dravia repeated. *"The public is on our side for a reason."*

180

The public is scared. I pointed out, falling into step beside Ryan and Kyle. *And the people I know, XXS, would never do anything remotely as bad as you.*

"You're a danger, and you fight back," Dravia shrieked. *"What else are we supposed to do?"*

Have you tried talking? I reached the end of the slope. *What you do isn't right. XXS, these people, aren't a danger. We want to survive.*

"You've made up your mind then," her voice faded. Dots danced in my vision. I blinked, breathing easier as Zack climbed over a log. I was right after him. The hair on the back of my neck pricked.

We aren't alone.

"How much longer?" Kyle questioned, placing a hand on my shoulder.

Mike huffed, "About another day."

The distant animal noises died. Flashes of light crossed my vision. A high whistle echoed, cutting through the air like a blade. I yanked Zack back, a dart embedding itself into a small tree, inches from where he had been standing. Another whistle followed, and another.

"Get down!" I shouted, crouching.

Letting go of my shoulder, my brother crouched at my side and then crumbled, a dart embedded in his shoulder. "Kyle?" Ryan called, balancing on a rock ahead.

"Out to our left, we're being followed!" I shouted, laying a hand on Kyle's neck. *He's not dead. Thank God.*

Right beside me, Zack folded next. "Zack?!" Luke called. "Wait, Ryan! Watch—" He darted in front of Ryan,

181

shielding him as a dart pierced his shoulder.

"Izzie, do you know where they are?" Mike shouted, the wind rushing at my sides. He faced Ryan. "Ryan, take cover!" I crawled to Zack, a dart protruding from his shoulder, and felt his pulse.

"Even if I did, they're moving around and are prepared. We'll have to look and get Zack, Luke, and Kyle to a safe spot!"

Night lured me as I slumped onto the ground with the others.

>>>

Bruises covered my body. Minutes ago, I awoke on the ground in the back of a van, unable to move no matter how hard I tried. A groan escaped my lips.

"Right, you're awake," one of the guards grunted. He wore a blue-purple uniform with a utility belt and a tag on his shirt that I barely made out. *Nemesis Umbra Regiment-Operative. Captain.* The man came over and lifted me onto a seat. Only Mike rode with me, not counting the three Umbra Soldiers in the van.

"Iz, you're alright!" he gasped, the tension in his pale, sweat-soaked face relaxed. His golden-rimmed eyes had bags under them. A wire ran from his arm to a box next to the feet of an Umbra Soldier.

"So." My vision blurred, a pinch in my arm signaling I was being hooked up to a similar device. Yet mine was smaller. "What happened? Where are the others? Where's Kyle?" The Umbra Captain laughed.

"Could you be any more pathetic?" the Umbra

182

Captain sneered, adjusting his sword. "Instead of worrying about your brothers, maybe you should do something useful and escape. Or ya know, shut up."

Okay, he's immature and rude. Wait a second— brothers? They're assuming we're siblings? Mike caught my attention, urging me to stay calm. I took a deep breath.

Even in this situation, I must keep it together. I do what Mike asks, drowning out the Umbra Soldiers' mocking laughter. The Umbra Captain sat next to me. For the next ten minutes, I listen to the road, the van rumbling beneath us.

Mike cleared his throat, drawing my attention. "Where are we going?"

"Wouldn't you like to know?" The Umbra Captain tapped the metal side.

I narrowed my eyes. "What's going to happen to us?"

At the back, a second Umbra Soldier leaned against his partner, who examined us with hawk-like eyes. "You'll see soon enough."

I need to do something. But how can we escape and save the others?

A while later, the van came to a halt. I was still immobilized as the back doors slowly opened, revealing an additional three Umbra Soldiers with guns poised. Mike scoffed as the Umbra Soldier with hawk eyes took him off the wire, handcuffed him, and hauled him out of the van. Next, they unhooked me and handcuffed me. The black handcuffs felt like a mix of wood and metal. They dragged me out, slamming my leg against the door.

183

As the Umbra Soldiers pulled me along, the effect of the drug began to wear off, and I regained control of my body. It tingled, still heavy to use, though I had little to no energy to do so.

They tossed me into a dark cage, and I hit the cold, hard floor as the door clanged shut. The air reeked of mildew as I spotted Kyle, eyes closed, slumped against the wall, hands also cuffed. His face was carefully neutral, yet I knew him well enough to know he was terrified.

We both knew showing that made it worse.

I sat next to him. The cage squealed open as Luke got thrown in. His eyes met mine, face and clothing plastered with dirt.

"What'd you do?" I asked.

He kicked the floor. "I tried to escape with my speed. Turns out that whatever they gave me slowed me down. So yeah, that's my bad. Now we have no chance, ebony weakens our powers."

"Ebony?" I gazed at the handcuffs. "Isn't that wood?"

Luke nodded, holding up his cuffed wrists. "Metal is intertwined with it, so we can't break free."

Kyle brought his legs close to his chest. "Did you get hurt?"

Shaking his head, Luke paced and sat against the side wall. "No, but we have to get out of here."

One of us could die. I tensed, squinting. *No, I won't let that happen.*

Luke wiped some of the dirt off his face. "Maybe we could get some rest to pass the time," he suggested.

"Yeah," I sighed, touching the rough concrete wall. "Though, there's only one bench in this cell."

"How about I take the floor, and you can have the bench?" Kyle offered, arching his back in a yawn.

"I'm too tired to argue with you. I don't want it, you take it."

"That's an idea," Luke ran a hand down his face. Kyle went over and flopped down. He shifted, trying to find a comfortable position.

I eventually go to the corner next to Luke. "Night, guys. This may be one of the last times we can rest," Kyle mentioned offhandedly.

The wall was uncomfortable, but exhaustion and boredom pulled me into a restless sleep.

>>>

I jolted awake by the creak of the metal bars.

Five Umbra Soldiers crowded outside. Entering the room, one of them grunted, motioning for us to exit. Luke twitched as I nudged him with my foot. "C'mon."

Kyle was already outside when I joined. The woman Umbra Soldier, who apparently thought we were taking too long, shoved Luke into me. He quickly backed away, brushing his shirt.

Shadows danced along the walls like they were following us as they led us through several corners. A sharp metallic scent hung in the air. We arrived in a room, overlooking a glass chamber. Inside, Ryan and Zack were tied facing the glass.

Mike wasn't anywhere to be seen.

Zack spotted us and shook his head. "I am glad you three are okay. We still do not know where Mike is."

Luke nodded, slowing his voice. "We're glad you're okay too. Do—do you think that—?"

A bang interrupted him. Inside the glass chamber, Mike appeared from a metal door, his brown hair a disheveled mess. *He looks exhausted.* Ryan abruptly rose, but one of the Umbra Soldiers shoved him back. Mike faced us, eyes wide and his chest rapidly rising and falling.

A low groan spread throughout the walls, with growing wind howling against them.

None of us could do anything to help him.

Zack's mouth pressed in a firm line as he stared intently through the glass. Luke's body tensed. My twin didn't move a muscle. Lights flickered in the containment, and Mike backed against a wall.

Ryan clenched his fists. "What are they doing to him?!"

A new Umbra Soldier, with a deep purple uniform cut in front of us, his eyes gleaming as he surveyed our expressions. His tag read *Agent.* "Experimenting with you! We want to put you all against your limits here! All to keep humanity safe from you freaks."

"You think we're freaks? We're stronger than you'll ever be," Luke shot back. "Hurt my brother and I'll prove it."

I went stiff. Mike knelt, eyes glowing white and gray. The noise of wind intensified, battering against the walls. The glass vibrated. He opened his mouth, tightly shutting his eyes. *It's forcing him to use his powers to their full extent.*

186

Can I break the glass? How do I get him out of there?

"Turn it off!" Kyle cried, pounding on the glass.

"You're hurting him!" I exclaimed, rising to my feet.

Strong hands shoved me back down. I struck the floor, rolling onto my back between Zack and Ryan. The Umbra Agent towered over me, his glare like ice.

Zack pulled me towards him without taking his eyes off Mike, who lay on the ground now, hands clutched over his head. He struggled less and less, growing still. A tear slipped down my cheek as I watched what I feared to be Mike slowly dying. The tension in the room became so thick I could cut through it like butter. His brothers struggled to keep it together, too.

. . .

MIKE

"That was inhumane," Ryan murmured, voice tight.

The agony of that chamber... *augh.* Mike's head throbbed from the memory. He'd never wish that pain on anyone. And he knew what he felt wasn't the worst of it. It was at *half.*

He lay on a cold, hard, metal bench. Probably inside the same cell from earlier.

"I could barely stop myself from putting us all at risk. I thought he died," Zack's voice broke off. "He still might."

Mike groaned as he pushed himself up, forcing a weak smile. "Nope, not dead yet. Were you hoping for something else?"

187

Ryan and Zack stared at him.

"Don't sit up so fast." Ryan stood, walking over to him.

"Mike, you are okay," Zack gasped at the same time, his voice strangled.

"Hey Zack, miss me?" Mike tried to grin, but it faltered, and he lowered his head. "What did you do? Is everyone okay?"

The thought of the Umbra Soldiers hurting any of them when he was trapped in there...

A metallic tinge lingered in his nose, enough to taste it. Scratching the back of his head, Zack replied hesitantly, "Do not worry, we are okay. That is all you need to know. How are you, Mike?"

He knew his brother well enough. They were not okay. They were just not telling him.

Memories seared his head— his wind lashing out, the horrifying realization of what he could've done clawing at him, twisting his gut. He can't let that happen again. Especially when the machine can get worse, and it most definitely could.

His stiff posture signaled to the others to drop the subject. "Get ready for tomorrow then," Ryan sighed, "Another one of us is up."

Perhaps it will be better. Mike attempted to convince himself. He shivered. *It was hopeless to stop it.* He couldn't prevent them, the Nemesis. It only made things worse for his group. Rubbing his thumb against his palm, Mike strained against the ebony ropes.

I'll have to search for an opening, any possibility for us to escape. And he had to do it soon, for who knows who's next? *Hopefully, it will be better for them than it was for me.* He had to believe that.

Chapter 15

IZZIE

I shivered, clouds of air forming before my nose. They were going to take us to the glass cage again. This time, it was my turn.

The door slammed against the wall, echoing in the cold, sterile hallway.

It already happened to Zack, Luke, and Ryan. Zack took out their lights, and Luke ran himself almost dead. For Ryan, they brought in numerous injured soldiers and hybrids, which he involuntarily healed.

An Umbra Captain, the one from the van, dragged me through a brightly lit maze of machines and gears. The clanking of metal against metal and footsteps rang in my ears. A faint scent of chemicals burned my nose. We arrived at a door, and my handcuffs were taken off. Sweat brimmed my brow, running down my back.

A girl in a white coat approached me, holding a vial. A glass full of liquid sloshing against the sides. She held it out. "Drink."

I declined. That was the wrong answer. Her hands

clutched around my mouth, forcing it open. She poured it down and waited. I swallowed and gagged, the bitter taste making me want to retch as it slid down my throat.

She smirked. The door unlocked with a click. The girl shoved me through, slamming it behind me.

Mirrors covered the wall where the glass should have been, showing my frayed, long black hair, torn clothes, and tan skin.

It's a one-way mirror.

The rest of the walls were pure white, with yellow lights on the roof and gray concrete flooring. I spun in a circle, waiting. The pit in my stomach grew harder to ignore. Low rumbling noises filled the walls, and the lights began flickering.

No visions or expected pain came. I scanned the room, then the door. *Isn't something supposed to happen?* The rumbling stopped, and the scent of smoke wafted to my nose.

"Huh," I breathed. *This is normal, right?*

The girl entered the room, another vial in her hand. "What's going on?" I asked.

No response. She held the glass vial out to me. I drank it and she left.

The rumbling switched on again, louder, and the walls violently vibrated. If I hadn't known about the machines, I would've thought it was an earthquake.

Lights swirled from the ceiling. I tilted my head back, a twitch slithering in my shoulders. Staggering to the side, I managed to keep myself from falling. High-pitched ringing filled my ears. *What the heck?! This isn't... foresight.*

The noise intensified. In the reflection was a girl with wide, cloudy blue eyes, mouth slightly agape. I can hardly recognize her. Her hair and loose-fit shirt billowed everywhere.

The walls proceeded to vibrate uncontrollably. A sharp pain stabbed and twisted my back, up my spine. Heat flooded through my veins. Folding my arms tightly against my chest, I shut my eyes.

The fabric in the back of my shirt tore open. I stumbled, slamming into a wall, something attached to my back bending. *Kyle...* My eyes watered, yet my body felt lighter and more energized. *I don't know if I can control it.*

. . .

MIKE

"What?!" Ryan confounded, stared at Izzie's raven black bird wings, extended in size to fit her exactly. "Wings? *Ikris* wings? I mean, yeah, I expected that."

Black feathers gleamed in the lights. Izzie thrashed her head, hands running through her hair. He blinked, rubbing his thumb against his palm. *How is she...?*

Umbra Soldiers around him shouted orders, frantically going about the room he was in, their voices becoming distant from Mike's thoughts.

She couldn't be. Ikris are extinct. It makes no sense.

The building groaned as an explosion reverberated nearby, sending Umbra Soldiers scattering. All of the Umbra Soldiers in the room vanished out the door.

Cowards. Mike stood, quickly making sure his

brothers and Kyle were still with him. The one-way glass separating them from Izzie collapsed, shards raining down and shattering on impact. The drywall around Mike burst into flames but managed to hold their form.

"Kyle!" Izzie yelped as he jumped to her.

Flames roared around them. The heat seared on Mike's back, sweat already brimming on his brow. A shard of glass hit his foot, skitting to Zack's foot. Picking another up, Mike used it to cut at the wood in the handcuffs, loosening it enough for him to slide it off.

His brothers and Kyle mimicked what he did. Mike skimmed the area for an opening. Flames arched from every side, smoke curling, filling the room. The ceiling above Izzie broke, part of it crumbling to the ground, missing her. *There.*

"Izzie!" Mike shouted, climbing over the glass and down to the broken room. A piece sliced his elbow. "We have to get out of here!"

"There's no way out!" She brought her hands to her face. He pointed at the sky, locking eyes with her. After a few moments, she shook her head. "No, are you suggesting I fly us out? Is there even enough room?" Warily, Izzie touched her wings, flapping them unevenly.

Mike scrambled, rescanning the building to find an easier way. "It's the only way out."

"What about your wind?" She raised an eyebrow, but he shook his head.

"It will feed the fire or kill us from lack of oxygen," his brother Zack coughed. The smoke thickened around them. "Unless Mike already mastered air control in tight

193

spaces."

Izzie's lips pressed into a line. "If it's our only option." She tilted her head to the sky. "I don't even know how to use these things." With a few unsteady flaps, Izzie rose off the ground, awkward and uncoordinated. She veered to the side, then the other before regaining control and landing roughly next to him. "Who's first to risk their life with a bird-human?"

Mike exchanged glances with his brothers. Luke stepped forward as Kyle raised his hand. "I'll go. I probably weigh the least, and if I fall, I can try to teleport myself."

"Wait, why can't you teleport us out instead?" Luke asked, placing a hand on Kyle's shoulder. "That would probably be a better idea."

"I've never teleported someone with me before, and it can only be within my eyesight, including a limited range." Kyle stepped next to his sister. "Plus, doing it too much gives me motion sickness."

Izzie nodded, breathing in deeply. Hugging him around the waist, Kyle wrapped his arms around her neck in turn. She took off. Shakily, they went through the gap in the ceiling, vanishing beyond the walls. More chunks of ceiling peeled off, the whole room became engulfed. Minutes later, she reappeared.

"Okay," Izzie panted, placing her hands on her knees. "Who's next?"

Luke volunteered. She went around his waist and took off with him, staggering before they ascended.

"Do you think this is too much?" Ryan arrived at Mike's side. "Is there no other way?"

He watched her and his little brother vanish. "I don't know. I think she can handle it."

Unconvinced, his brother toed at the dirt. A soft landing puffed the dust into the cloud as Izzie landed. The fire crept closer and the smoke grew lower. She quickly grabbed Ryan, slightly higher than the waist, and took off.

The hot flames made a deadly circle around them. Zack stumbled into Mike, eyes streaming from the smoke. "I do not think she will get us both in time," his brother wheezed.

"Then you go without me," Mike insisted without hesitation. *Please hurry.*

He wiped his eyes. "Not happening. They need you more."

Finally, Izzie reappeared, hovering above them. Zack's wheezing switched into coughing. Mike's own throat felt like sandpaper rubbing against it.

Dropping between them, she clenched her teeth. "If I take one of you, the other will die."

"Take Zack," Mike rasped.

His brother shook his head. "No, take Mike." Zack pushed Izzie toward him

Looking between them, her ear twitched. "Stop it. Both of you come here. I'm going to try to take both of you."

Mike held up his hands. "Look, we'll be too heavy! It won't work. Take Zack—"

The second wall from the right started to crash. Almost immediately, Mike felt himself lifted into the air, Izzie's grip tight around his wrist. Wind brushed his face, welcoming him.

With a strong start, she cleared the now large gap and hovered two inches above the tip of the inferno. Her grip faltered for a second as she tried to fly them to the side.

How is she carrying both of us? Did she get strength too? Mike glanced up. Izzie's brow furrowed, her nose scrunched, and her teeth clenched. Air ripped between them. She struggled to keep them aloft, her wings beat slower, and a tremor ran through her arm.

The heat rising from below licked at his feet, the flames napping closer. Izzie's breath hitched, barely audible over the wind. She regripped Mike's wrist, sweat already loosening her hold as they dipped lower.

She can't keep this up for long. We're too heavy. It's either none of us or two. I know what I have to do. Her and Zack's hands slipped before he initiated his plan.

"Zack!" Mike cried, reaching out as his brother plummeted. Almost in slow motion, his brother with outstretched hands, back facing the flames as he fell.

Mike instinctively arched his hand, bending the air to slow Zack's fall. It was not enough. Izzie hovered lower, hesitating as the flames consumed Zack. His feet touched the ground, and he dropped to his knees. A hand stuck in the air, waving them off.

Please get out of there! Please, don't die... Zack—

The land shifted underneath Mike as Izzie frantically tried to clear the building entirely.

"No! We have to get Zack!" Mike shouted. She didn't respond, but the altitude faltered again as they sank lower.

196

We have to go back. We need to save him. Mike clenched his teeth, extending his arm where he last saw Zack.

No, it's useless. His brother is as good as dead.

Tears broke free, and he swept his hand, bringing the wind up. Her eyes met his briefly as she ascended and crossed over the flames, slowly gliding over the other side.

He failed yet another person.

. . .

IZZIE

We made it.

But I dropped Zack.

Exhaustion coursed through my body like a stone as I landed. Letting go of Mike, I stumbled backward, collapsing onto sweet dirt. I gasped for air, recalling Zack's hand slipping from mine. Over and over. The times he reacted to our pranks. Our conversations. How he cared about me, us, and had our backs. And now...

"Where's Zack?" Luke asked. His wide eyes darted between me and the fire raging in the distance, hands trembling. "Izzie, you have to go after him!"

My wings trembled, folding at my sides as my throat closed. It took a second for someone to respond.

"He— fell," Mike admitted, hacking into his hand. His voice broke, and tears streamed down his cheeks. "There's too much fire now. It won't be safe."

"N-no," I coughed, pulling myself to my feet and bracing against a tree. "You guys go farther from here to be able to breathe and be safe in case there's an explosion. I'll head back and find him. I have to." I spread my wings. *I can't leave him there.*

"No, Izzie," Ryan said sharply and caught my wrist. His brown eyes flicked over my face, teeth clenched. "You can't. There's too much smoke, you won't be able to breathe."

"Neither will Zack," I argued. I yanked back my hand. "I have to get him. I left him there, and he will die because I…"

Mike wiped ash from his face. "She's right. His chances of survival are slim." His voice softened, lowering his gaze to me. "I can't let him die, but going after him is too risky."

"I'll be fine!" I prepared myself to take flight, my wings aching. Smoke stung my eyes, and each breath clawed at my throat. "I won't leave him!"

"Iz, wait!" Kyle approached me. I lowered my wings. "No matter how much you think you need to, you shouldn't go after him. You heard Mike! There's too much smoke and the fires are too hot! You'll die too. Please, I can't have you die. I need you."

"It doesn't matter if—" I coughed again, folding back my wings and staring at the flames. "If I die too. I have to save him."

Luke stepped forward, his hand trembling as he placed it on my shoulder. His eyes were puffy, avoiding my gaze, tears streaking down his face. "You've done enough. We just have to hope Zack gets out safely." His voice cracked as he turned to the fire. "Zack's strong. He'll find a way."

I shook my head, blinking back tears. *It's your fault.*

198

Your fault if he dies. You didn't save him.

I'm so sorry, Zack.

Mike hacked and I faced him, seeing his eyes redden and watering. Ryan stood next to him, his freckled cheeks blushed. Behind, dull dark gray smoke floated out of the building.

I glanced at Kyle, who looked as worn out as I felt. Luke, still next to me, sniffed, face blank, tears streaming down his cheeks. He wiped them away with his arm.

"What do we do?" Kyle whispered, his voice cracking as Mike's hacking increased. "Zack is gone. We have no medicine, immediate food, or weapons, no idea where to go."

Luke forced a tight smile. "At least we don't have to worry about dinner. I think my lungs are full enough of smoke to last a week."

An explosion erupted from the building, sending debris raining down.

"Let's get out of here," Mike said curtly, his voice catching. "After it dies down, we will look for Zack."

Luke walked past me, adding underneath his breath, "And he better not be dead."

>>>

Clutching his throat, Mike climbed after Luke down the rocky slope. None of us had said a word for the past hour, our shoulders slouched and heads bowed.

My wings shook. They felt large, and my back ached. Well, my whole body ached, but it stayed more prevalent there. Dust and brackish wet stone crept into my nose as I shuffled after Mike. Right by me, I hear a rip from Kyle's shirt.

"Dang," he muttered, frowning at it.

"It's not that bad." I tried to reassure him, rolling my shoulders and leaning back against the stone for a second.

"Not that bad," he repeated with a huff.

"My shirt ripped too. At least you're a man, so it's no big deal."

"I guess, yeah," Kyle agreed, stepping off the last few rocks. He reached to touch my wings. "If it's cool, I want to examine your wings more closely. They look sick."

Without a word, Ryan nudged me forward.

Is he mad at me? I wouldn't blame him. Crawling down the last few rocks, I stood under the shade of a tree. A burnt smell lingered in my nose. *If Zack somehow survived, do you think he would hate me too? Why wouldn't he?*

What use am I if I can't save everyone?

Mike and Luke were already further along the path as we caught up to them. Mike's coughing subsided, though his breath still rasped, coming in gulps and mimicking a cat's hiss. Blood painted his elbow. His lips wavered as he stopped to wait for us.

On the other hand, Luke ran his fingers over his face with measured breaths. His dark gray, golden-rimmed eyes focused on the ground, his blond hair sticking out all over.

Ryan moved behind me, instructing me to lie down on my stomach. His hands gingerly touched my wings, moving around cautiously. I flicked them a little bit, causing him to flinch.

200

"These are bird wings, but stronger. Ikris wings..." he observed, his voice distant.

"Ikris wings?"

"It's—" Ryan gulped, taking a second. "It's like humans with bird wings... I'll tell you later. How are you feeling?"

"I don't know," I said, sitting back up and straightening what's left of my shirt. "I'm better than Mike and Zack. Then again, I'm still alive."

Ryan's breath caught, and he leveled his face. "No, not that, I meant from the machine. Are you okay?"

"Oh," I paused. "It didn't work on me, well, in the sense of having no visions."

"Huh," he wiped his nose. "Perhaps the wings make your powers stronger."

"The first time it wasn't full power," Luke added, coming in front of me and squatting. His golden-rimmed gray eyes didn't hold the same light they once did. "The second time, Nemesis went all in. That's why your wings came and it overloaded, causing the explosion."

"Does it hurt?" Ryan pushed, giving Luke his look.

"Like hell, but not anymore," I lied, standing back up. I lowered my voice so only he could hear. "Please check on Mike. I'm worried about him."

"I will," Ryan sighed, blinking away a shine crossing his eyes. He placed a hand on Mike's back and guided him away. Luke tilted his head but left to join his brothers.

Kyle touched my shoulder. "Let me look at your back again." I turned, and the light touch of his hands froze.

"How did Ryan not notice?"

"Notice what?" He didn't respond. "Notice— what?" I repeated.

"You have a decent cut along your back. My guess is it's from the glass. Your shirt's barely covering it."

He probably was distracted by Zack.

"Is it bleeding?"

"Slightly. I'm guessing it doesn't hurt then?"

"It should be fine. It is not the most important thing right now." I brushed my shredded shirt and jeans. "We should go check on Mike." Without waiting for an answer, I strolled over.

Kyle jogged a little to catch up. "Wait, didn't you breathe in smoke too? How are you?"

"Don't worry, I'm fine," I insisted, brushing off his question. *At least I'm not dead.*

"Even with what happened to Zack?"

"I tried to go back for him."

"I know," Kyle fell silent for a moment. I forced my shoulders to relax as he scratched his forehead. "I wish I could've done something back there. To save or help anyone."

I slowed and touched his arm. "Are you okay?"

"Yeah," Kyle answered absently.

"Not convincing."

"You already know I'm worried about you. About all of this. And that's obvious enough to go without saying."

In the distance, Mike and Ryan sat across from each other. Ryan felt his brother's chest, while Luke held out a few different leaves.

"I'm good," I insisted, heading to the brothers. "Let's worry about one thing at a time." My brother fell into step with me, and I caught his hand. "Look, I'm sorry I dragged you into this mess. I'm sorry I wasn't able to save Zack. I'm especially sorry for you getting hurt. If I had been..."

"Anything's better than that place. Thank you for getting me out of there." He shuddered. "And don't give yourself so much credit. I know you wanted to save him as badly as any of us."

We reached them. Mike pinched the bridge of his nose while Ryan sat back.

Kyle adjusted his collared shirt. "How is he?"

"Good for now. We have to go a little farther before we can rest. Then I need to inspect everyone to make sure we're good after—" Ryan closed his eyes, a single tear streaking down his cheek. He quickly wiped it away.

Luke helped Mike to his feet. "Where do you suppose we'll go?"

"I-I'm not sure," Ryan sighed. "We need a plan, though we have to keep getting away from the building."

"Then let's keep going in the same direction." Luke paced ahead.

"We can't just wander without knowing what's out there," Ryan pointed out.

I glanced between the two. Mike shook his head but didn't speak, his breathing still heavy.

"You said it yourself, we can't stay here. They'll find us." Luke narrowed his eyes. "We don't have much time."

"What happens if we aren't careful and run into another disaster?" Ryan's voice broke. "We aren't prepared."

"We've managed so far," Luke snapped, folding his arms. His posture softened, and he raked his fingers through his hair. "I get you're worried. We'll try to be as careful as we can. But we need to go."

Ryan narrowed his eyes, then nodded. I began the way through a trail, weaving every so often. We veered off it yards later, so it would not be easy to follow us if the Nemesis ever came looking.

We went by a few streams leading to a river. It was beautiful, yet the river's current pulled itself toward the ruin behind us. The air around it carried a bitter staleness like ash long settled. Luke tried to lighten the mood. "We should try and jump over it. Backwards river, right?"

Ryan and Mike declined. So, tracking the riverbank we went. The sun fell from high in the sky to setting by the time we slowed our pace. My twin eventually claimed we've gone far enough, and we found a cut-off hidden from most angles. A stiff tinge of mud by the river hung in the air.

Mike slumped against a tree, his breaths still like an old grandpa with a sore throat. He tucked his head into his arm. Ryan stood at his side, eyes vacant of emotion as he crouched and fiddled with some bushes that had berries.

Luke stuck with them, a few feet away. His brows furrowed, mouth pressed in a line. A stick firmly in his hand, Luke dug at the dirt, revealing several scratches on his face. One had a line of blood trailing down it.

Kyle and I were left to ourselves. I tucked my wings against my back with an exhale, recalling the fire. My sweaty hand slipped from Zack's. Despite how hard I squeezed, I couldn't hold on. He was inches, then feet away. Mike's cry as his brother fell, pleading to get him.

Yawning, I rubbed my eyes. *I can't forgive myself for leaving him.* The numbness in my arms and back left, leaving my body in pain and pressure in my chest. The cut did hurt, and I was light-headed, but I didn't deserve to take a break. Not with Zack still out there.

I mean, we have no food, and they need rest. I can cover more ground alone and know the area.

No, I shouldn't leave them. Kyle, the brothers. They'll never forgive me if something happened. But Zack... what if I miss the only chance to save him? I will take the blame and the consequences for losing him. And, to make up for it, I will go back to search. If the fires are still going, I can fly above the flames. He won't die, not if I can help it.

Kyle sat on his legs across from where I stood. Scratches stretched across his arms, a few specks of glass still shimmering on them.

I squatted next to him, using my arms to steady myself as dots spread across my vision. "I'm going to go look for some more food. If the guys ask where I went, tell them I'll be back in a minute."

He caught my leg. "Wait, I should go with you."

"I need time alone. I'll be back soon." I took off, taking care to go in a straight line.

I ended back at the trail, full of abnormal pitch-black rocks jammed to fit the path, unlike the regular

205

gravel picked one up and turned it in my hand, rubbing my thumb over its smooth surface before dropping it back to the ground. *Don't get distracted. I have to hurry.*

Bright light flooded over my eyes. Like a haze, Nemesis gathered next to their burnt-down building. One of them, a scientist I guessed by the labcoat, pointed to some of our footprints, leading the way to the rocky hill. Another, with a dark purple trench coat lined in gold, stood next to someone tied up with a bag around their face. He had neck tattoos with his hair that looked like a black mop. I focus harder on the trail. The one I was on now.

"Yeah—Gone down—Probably right— Dangerous— Didn't know—"

Gone down? Do they mean—? *Heck. Which direction did I come from?*

The scene shifted into two very different areas, fading within one another. Part of it was the brothers and my twin getting attacked with the darts, yet I wasn't there. The other showed me getting captured, but they went uncaught.

I rubbed my eyes, being brought back to the pitch-black rocks under my feet. *What was that a vision?* A thick burning smell crossed my nose. *Probably. I have to move, but I also need to find Zack.* Twisting, my already ruined shirt got snagged on a rock, tearing half of it off. A gunshot pierced the air, a cold dart pinching my arm. It was the last thing I remember before I blacked out.

. . .

MIKE

Mike chewed the berries as Ryan handed them to him.

206

His chest and shoulders weighed in on him, tears constantly threatened to break free. *Nemesis took all our supplies. Took my brother.* All he wanted now was sleep. After all that happened in the Nemesis's second headquarters, he wanted it over with. *Please, please let Zack be alive.*

Kyle went to Ryan, whispering. Ryan replied, then told Mike to get some rest. No protesting entered his mind as he drifted off.

A gunshot snapped him awake from his dream. Ryan was already on his feet, scanning the trees. Luke blurred to his side. They crowded around the tree, bewildered. Mike pushed himself up; the roughness in his chest there yet lessened during the night. Kyle fidgeted, squinting, and suddenly bolted toward the sound.

"Kyle, stop!" Luke went after him, catching his shoulder. "Do you want to get hurt or caught?"

"I-I," His voice cracked. "We need to go get her. This can't happen. Why did I let her go alone?"

"We don't even know it's her, but I know it's hard," Luke's voice broke, and he quickly wiped his eyes.

Ryan caught Mike's attention. "If they already have her, there's a good chance they'll get us, too. We have to leave."

"B-but what about Izzie and Zack?" Kyle's voice trembled. "Let's go get them. Or I will."

"Kyle, stop running off blindly. If we go after her without a plan, we're putting everyone at risk," Ryan pointed out sharply.

Mike tugged his hair, torn between saving his

brother and Izzie, and the responsibility for everyone's safety. *Damn it, Izzie. Why didn't you stay?*

Mike knew Izzie was strong, but they couldn't lose her either. "We can look, but we're not rushing in or attacking. If we find her, then we get the hell out of there. If she's gone, we'll regroup and carefully search the base. Remember to be quiet and careful, or else we won't have a chance at getting them back."

Chapter 16

IZZIE

My wrists were tied tightly behind my back, cutting into my skin. My wings were missing, and a strange emptiness settled between my shoulder blades. *Where'd my wings go? Did Nemesis…?*

The metal chair dug into the back of my legs, its surface slick with condensation. Across from me sat a man in a crisp purple and black uniform, his silver Nemesis insignia catching the faint overhead light. His smile was thin and calculated.

"Ikris huh?" he began, his voice smooth like oiled leather. "Special, that. Do you know why?"

Special? I stifled a snort. *I'm tied to a chair in a room that reeks of damp metal with no wings, and my brother and friends are in danger.* I bit the inside of my cheek, refusing to meet his eyes. His tone hooked the edges of my thoughts, tugging at a small, unwanted thread of curiosity.

"Come now," he coaxed, leaning forward. "You're Ikris. But you've been lied to—hunted, manipulated. We're not your enemy. We're the only ones who can help you."

"Help me? By kidnapping me? By threatening my

brother and friends? What about that says you can 'help me?'"

He chuckled softly, shaking his head. "We're not the monsters those brothers made us out to be. Magic is dangerous, yes, but only when left unchecked. If you let us, we can teach you control. You'd never have to fear hurting anyone. In turn, you'll help us round up other dangerous scum with no control."

He spoke as if he believed his words, as if Nemesis wasn't responsible for the destruction and terror I'd witnessed.

"I don't believe you," I stated firmly, twisting my wrists and feet to test the rope.

"You don't have to believe me. But you will see. Soon enough." He exited.

The gray ceramic walls had only one door and a black window to my right. Pressing my feet back against the chair, I managed to stand. A headache built as I looked down, a wave of spinning images washing over me. Half of my shirt was missing, looking like a crop top with holes in the back.

The door swung open, and Jane entered, her white lab coat swaying. A blue tablet was held in her hand. She glanced at me, then back down at it.

"Good, now that you're awake, we can begin," she said flatly. She retreated to the exit.

"Wait—"

"It would be a good idea for you to sit. Or don't, I don't care."

The door slammed before I got another word in. I sank back into the chair. Lights powered on and flashed. The walls hummed to life, sounding more like an AC unit than the earthquake roar where I got my wings. A strange sensation slithered inside me, tugging away a piece of energy. I clung to it, strained, but it slipped through my grasp. It escaped, leaving me breathless. An emptiness replaced it. The machines groaned and switched off, along with the extra lights.

Minutes later, footsteps echoed from outside the door. Jane reappeared, smiling. Typing on her tablet, she went to a far wall and opened a latch, revealing a panel with buttons. She clicked a few. A glass-like feature went over the black window, revealing a man on the other side, his bronze hair spiked and wild.

His crystal light blue eyes lingered on me, somewhere between weariness and curiosity. Jane left again, slamming the door behind her.

The noise engaged once more, switching between high and low frequencies. That part of me that was taken rushed back, holding additional energy. Power ran through my veins with a rush of coldness, like taking an ice bath. The familiar part surged against the new, striking it and then resettled. The man on the other side slouched, his frame frail.

I squinted, focusing my eyes. The door felt way further away than it was moments ago. The walls stretched up higher. *What the… how long have I been here?*

The clanging of metal echoed, followed by the door within the man's room opening. Umbra Soldiers surrounded him, all in blue-purple uniforms, two of them

211

yanking his arms and then pushing him out of the door. My door swung open after, revealing more Umbra Soldiers.

They roughly freed me from the confines of the chair and added black ropes to my wrists. Escorted down a long hallway, I swayed with each step. Each cell we passed held thin prisoners, some barely recognizable as humans, others more like me, all of them with glassy eyes.

One of the last cells held the man, about early twenties, if that. His brown hoodie stuck out against the light gray wall he leaned against. An Umbra Soldier opened the cage, motioning for me to enter. I stepped in, flinching as the bars rolled closed.

"Oh, it's you," the man sighed, hugging his knees to his chest. His slender frame made the hoodie and dress pants baggy.

"Hi?" I responded, thrown off by his tone. "Who are you? Are you okay?"

"Yeah..." He tilted his head, narrowing his crystal blue eyes. "Don't you know what happened over there?"

"No, not really..." I rubbed my forehead. "Do you mind telling me?"

Shifting from the wall, he scanned my ripped shirt. Something about the way his eyes quit shining sent a shiver down my spine. "Figures. The first time the machine took your powers and gave 'em to me. But I couldn't handle all that extra power, so they switched it back. In the end, it all went back to you."

"Why would they do that with you instead of anyone else?" I asked. I raised my eyebrows. "Wait, you said you have magic?"

"They're trying to keep me from running away again, and to test if that machine does what it's supposed to do." He looked away. "And yeah, I used to— They handed it over to you, don't you remember?"

"Can I give it back?" I placed my hand over my stomach.

His ears drew back, his mouth slightly open, the scruff on his jaw sharpening. It was a carefully shown surprise as if he didn't expect such an offer. "Seriously? You don't wanna hang onto those extra powers? To be stronger than everyone else and prove to Nemesis that you're worthy of them?"

I leaned against a wall. "What? Listen, I don't work for Nemesis. And no, it was your powers in the first place. Why would I want to keep it if I have my own?"

"It's not so easy," he laughed, hollow and lifeless. "You don't understand. My powers were everything to me. I really thought I could protect my clan, take care of my friends, but I messed it up. Without them, I'm nobody, and even with them... I couldn't save anyone."

"I'll give them back," I insisted, rolling my shoulders. "Just tell me how."

His tan expression darkened, melting into creased eyebrows and a tense jaw. "You can't. Not until we get outta here."

"Then let's leave. I don't want to be in here any more than you do."

"What's the point?" The man gestured around, refusing to meet my gaze. "You're just as screwed as I am. You don't know a thing about this building, and you're like, what, thirteen?"

"Fifteen. And you do, so if I can somehow help with all—"

He pinched the bridge of his nose. "I don't know. Every time I've tried, I failed and got punished for it. How do I know you can do better?"

"They punished you? Why—?" I trailed off. "Don't you want to get your powers back? We can get out." I bit my lip. "Will you come if I try?"

"I've told ya, I've already given it a shot. They've thought of everything around here."

"Well, this time you have help," I pointed out. I scratched the back of my neck. "Look, again, I'll give your powers back. Just help me out of here."

The man stared at me for a moment, bringing his arms closer to his chest. "Alright, you ain't gonna drop it," he sighed reluctantly, running his hand through his hair. "I'm guessin' since you're stuck in here with me, neither of us really matters much to the Nemesis. It'll be smoother without all the constant looks, but if we screw up— it's on you. All the blame, consequences, everything."

"That's not going to happen." I straightened.

He scoffed, slowly moving to the lock and motioning me over. "Come over here. If you use my powers right, you might be able to figure out the code and make a key."

"Find a code and make a key?" I felt the lock with my fingers. The lock was like the one you would use for a bike, yet the key for a large door handle. "What are your powers exactly?"

"Hold on." He pulled my hands away and twisted the rope on my wrist, loosening it and sliding it off. "Alright, you should be good to go now."

Why was that so easy to take off for him?

The lock clicked and slid with such ease that I tripped, unable to prevent myself from sprawling out of the cage. The man chuckled and held out his hand, stepping after me. I used the wall and stood, holding his gaze.

"What *are* your powers anyway?" I repeated, brushing past him.

"They're… kind of tough to explain. I mainly use 'em for codes and locks."

"So you can pick locks and do what with codes?" I asked. We began walking.

"Best to tell you later." He waved me off.

I squinted at him then shook my head. We rounded the corner at the end of the hallway and I lowered my voice. "With a power like this, why did your previous attempts fail?"

Silence. *Why is he refusing to explain his powers?* I shook my head. *Whatever, I need to focus on getting out of here.*

I examined the hallway we strode down. *No Umbra Soldiers or cameras?* That was really unsettling. Our steps felt too loud and exposed. *There has to be something, right? Was it intentional?*

"You really think this is gonna work?" he asked quietly, adjusting his bronze hair out of his face. "I've been here forever. Folks probably think I'm dead. Hell, I might as well be."

"We're not going to get anywhere if we don't try."

Cries and begging erupted every time we passed a cell. The people and hybrids inside had scars across their bodies, their eyes wide. I suggested freeing them, but the man said we shouldn't acknowledge or let them out. *"We don't know who they are or what they're doing here. They could end up killing us after all they've gone through. Anything to make their lives easier and free."*

What have they been through?

"Please save me! I'll do anything!"

I breathed in deeply, staring ahead of me.

"Don't leave me to die here!"

"Are you going to let us get tortured while you walk free?"

We turned around another bend and his pace slowed. "You gotta erase us from the camera footage up ahead."

"How do I do that?"

His eyes glinted, a smile tugging the edges of his lips. "Put your hands out and pray."

I smirked, rolling my eyes. "Thank you. Tell me how you really do it."

The man snorted, "You'll be able to see the code if you want, but tell it to keep us hidden, and the cameras won't catch us at all. I tampered with them before. But we still gotta watch out for Umbra Soldiers."

I went where he pointed. "Isn't it odd none of the

soldiers are patrolling?"

"What do ya mean?"

"Aren't they afraid someone will escape?"

"Nobody's ever made it outta here. I was the last one who tried, and that was two years ago. If anyone did get away, Nemesis didn't seem to care none. Also, they ain't completely got my powers figured out yet." He slowed more, throwing his head over his shoulder. "As for where they're at, I can only guess they're gettin' ready."

"Ready for what?"

He shrugged.

"Look, if we're doing this, I'll need more than vague instructions." I narrowed my eyes. "What are your powers exactly? How do I use them? We need a plan."

At the end, rows of cameras and speakers lined the ceiling. The lights flickered as he arrived at the door first and tried to open it. Locked. I sighed and touched the keyhole. The hairs on the back of my neck stood. My ear twitched.

We're being followed.

Familiar heels echoed. Jane broke through a side door, her dragon staff splitting in half to reveal two swords in her hands. "Leaving so soon? You didn't really think it'd be that easy, huh?"

Her again? When we first met, she caught me in a net. This time, I wouldn't allow her the upper hand. *She's perceptive, yet acts on instinct and is quick to jump to conclusions. Could I fool her into trapping herself?*

I stepped in front of the man with a long sigh,

217

bouncing on my toes. "What is this place?"

"A temporary arrangement until you've proven your worth." Clicking her tongue, she extended a sword to point over my shoulder. "Say, aren't you the troublemaker? I thought I clarified last time that it was your last chance. Do you want to be in the Irie until death?"

"Sorry about that." He held up his hands. "I can—"

"No—" I cut him off. "This is between you and me."

"If you say so." Jane shrugged and stomped on the tiles. A thick purple cloud from her ankle motor spilled over the floor, clouding up and covering my waist. "You think you're special, don't you? You think XXS is innocent? You think Nemesis is the worst thing out there?"

Blinding light seared into my eyes, paired with the scent of burning metal. The faded background mixed with a second scene. Jane either planned to attack with her swords or—

Blue numbers interrupted the vision, expanding from the cameras above me. She charged at me, side-swiping with the hilt of her sword into my side. I folded over, biting my tongue to keep myself from speaking. The wind shifted as she moved away.

"You're nothing more than a failed project," Jane sneered, her voice quiet but sharp as if in my ear. "Nemesis studied and fixed you—and we'll take it back."

What? The purple smoke rose above my head. It was so thick I couldn't see. A whoosh of wind indicated a swing to my left. *A failed project?* I dodged, backing into a door. *No, I have no memories of anything Nemesis. Only Kyle and my 'Mom'. That makes no sense.*

Taking the handle, I opened it and sidestepped as she ran forward and slashed, entering with me.

Does it? Does she know about the wings?

"The code! Use their defense systems against her," the man shouted. "The lasers!"

He didn't hear her? The blue code was still very distinguished from the purple fog. "How do I use the lasers?" I called, moving around the room.

"Figure out the code linked to them, then write a command in your head!"

My mind mapped out the sequence of commands. I touched a far code, one with attack commands strung throughout, mimicking his instructions. Jane struck the wall next to my neck with a *clang,* the metal dragging down the stone.

"Magic like yours doesn't belong!" she shouted.

Danger immediate: True. Description and command: Draw lasers for a woman with golden-brown hair, a white lab coat, and high heels. Only shoot if she leaves the room.

Red lights pierced through the smoke, evaporating it and focusing on Jane. Two on her head, three at her heart. Her eyes widened as she jumped away from me, dropping her swords.

"You won't get away, *Izzie.* Finding and taking you will be easy. Then I will make you suffer. You have my word."

Tucking my hair behind my ear, I left the room, calling over my shoulder, "Yeah, right."

The man waited beside the door. I quickly unlocked it, leading us to the side of the building. Security cameras and machine guns mounted along the perimeter brick wall. Umbra Soldiers lounged at the front gate, about fifteen in total, all armed. Occasional electrical and maintenance boxes dotted from here to the end.

The man placed his hand on my shoulder. "That was crazy, but this is the tough part." His voice went cold. "If you get caught or hurt, don't expect me to hang back. I makin' a break for it and leaving you here to rot and suffer in this hell hole."

"Jee, thanks for the vote of confidence." I scratched my hand. "Especially after I just saved us. So, genius, have any brilliant ideas on how to get past these Umbra Soldiers?"

Removing his hand, he tapped his chin. "Yeah. We duck behind the closest box and then keep moving until we're close to the gate. There we make a break for it."

"I guess that could work... up until the last part." I rub my arms, peeking around the corner. "Running seems like the easiest way to get caught. Shouldn't I use your powers?"

"There's only cameras and guns from here on out. The guns don't have any smart tech, so it won't do much good."

"Okay then." I nodded. "Let's try it."

"I'll go first." He shifted around and darted to the first box, squatting and facing me. I followed, practically sliding beside him.

"Dramatic, aren't you?" the man muttered, slipping around the box and then sprinting to the next.

I repeated the action. Before I reached his side, he

made his way to the next and then faced me.

As I reached him, his head poked above the electrical box. In the distance, an Umbra Soldier pulled out a tranquilizer gun, aiming directly at him.

I lunged and tackled him to the ground as the first shot fired. The dart flew overhead, ricocheting off the building's wall.

His breath was warm on my ear. I pushed off, squatting as he knelt.

"You saved me," he gasped, focusing on the dart. "Why?"

"Yeah, well, now we must make a break for it," I responded lightly. "They know we've escaped."

"Look, I wasn't gonna to tell ya this," the man said, shaking his head as he crouched. "But, I owe you one. I've got two shivs strapped to my legs. Made 'em during my time here."

He rolled his pants, revealing shivs hidden in the folds of his socks. Quickly, he held one to me and unstrapped the other. *This would've been useful earlier.*

We sprinted on opposite sides of the next box, using the maintenance containers as shields. When reaching the open space, we weaved across it, the cold wind stung my face. As the man and I reached the gate, I fumbled with the lock.

"Come on!" The man urged, lunging at an Umbra Soldier and countering two more. Their name tags held the title *Enforcer* instead of Operative.

Three Umbra Enforcers surrounded me. I took the

shiv with one hand and faced them, my left hand still fumbling with the lock. The Umbra Enforcers pointed different guns at me, instructing me to lie down while closing in.

One went at me with a knife. I blocked him, twisting the knife away. My fingers felt numb from the cold, still fidgeting with the lock. He dropped, aiming for my leg, and I sliced his arm.

With a final twist, the lock clicked and the gate swung open. All of the Umbra Enforcers straightened. I kicked the one lunging while the man shoved the rest of them into each other. We tumbled through, immediately entering a forest, and kept running.

>>>

I don't know how I got past all those Umbra Enforcers. How either of us did. But we did it.

I did it.

The Umbra Enforcers pursued us for a while, gunshots ringing out. We weaved and ran for hours after losing them.

Breathless, I stopped to catch my breath. The man joined, his face flushed, and his hair was a mess.

"That was a close one," he gasped.

"We made it."

Dried blood crusted on my arm, his forehead, and both of our clothes. I'm not sure if any of it was ours.

My attention turned to the high-peak mountains, tops covered with a blanket of snow. I could only guess that's where XXS is. Or maybe—

"Hey." The man grasped my attention, still breathing heavily. "You really didn't have to do that. I don't expect folks to help me. But… I appreciate it, I guess."

I managed a small smile. "That's what I do."

He avoided my eyes. "Guess I might've misjudged you. Look, I know I wasn't the friendliest person you've met, but I hope that doesn't mess anything up. Name's Atticus."

"It's fine," I replied, my breath clouding. "My name's Izzie." I rubbed my arms. My ripped shirt did nothing to keep me warm. It was like a crop top for summer teenagers.

"You cold?" Atticus ran his fingers through his bronze hair. He shifted the sleeves of his hoodie then grabbed the hem. "Here, take this." He took it off, revealing a gray tunic with a white circle logo underneath it, and handed it to me.

"No, I can't." I raised my hands, goosebumps spreading over my arms.

"Please," he sighed. "I want to make up for being a jerk to you earlier."

I slowly take it. "Okay. Th-thank you."

He nodded and lowered his crystal light blue eyes to the ground. "I don't have anywhere to go right now. My goal has always been to get away from that place for as long as I can remember. Unless…" Atticus trailed off, scratching the back of his head. "Forget it. What about you?"

I recalled my twin Kyle and the brothers who allowed us to join them. Zack. *Did they or XXS try to find me at all? Did they go look for Zack? How long have I been gone?*

"I do." I stretched, my back oddly warm.

"Oh." His smile deflated. "Where to?"

"My brother and some boys I've been traveling with. We have this Clan I'm a part of."

Atticus turned, expression blank as I put on the hoodie. "Well, I suppose I'll see you around then. Thank you for getting us outta there. Have fun, Izzie."

"Wait!" I grabbed his arm before he left. "You can come with me."

He looked over his shoulder, eyebrows lifted. "If you want me to come?"

"We could always use the help." I smiled and let go.

The lines on his face softened, a faint smirk played on the edge of his lips.

Where do we go first? Those mountains... It's a start. We picked a direction that wouldn't lead back to the facility. The mountains gradually grew closer, and soon enough we reached their base, where I realized my initial thought of it being XXS was wrong. Atticus decided to move south.

Bees whizzed past, landing softly on flowers while we trudged along. We arrived at a little shallow river that Atticus jumped over. I waded across, my feet getting soaked. We kept going. Time blurred into the sixth night, the soft grass swayed around a lonely tree I brushed past, making it a good spot to hide if it got windy.

"You're nothing more than a failed project," Jane sneered. *"Nemesis studied and fixed you—and we'll take it back."*

What does that mean?

Atticus abruptly halted. He scratched his ear,

meeting my eyes. "Oh man, we forgot to have you give my powers back. If you were serious about what you said."

"Oh right." I stopped at his side. "One question... How do we do that without a machine?"

His hair blew over his face as he smiled, his light blue eyes shining. "Hold out your hands and grab mine." I did. His tan hands were warm. "Now, I'm not sure if this'll really work, but some research suggests it could. So I need you to concentrate on all that extra power you've got, that your body knows it's not yours, and just, uh, transfer it."

The world slowed as time stilled, then a gust of wind hit. Our hair whisked around like a tornado.

<p align="center">~~~ ~~~ ~~~ ~~~</p>

OTHER

Inside his office, he breathed in deeply, struggling to keep his composure. "If that girl is so valuable, how'd you manage to let her escape?!"

"I'm sorry, sir." Jane swallowed hard. "We didn't realize they'd attempt to escape the same night after exhausting them with the machines."

Hitting the table, his vision turned red. "And you were wrong! I want her back *now*. No more of your foolishness."

"Yes, sir. Don't worry, I'll see to it. The guards who failed have been executed. We'll have her back in no time. And you should talk to your followers soon, they're eager to hear from you."

"I know. I don't have time for your failures, Jane. Fix it." He spat on the floor. "Ikris are supposed to be extinct. By *us.* What would happen if *she* found out otherwise?"

"Our leader, if she doesn't already know, will be enraged," Jane warned. "Don't worry, I will see to it."

He turned, his voice deadly serious. "You better. And if there are others... God bless you, Jane."

~~~ ~~~ ~~~ ~~~

IZZIE

Cold, moist grass seeped into my clothing. My back was strangely hot. I lay next to Atticus, his eyes closed and breathing steady. I rolled further, my body aching. Night passed on, fading into the day.

My hands moved sluggishly against the ground. I groaned as I moved, a razor-hot pain slicing my back. Heat radiated from it in waves. My cold hand brushed my head. It felt great. *It's okay. I'm fine.* The thought kept me level-headed. Atticus stirred next to me as I shifted against a tree.

He lifted his head, eyes darting back and forth before resting on me.

"You're okay," he exclaimed, sitting up and wiping his forehead.

My lips pressed together. "Odd first words. What happened?"

"I don't really remember. The last thing I recall is it getting dark as the wind kicked up. I was kinda worried that something had gone wrong."

"Do you have your powers back?"

Nodding, he held out his hands. "That part I was

missing finally came back to me. I feel a whole lot better now—Thank you."

"Well, that's great." Trying to shift, I retracted my breath sharply. My sight blurred as I went back to my original position.

"Were you hurt?" Atticus asked.

"N-no. Don't worry." I reached back a hand, tracing the lower part of my back. "I-I'm just sore."

"Everywhere?"

"Yeah. I'll walk it off."

Atticus hesitantly brushed my arm, sending invisible sparks across it. Taking in a deep breath, I shook out my arms and legs. He stood and offered his hand, which I took with a shrug.

Smirking, he pulled me up. Blood rushed through my head as I examined our surroundings. *Where the heck are we?* A small tree sprawled ahead, alone amidst the many large trees extending to the sky. There were no more hedges or bushes, just a carpet of twigs, pine needles, and leaves.

"So, where are the people you're searching for supposed to be?" Atticus scratched his head.

"Maybe at the XXS's base? Either that or I don't know."

"XXS?! You're with them?" He drew his head back, mouth hanging open.

Another spike of heat sliced my back. I grimaced. "Yeah."

"What was all that?" He stepped closer. "Are you alright?"

"My back..." I pulled the hoodie down. "My twin said he saw a cut down on it, b-but I haven't really noticed it until now. When we escaped, it might've gotten—"

Atticus spun in a circle, fixating on the distance. He pointed at the dwarf tree. "If you can push on, I think I know where we're at. That little tree over there, I should've guessed it earlier. My memory's not great after being away for so long... Do you think you can keep going until we reach XXS? It'll only take a few days if we take some shortcuts."

I breathed deeply, rolling my shoulders. "Yeah, I can."

Time slipped by as the mountain hiding XXS loomed ahead. We made our way past the trees, into a desert with close to no life, that bled back into the moorlands. Throughout the journey, my head grew hot and stuffy. Atticus also explained he knew some of the people there. They were with him before he got captured.

"They were always real protective of each other. It's tough to wrap my head around the fact that they never returned. I can't figure out why; thought we were like family. Maybe they couldn't find me."

"What did they look like?"

"One thing they all shared was those golden-rimmed eyes."

My brow furrowed. I gestured for him to continue.

"Four of 'em in total, all and very tan... uhm." He

tapped his chin. "Oh, and they couldn't stop talkin' 'bout their lost siblings. I think they were twins."

I stopped in my tracks, eyes going wide. He paused a few feet away, glancing back with a look that asked me, *What's up?*

"Wait a second. Are you talking about Mike, Ryan, Zack, and Luke?"

He nodded slowly. "Yeah, you know 'em?"

"Know them? They're the people I'm going back to. Well, and Kyle." I walked over to him. "They mentioned you before, saying you were killed by Nemesis."

"Hold on a second... Let me get this straight. They thought I was dead?"

"Yes. Zack stayed quiet about it, but Luke was incredibly upset at the topic, so I changed it." I bit my lip. "Hopefully, he'll be happy when they see you again. But..." I tucked a strand of my hair behind my ear, looking at my feet. Black fuzz edged my vision. "I must warn you, Zack is... potentially dead."

Atticus carefully masked his reaction, leaving it neutral, but hurt still shone deep in his eyes. "The brothers had a slight rasp when they were tired. If I hear it again, maybe I'll be sure it's them."

Silence came between us as we broke out of the moorland back into the forest and onto the familiar plains. The moss expanded on every surface. Reaching the crevice, Atticus removed a rock and spoke into the side. I steadied myself against the wall.

The camouflaged glass door opened to XXS grounds

with a faint swish. The sound caused my head to pound harder. I let go of the wall to go forward, but my legs gave out. Atticus caught me, lowering me to the ground, saying something in my ear.

What's wrong with me? Is the cut infected? I winced as he lifted me, my thoughts spinning. He said something else, but I couldn't make out the words. *I can't be a burden. I can't be weak.*

Then a quieter voice whispered back, "*Let him.*"

Something brushed against my skin as Atticus helped me inside. The voices floated in and out of my mind. *We are back, aren't we? I am with my brother and my friends again.*

Chapter 17

MIKE

Mike, Kyle, and his brothers combed the area. The high-altitude air was brisk, carrying a scent of damp soil and the tang of ash. The remains of the building smoldered, burning embers dotted the ruins, flickering amidst the wreckage. Spirals of smoke curled upward, dissipating into the grayish-blue sky. The ground was littered with scorched debris, but there was no sign of Zack—or their bags and weapons. They didn't find anything or any sign of Izzie except for a torn section of her shirt, fluttering in the wind like a ghost.

Mike sighed as he surveyed the devastation. Going back to XXS was the only option. They needed to heal, replenish their supplies, and figure out where Nemesis had possibly taken Izzie—or Zack if he had survived. Not to mention, it was the best way to formulate a plan. Most of them like the idea, except Kyle, who wanted to keep searching for his sister, though even he eventually agreed when their search yielded nothing.

The journey back spanned four days, trudging through dense forests where sunlight barely filtered through the canopy of twisted trees. The air in the wetlands was thick and heavy, buzzing with the hum of unseen insects as their boots sank into soggy ground.

From there, they crossed an expanse of rolling hills cloaked in mist, where the wind howled like a mournful spirit. The vast openness was disorienting, the endless stretch of grass and heather broken only by the occasional jagged boulder. Finally, the landscape shifted to the craggy cliffs and winding trails of the mountains. By the time they reached the entrance to XXS, Mike felt his body ready to collapse from sheer exhaustion.

Instead, they broke the news of Zack's potential death and Izzie's capture. Whitney searched for everything they had, meticulously pulling up Nemesis's bases, plotting with intel around each known building. Afterwards, Mike ate dinner and went to his room, hoping that at least Whitney had somehow found something— anything— that could lead them to Izzie or Zack.

Another four days went by of Mike, Kyle, and his brothers kept to themselves. Zack's absence was a gaping hole in their family. Mike was close to Zack. He was a strength Mike could never be, always there to listen and reassure them in the hopeless of cases. Like him and his brothers, Zack was very protective and kept them together when they fought. Or when Mike grew overwhelmed and needed a second to breathe, Zack stepped in.

It wasn't significant, but Mike held onto a glimmer of hope that Zack didn't die. If anyone could survive, it was Zack. And if that was the case, he'd do anything to save him.

But until then, Mike had to keep himself together. His brothers needed him now more than ever. And he could only focus on what he could control.

By the ninth day, the team prepared to leave. Dust motes puffed in the air, disturbed by the occasional draft. Mike and Ryan stood at the front, waiting for Luke and Kyle when XXS's heavy doors creaked open. A man strode in, supporting someone. As they stepped into view, Mike's breath caught in his throat.

Izzie. She leaned heavily against the man, her brown hoodie damp with sweat, her face flushed red. *Is she okay?* Mike's heart skipped, and he took a double look at the man. Wait, *Atticus*? *Could it really be him?* For a moment, Mike's mind struggled to process what he was seeing. The man's expression was weary but unmistakably alive. And undeniably Zack's and Luke's best friend.

Mike's mouth opened.

"No freaking way. Atticus is alive? Luke's going to be so happy," Ryan muttered, placing his hand over his mouth. "Good timing, we could use it."

Mike's brother ran up to the duo, saying something to Atticus and feeling Izzie's forehead with the back of his hand. Over his shoulder, he waved Mike over. "Can you take Izzie to the medical room, please? I'll be there soon."

Nodding, Mike took her from Atticus, placing her arm around his neck and picking her up. Her frame was alarmingly light, her body radiating heat against his arms. "We'll talk when we get back," Mike called to Atticus.

Back from the dead. Let's hope Zack can do that too. If I knew anything about my brother, it's that he wouldn't stop fighting, especially for us.

Inside, Mike took a left and nearly collided with Luke and Kyle. They both stopped dead in their tracks, backpacks strapped to their shoulders, eyes pinned on her.

"I got her," Mike explained quickly. "Luke, get outside. There's a surprise for you."

Luke's brow furrowed. He opened his mouth and closed it, a shine crossing his eyes as he hesitantly strode off.

Kyle's hands trembled as he rubbed his eyes. "What happened?" he asked softly, as he trailed behind Mike, sticking close to Izzie.

"I have no idea," Mike admitted.

. . .

IZZIE

I drifted in and out of consciousness, aware of murmuring beside me. Ryan and Kyle, maybe? I lay on my side. The door squeaked after some time, signaling that either someone left or entered the room.

"Do you need any help?" Atticus inquired.

"Yes," Ryan responded immediately. "Can you tell me what happened before she collapsed?"

After Atticus explained, I felt a hand touch my back. *Atticus's hoodie is still on. I must've not been out very long.* Forcing my eyes open, my vision slowly went in and out of focus. Windows and a few chairs lined the walls to my left.

Bracing myself, I tried to sit up using the bed's edge. My brother was there in an instant, his hand on my arm. "Woah, Izzie. Take it easy."

I chuckled. "I'm just a little dizzy. Perfectly fine. How are you guys holding up?"

"I mean, we're fine." Ryan pushed his chair to the bed, a cup of water and a pill in his hand. "Mike's coughing stopped, and he got cut from the glass, which got slightly infected. Luke got burned on his leg, but it's treated now." He sighed, handing me the pill and water. I take it. "That's for the fever. Now I want to see the cut on your back that both Kyle and Atticus told me about. Please hold still, Iz."

I slowly turned. He lifted the back of the hoodie. Cool air fluttered onto my skin, replacing the heat. I flinched.

"There's an infection, alright."

Why does he sound puzzled?

"How and where did you get this?"

"I don't know, glass?" I rubbed my forehead. "I can't remember. I was more focused on the wings bit."

Ryan grabbed a tube and slid on gloves. "I'm going to clean it and apply antibiotics. Then we'll put a small dressing on it. You'll be fine within the day, just take it easy, okay? I'll need to check in on it again later, along with that fever."

About an hour later, an unfamiliar person knocked on the door and said, "Lunch is ready."

Atticus opened the door and left. After Ryan finished, my twin helped me up and we headed out.

"Where'd you get that hoodie?" Kyle wondered, running his finger down a scar on his arm. "And where'd your wings go?"

"Oh." I brushed the soft fabric. "Yeah, most of my shirt ripped off and Atticus gave it to me after we escaped.

The wings, not sure. They were gone when I woke up in a Nemesis facility."

He raised an eyebrow. "Atticus gave it to you? That's all?"

"I was cold," I admitted, entering the cafeteria, the smell of food making my stomach growl.

On the table displayed a variety of options. Sandwich, fruit trays, soda... I took a handful of cookies alongside a roast beef sandwich and settled by Kyle. He gave me his look and rolled his eyes.

>>>

After we ate, Kyle forced me to rest. During which, Ryan examined the infection and my fever again. The fever vanished, and I didn't need anything else. He reapplied some antibiotics, which stung, but the inflammation died down. The odd warmth in my back vanished.

The infection wouldn't have gotten that bad if I'd been more cautious. I was careless, trying to shove aside a small problem that just became bigger. I should be able to trust Ryan and his brothers. I should've told him about it before I left in search of Zack. Ignoring my problems hadn't helped anyone, it'd ended up being an inconvenience instead.

With the Unicorn too... if only I had trusted the brothers and hadn't been so prideful and scared of their reactions. I tried to only rely on myself, yet we needed to work as a team. I won't fight help anymore if I truly need it. Physically, of course.

Days passed as we planned our next move. We decided to leave after everyone healed in search of any

236

signs of Zack and to retrieve the vials from the blood I left. Atticus asked to come too after he caught up with Whitney.

While they packed, I had to get answers. A plan formed in my mind, not yet fully grasped, to execute in the battle. From where it began, I had no idea. Maybe a thought or something someone said.

Was all of Nemesis truly the enemy? Or were they lied to by their leaders, who wanted us dead? Dravia made me think it was the latter. I shut my eyes. *My Ikris powers have to have something to do with the final battle.* I had no idea where the thoughts would take me.

I stood in a hallway, arms folded, a bag at my side full of food, water, and two changes of clothing. I had two daggers in my jeans pockets. My brother exited through the doors, his backpack bouncing with each step. *I should head outside with him.*

The backpack pulled back my shoulders. I opened the door, and the sun immediately blinded me. Shielding my face, I squinted to see Atticus and Luke leaning against the wall right next to the entrance. They talked quietly, Luke smiling for the first time in a while.

I will be more careful. I won't hold them back. I forced a small smirk as I walked over. *I will take care of myself, not be someone they have to protect.* I pinched my arm.

Luke glanced at me as I arrived between him and Kyle. A half-smile formed on his lips as he nudged my shoulder. "Don't look so serious," he said lightly.

I shrugged. "Sorry, lost in thought."

Kyle grabbed my wrist and shook it. "Ugh, how long

do they take?! It's been like, almost an hour."

"Hang in there, man." Atticus's mouth twitched upwards. "They'll be here any second."

"We could always let them catch up." Luke tilted his head, receiving a nudge from Atticus.

Kyle's gaze bore on the door. As if his stare signaled it, it opened, relieving him from his glare.

At first, Mike exited, appearing pale. I rose to my toes. *Is there something wrong with him?* Ryan trailed behind him, talking animatedly. Both held backpacks full of their gear. *Oh. Mike's tired.* Even from here, I could hear Ryan talking about a new medicine they created.

"Whitney wants us to hurry. With all the tension going on between us and Nemesis, she doesn't want anyone to be away for too long," Atticus said as they approached. "Especially with Zack *missing.*"

>>>

Nights and days passed since we left. The sun was bright and we made good time, though my legs ached. They were all taller than me, even Kyle, who grew about an inch in the last month. I did my best to keep pace, hiding any signs of strain despite my muscles screaming at me. At last, Mike called for a break.

I tossed my bag and sank onto a tree root, uncomfortable but too exhausted to care. Luke strode over to me, tossing a pebble between his hands.

"You know. I used to think being fast was all I needed. Turns out running doesn't fix everything, but it sure does allow me to win a lot."

"Good thing you've got us to slow you down and keep your ego in check." I rolled my eyes.

He dropped the pebble and laughed. "Yeah, I guess I do."

Luke left to Atticus, patting him on the back. I sighed, tilting my head back. The distant crunch of twigs and leaves made me tense, my ears strained. Everyone had already stopped walking.

I'm being paranoid. I squatted and ran my fingers through the grass, pulling at the blades.

Roaring pierced the trees. There's only one thing that roared like that.

The Pig Morph charged out of the underbrush, its one swinging horn had broken off, and its eyes were cloudy from when I stabbed it in the eye. The pig had tiny cloud angel wings and a type of halo hovering above its head.

Ryan said he would tell me about it later, but he never did. The Morph spun in a circle until its eyes locked on me. *How did it find us?*

"Why's it paying so much attention to Izzie?" Atticus questioned, and then it charged.

Instinct kicked in. I dropped into a crouch. *After your first meeting, the Morph can predict everything you are about to do.* Mike said in one of his never-ending conversations. *It's why it took us out so easily.*

So it never met Kyle before. Or Atticus.

A shriek sliced in my ears. A bacon scent wafted through my nose, almost taking me off my feet. Luke slashed its side with his katana, returning to my left. A spurt of dark blood stained the ground. Doing a 360, it faced me again and barreled forward, tearing up grass in its wake. I dove behind Ryan, who angled his dagger and pierced its hind leg.

Digging into my pocket, I pulled out the dagger and knife Luke lent me. Mike was past a few trees between the Morph and me, next to Kyle and Atticus, a glass glaze in his eyes.

"Kyle, Atticus!" I held up my weapons. "It can predict everyone except you!"

The Morph's eyes darken, a strange, unsettling feeling washing over me. Dots floated in or out of my vision. I backed into a tree as it slowly trotted closer.

"Don't fret," the voice informed me. *"It's merely blocking your foresight."*

What? A wave of nausea crashed over me... One that couldn't have been from the Morph. My twin teleported between the Morph and me, taking out his dagger and impaling it in its nose. The Morph cried and snorted, backing up.

Clutching my fists, I refused to let my legs give out. The Morph threw its head and flapped its wings. Atticus crossed beside it at the same time as Luke.

A humanoid shadow appeared at my side. I crossed my arms to it. It was the outline of a human figure, but everything inside was a complete void. Like it wasn't physically there, but I could see it. *My weapons can't do anything against a shadow. I wonder if it's working with the Morph.* Or controlling it.

Distant voices shouted over each other.

"If hurting the Morph makes it more powerful, how can you stop it?" the voice prompted. It came in the direction of the shadow.

Who and what are you?

No response. The shadow didn't move. The outline rippled like static back and forth. The Morph charged at Ryan and Atticus, who countered it with slashes at its sides.

Okay, hurting the Morph makes it more powerful... Wait, this had been in movies before. There were some creatures you'd have to heal to defeat instead. Is that the same with the Morph?

The Morph went at me again. I used the tree next to me, climbing and landing behind the Morph as it barreled into its wood. It spun quickly, throwing its head and snorting. I slashed its nose while backing away.

Kyle, I reached out to him. *Get Ryan to heal the Morph.*

"What? I'm not doing that!"

"Luke!" I yelled, and all the colors turned black and white. The Morph reared, shoving someone aside and circling me. *Please don't hurt them.* "Distract the Morph and the shadow if possible. Atticus, defend Ryan. Ryan, heal the Morph!"

"Heal it? Are you out of your damn mind?" Ryan said. "Mike? What do you think?"

No response.

"I got you, Izzie!" Luke shouted. "Guess bacon's on the menu tonight!"

Last time, the Morph took them out before they could

react. All except Ryan. This time, since it's focused only on me; Mike, Ryan, and Luke should still be able to fight it. The shadow must be connected to the Morph. We take it out, we take the shadow too.

Trying again, I reach out to Kyle as I'm barely able to make out the pig leaping at me. *Do it!* Wind rushed from above, knocking the pig back enough to miss hitting my side. Two figures jumped it and it reared, throwing them off. Another blurred in front of it and past the shadow, as two more figures ran to it. I stood my ground. An incredulous white light overtook its body, a *boom* vibrating throughout.

Chapter 18

IZZIE

Crickets chirped incessantly. I covered my ears. Some time ago, I got knocked out. But whatever attacked us was gone. I tried to piece together my last memory: the black and white Morph lunged at me, but a rush of wind knocked it aside. Two figures attacked it as it reared... Another one blurred around it, past the humanoid shadow. Then, the incredulous white light overtook everything... There was a deafening boom... and I blacked out.

The metallic tang of blood hit my nose as I lay in the soft dirt. My eyes flew open, and a green leaf drifted past my ear. I sat up. The grass was slick with red. Moonlight cast long shadows over the wreckage. I located my brother, unconscious, next to Mike. Kyle's arm bent at a horrifying angle, and Mike had a black eye with dried blood smeared across his cheek.

What the heck happened? Nemesis? Did we kill the Morph? Why didn't they take us?

Luke lay pale in a pool of blood. I couldn't spot an injury, and his chest still rose and fell. A wave of cold rushed through me. *Ryan, I have to find Ryan...*

Tearing my eyes from him, I located Ryan, slumped against a tree, whose skin was washed out in the moonlight. He seemed unhurt.

I exhaled sharply, the tension in my shoulders easing, and approached. Next to him lay Atticus, his arm slashed open with dried blood crusting around the wound. His shirt was tightly wrapped around his arm, acting as a makeshift brace to suppress the bleeding.

A dull pain pulsed through my ribs. I pressed my hand at my side. The air felt thick, and the crickets— those dang crickets— kept chirping like nothing happened. Below them, Kyle twitched, letting out a low groan as he stirred. His lips twisted.

"Kyle?" I asked. "Are you okay?"

His eyes fluttered open, glazed. "Wake… Ryan."

I rushed to Ryan and shook his shoulder. He groaned and swatted at my hand.

"Kyle needs help," I began.

He sat up quickly, blinking. "Is he okay? I don't remember-" Ryan rubbed his eyes, wincing. "Why do I feel so sore?"

I gestured to my twin. Ryan scrambled over and dropped to his knees. "Kyle, do you remember what happened?" My twin shook his head. Sighing, Ryan placed his hands on Kyle's arm. "This could backfire or do absolutely nothing, but let's hope this works."

"Hope it will—" Kyle cut himself off as a blinding light erupted from Ryan's fingers, expanding outwards. Kyle grimaced, biting back a groan as his arm shifted, bones knitting back together with a sickening crack. Ryan's face drained of color as the light vanished. A smell of vanilla hit the air, and Ryan collapsed against a tree, panting heavily.

Stepping back, I tripped over Atticus's legs to the ground. "What—" he mumbled with a hoarse voice. I quickly rolled back to my feet as Atticus used one hand to lift himself, grimacing.

"I don't know and s-sorry," I stammered, dusting the dirt off my shirt. *Idiot.*

"It's okay," Atticus mumbled, seeing the others. "Are they alright? What in the world happened? I don't remember anything."

"Neither do I," I told him, helping Ryan and Kyle up.

I took in a sharp breath as Ryan leaned against a tree, running his fingers through his hair. "Okay, I'm going to get Mike and Luke then. Maybe they can recall—"

Luke. I pulled Ryan's arm, showing him his brother. He sharply inhaled at the sight of the dark puddle of blood around Luke's neck and rushed over.

Kyle brushed past me as Ryan left. "Are you okay now?" I asked, touching his arm gently.

"Yes," he said with a hint of awe in his voice. "Ryan didn't hurt himself healing me... Did he?"

"He'll be fine," I assured, biting my lip.

"Did you get hurt?"

"Bruised." I shrugged, adjusting my bag.

Comparatively speaking, all of them were injured worse than me. If it was as bad as it looked, we all had to return. Already. Or Kyle might suggest he continue alone. I obviously won't let that happen, especially since part of this mission is my fault.

Our eyes met. He had a kind of calculating look as if he didn't believe me, but I broke eye contact and faced Mike, who sat next to Ryan and Luke.

"No really. I'll be fine," I insisted, straightening. He narrowed his eyes. My twin and I could read each other like an English professor reading a children's picture book. "I-I think we should check on the others."

"Sure," Kyle said.

Luke pressed his hand against his head as Ryan talked to him. I could barely make out some of Ryan's words. "Damn, you look like hell." The grass beneath Luke rustled, undisturbed despite yesterday's attack.

"Feel worse." Luke managed a weak smile.

Atticus slowly joined us, his arm wrapped in a spare shirt from his bag. He held it carefully, breathing slowly.

"We need to return," Mike said. "My powers are depleted, and none of us are in good shape."

I glanced around at our group. The brothers and Atticus barely kept themselves upright. Ryan shook his head. *They sacrificed so much for us.*

"The vials... We need to get them. Not just Izzie's, all of them. It's time-sensitive." Ryan gritted his teeth. "We can't just abandon it."

They deserve a break.

"I know," Mike acknowledged, swearing under his breath. He touched the dry blood on his cheek and gestured to Luke and Atticus. "But we can't."

What if Kyle and I were to go?

"Kyle and I are fine," I said abruptly. The attention shifted to me. "If there's only a certain amount of time, we can go."

"No," Ryan immediately snapped. "Not a chance. You can't do it by yourselves."

"We can't ask that of you, and Atticus might need to be there," Mike added. He bit his lip and straightened, a glint crossing his eyes. "Ugh, I know about the time limit."

I want to help them as much as they helped us.

"Let us try," Kyle interjected.

Dark circles shadowed Mike's eyes. He sighed. "Do you guys think you can do it alone?"

Ryan tensed but said nothing as Kyle nodded, shooting me a look. "I think we can."

"Are they going without us?" Luke asked absently. Some of the blood he lay in earlier came from his lips, which were split open, along with a trail in his ear.

"Unfortunately, yes." Mike clicked his tongue, touching Luke's shoulder. Ryan muttered to Mike as I helped Atticus to his feet. After some back and forth, Ryan summoned his dagger.

"Here," Ryan stood, holding out his dagger. "Protect yourself and your twin for me."

Kyle's mouth opened to protest, but I nodded. "I already have two, but I'll take it and give one to Kyle. Thank you." Ryan went back to squatting next to Luke.

"Take care of them, Ryan," Kyle mumbled as they collected their stuff.

. . .

MIKE

A persistent ache pounded in Mike's head. None of them looked good, not even Ryan, fatigued from healing Kyle. *He's used his powers too much. It's going to be a few days back.*

As days dragged into the nights, they stopped to rest quite a few times. At the end of day two, Ryan confirmed that he was ready to heal one of them.

"Do Luke or Mike," Atticus insisted, holding up his hands. "Mine doesn't need to be magically fixed."

The last two days had been rough. Luke had to be led by Ryan for the last hour, stumbling into relatively anything. He was the obvious choice. Ryan touched his shoulders. "Ready?"

Luke gave a slow thumbs up, the familiar bright light engulfing their figures, a scent of vanilla taking the air. Ryan abruptly fell to his back as color partially returned to Luke's face. *His magic is drying up, but he's pushing himself for our sake.*

It would take a while for them to get home.

. . .

IZZIE

I ducked after Kyle as he went underneath the last few branches leading to the moorlands. Silence hung dry between us, nagging at me to say something. Anything. At least the dull ache in my ribs eased. He stopped short, and I

248

nearly ran into him.

"Tell me," Kyle demanded, arms crossed. "Were you hurt? And don't lie this time."

Reluctantly, I scratched my head. "I guess my rib cage was. It's only bruised, so it isn't a big deal. I barely feel it now."

His ear twitched. "Will you tell me if it hurts worse?"

I returned to walking, pausing when I realized he hadn't moved. "Of course, I'll tell you. You're my brother."

"And yet, I thought we promised to never lie to each other." He jogged to catch up to me, eyes trained on the ground.

I opened my mouth to respond but didn't say anything. *I'm not trying to lie to you. I don't think it's a big deal.*

In the distance, a building appeared over the rolling hills. For a base, it looked small, barely the size of a house.

"We'll have to take it and leave." Kyle touched my shoulder.

We were here for the vials. A few of which were from me. I should have been more careful rescuing the brothers. They had my blood; who knew what they'd do with it? Luckily, Whitney's assistant found out where they took it. Unluckily, we had no idea what they planned.

I crouched in the long grass, the rough blades whispering against my legs. "Let's look for a side entrance."

"Okay." My brother crouched too, creeping closer. "I don't see any big enough on this side."

249

And I don't see any guards. I stood and meticulously went toward the front of the building.

Kyle trailed after me and hissed, "What are you doing?"

"They won't expect us from the front. Look, it's completely unguarded." Stepping against the wall, I inched toward the doors.

"Maybe that's exactly what they want us to conclude."

Ignoring his warning, I pushed open the door and slipped inside. For such a small place, the interior was surprisingly spacious and vacant of life. To the right lined rows of vials and the left held a mess of wires and chairs.

"I can't believe that worked." Kyle strode in. "Why is no one here?"

"That is worrisome." A chill crept down my spine. One of the computers resting on a desk had its light on. I squinted at the words on the screen.

Twelve days until we raid. Twelve days until we save the humans from those monsters. My stomach dropped. *Oh, that's not good.* "Come see this."

Kyle read the screen out loud over my shoulder. "Twelve days? They're prepared much more than we thought. We have to get leave *now* or it'd be too late to warn them."

I located the date last edited. *Three days ago.* Kyle and I would barely even *make it* before they attacked, let alone warn XXS. Mike, Ryan, Luke, and Atticus had no idea what was coming.

Circling the rest of the room, I checked we didn't

miss anything. We stuffed several vials in our pockets and backpacks, and within minutes, we were out.

"It took us almost a week to get here," I muttered. "When we get back, there won't be time to prepare. They'll already be under attack."

The dagger Ryan gave to me clacked against a vial. I took it out, which drew Kyle's attention. The calculated look returned, eyes lighting up.

"That dagger can return to Ryan if you throw it in the air, right?"

"Yeah?" I replied. "But why would I do that?"

He took a crumpled piece of paper out of his pocket. I raised my eyebrow. "We need something to write on and stab the dagger into it. If we're lucky, it will take the paper with it when returning to Ryan."

Shaking my head, I hid it behind my back. "That's a good idea, but if it doesn't work, we lose one of our weapons."

"It's a risk we have to take." He held out his hand.

I chewed my inner cheek. *It's worth trying to warn them.* Giving in, I bent and picked up a stick. Kyle caught on, picking up more and dropping them on a nearby stone. Later, we were able to start a tiny fire and let it burn for a few minutes.

As it died out, Kyle took another stick and stuck it into the charcoal. "Hopefully, this works." He clenched his teeth and began scraping on the paper. After reburying the stick in the charcoal a few times, he finished. The rough words were messy and light, easy to fade away. "That should be good enough. Give me the dagger, Iz."

I passed it to him. *That was smart, Kyle. You've grown a lot.* Ripping the paper, he threw it into the air. The dagger shimmered for a moment before it vanished, paper and all.

"It worked!" Kyle pumped his fist in the air. I smiled.

"Not bad. I always knew you had a few brain cells," I teased. He playfully shoved me.

We continued until nightfall, with the stars twinkling at the new moon. We settled for the night, almost emptying our backpacks of the rest of the food. Exhausted, I drifted into a deep sleep.

>>>

The dagger's success left us both some relief, yet it didn't last long. Three more days melted by, with occasional conversation and the looming attack on our minds. Nothing much happened except for a run-in with a snake. *But Kyle made me promise not to tell anyone about it.* I chuckled, distracted enough to miss a small stone in my path. I stumbled, easily fixing my stance.

"You, okay?" Kyle asked offhandedly, yawning.

A low growl answered for me. A wolf broke out of the shadows, its head down. Its yellow fangs bared, dripping with saliva.

"Nice doggy," I backed slowly. Each step felt loud.

Its growl deepened, and the wolf's saliva dripped onto the dirt. My brother linked my arm with his, and with my other hand, I grabbed my dagger. Under my breath, I asked, "Kyle, can you teleport us out of here?"

"I can try," he gulped. "I've never teleported two people before."

My heart leaped as the wolf lunged, and we were gone.

Chapter 19

IZZIE

I plummeted, the air whipping my face. The impact hit me like a freight train, pain exploding in my rib cage, threatening to splinter bone. I choked back a scream. Kyle staggered to his back next to me, his skin pale, reflecting more of a sickish tint.

I rolled to my side, eyes locking onto the mountain in the distance, our destination. It's closer than before. Four days. *He can only teleport where he can see— how far did we go?*

"Are you okay?" I croaked, cringing inside as I watched him. My voice felt raw.

Kyle coughed, "Yeah. Just a bit dizzy. You weigh a lot."

I rolled my eyes. We lay there for a good hour. *I should be fine.* Pushing myself up, I used a tree trunk to stand. Kyle mimicked me, placing his hand on my shoulder. I couldn't tell if it was to help him or me. I tried to suppress the constant ache in my chest, wrapping an arm around my ribcage.

The sun had long since vanished, dissolving into days and nights as we traveled through the forest, around a mushy pond, and the moorlands as we arrived. The pain in my ribs receded to a manageable throb, and Kyle's color returned to be more tannish than ghost white.

My stomach growled. Yesterday we ran out of food, but since we were close, we decided to push through it.

Tapping the sidewall, I said my name, and it opened. Atticus was there, arms folded. "Figured you'd show up tonight. I mean, maybe a little later, but I'm not gonna complain."

He winked and then went inside with us, informing us what they did while we were gone. Ryan intercepted us in the building, preventing Atticus from continuing, and confirmed that the dagger with the note worked.

We emptied the vials into the laboratory, and not long after, I ate, took a much-needed shower, and collapsed onto my bed.

My ribs didn't disrupt my sleep that night. As usual, my dreams did. This time, it wasn't even a nightmare. It was more like a vision rather than a figment of imagination.

I wandered, drifting through this cold, well-lit hallway, ending at a door where distant voices overlapped. I opened it, revealing a massive gym, packed full of people in lab coats or regular clothes, all armed with weapons or strange gadgets. A few hybrid animals lurked between, coexisting peacefully. Two microphones were stationed at the front, one manned by Jane, the other by someone I didn't recognize.

Unlike those in the crowd, the man wore a black and dark purple lab coat, trimmed with gold. Shades rested on his pointed nose. His neck was adorned with tattoos, barely noticeable underneath the dark purple wing-tipped collar.

His sleeve caught my eye, with a large black badge with gold cursive writing.

Inching closer, I could barely make out the words: *Nemesis Dark Hope.* My dream *was* becoming a vision.

The man tapped on the microphone, silencing the chatter. "Our mission went exceedingly well, thanks to Jane's hard work." Hatred crossed his eyes, fading back into the never-ending black as the applause died. "Now, people of Nemesis, it's time to win. Those XXS murders and traitors will be done with! Humans will be safe at last, all thanks to us!" The room erupted into cheering again, dying quickly as he raised his hand.

"There's one more thing I must discuss. Recently, I've received new information about a girl who may have wings. Her alias name is Izzie. She recently joined the XXS after an attack on her school. We have reason to believe that she is *extremely* valuable and must be captured. I'm asking you to leave her unharmed and assist us with her and her family's capture."

Cold sweat clung to my skin. The vision abruptly cut off. I glance at the digital clock. 4:00 A.M. *He said my name... He described my past.* I tried to make sense of it, but I was too tired to think. *I'll tell Kyle and the brothers in the morning.* Exhaustion pulled me back into a fitful sleep.

>>>

Sunlight danced directly into my eyes. I grimaced and rolled out of bed to get ready. *Today or tomorrow, the Nemesis will arrive.*

In the cafeteria, I picked out some cereal and sat down. My brother joined me a second later with a muffin, poking at it absently.

Across from us sat Mike, in the middle of a conversation. "Look, I've been thinking. You could stay inside when they come—"

"It was never safe!" Kyle rolled his eyes, slapping the table. "We joined, didn't we? It won't be safer with us locked in here. This is a fight for our lives and our friends. You have to let us be a part of it. We've already proved ourselves."

"They're right, Mike." Whitney walked up, putting her hand on his back. She leaned in. "Even if they're young, they're a part of this. You don't need to protect them now."

"Yeah." He looked up at her, placing his hand on hers. "Yet they feel like our little brother and sister. And I can't let that go."

>>>

Whitney lifted another curved sword. I shook my head. We stood in a training-storage room, and so far none of the swords suited me. It was either too long, light, off-balanced, or too heavy.

A few people spread throughout the room. Weapons clanked with hushed voices. Picking two more, Whitney set them out to me, naming them *Nightfall* and *Python Strike.* I tested them in my hand, with a swing back and forth. Both were oversized and clunky; I'd trip before I could swing properly. I declined, and she placed them back. *Why can't I find one?*

A sword I had seen since we entered the room lured me. It stuck inside a rock, not exactly unique. The silver hilt caught the lights, making it almost wanting. Whitney smiled, noticing my interest.

"Oh, do you want to try that one? Only one person I know of was ever able to pull that out... She surely was special." Her voice betrayed her calm demeanor. She flinched, sensing my gaze. "The Nemesis killed her. No one's ever been able to pull it out since then."

"I'm sorry," I said softly. I went to it and touched the handle. "Do you mind if I try?"

She shrugged, sliding her hands in her pockets. "Sure, if you want."

I grabbed the hilt and pulled. It didn't budge. I sighed, letting go. *Of course, it wasn't going to happen.* "Maybe Kyle should try it," I suggested as he walked in. "Speaking of the devil."

"Want me to try what?" he repeated, eyes landing on the sword. "That?"

He took the hilt, giving it a hard yank. His hands slipped off, and he fell. A quiet laugh escaped me before I could stop it. I offered my hand.

Scratching his head, Kyle stammered words under his breath, taking my hand and heading to the other swords. He picked one with a bronze hilt and swung it, confirming in approval. My jaw dropped. *Okay, now that's unfair.*

"There are two more swords that I think you might like," Whitney said pointedly, briefly waving at him.

She led me farther back to a closet. Varieties of weapons dangled on the walls. On the left side hung two swords, one glowed red, and the other pitch black. Both had decent silver hilts. I reached out and tested the red's weight. Taking a couple of swings, I stumbled. *So close, but its*

258

balance is off. I set it down, picking up the black sword. Weighing the sword in my left hand, I smiled. A few swings later, I inclined my head.

"That sword is called *Tri-thum.* No one has liked it yet, but there's a first time for everything."

"Wow, alright then," I muttered, walking to Kyle. The one he held was called *Sonar. Why do we even need to know their names?*

"As soon as we received your message, everyone was informed of the attack," Whitney said, striding past us and out of the room. We followed her. "Many of our members will be arriving throughout the day. Of course, most should be armed, but others will have to come here and get their weapons like you. It's common for people to return with nothing, become lost, hurt, or worse."

She paused, her posture deflating. "Speaking about Nemesis, our scouts expect them to come later today or early tomorrow, equipped with high-tech weapons. They aim to kill or capture us for experimentation. Hopefully, none of us will be, but that's unlikely."

"Is there any way to stop them without anyone dying?" I sheathed the sword, letting it swing by my side.

Whitney's expression softened. "I doubt it. A goal like that is unrealistic. If there was a way, I couldn't tell you. People will die."

Kyle scratched his head, still holding the hilt of his sword. "Perhaps we could try."

She tilted her head at him. "I'm sorry. As much as I don't want it to be, we can't stop it."

"If you want to stop the blood and death." I froze. The voice that helped me find Mike and his brothers when they were captured and guided me to Kyle returned. Where had it been? *"You must be there at the center. You and Kyle can save this land— only if one of you is willing to take the stand."*

The voice had only helped me, yet I still didn't know where it came from. If it came down to it, I was willing to risk myself for thousands of others. Taking a shaky breath, I slightly nodded to myself. "I have an idea of what to do, but you will not like it."

. . .

MIKE

The field was packed with people. Mike got to reconnect with old friends, some bearing new scars from the last time they met. Others were missing friends entirely. Mourning for the dead would come after the battle. The end of the war. And Zack would get the burial he deserved. There were also new members, faces he'd never seen.

Leaning against a wall, Mike overlooked the grassy space, rubbing his thumb against his palm. Soon, it was going to be full of blood, cries, weapons, and magic. On his right extended a steep cliff leading to the familiar lake, the left was thick with trees. In between spread out the sizable field to the mountain entrance.

His brothers would fight in that battle. Should he watch Ryan and Luke to make sure they don't die also?

Neither was in sight; maybe they were catching up with their friends. Glancing over his shoulder, Mike spotted Izzie and Kyle walking out the doors with new swords strapped to their sides, arguing. Kyle's face was red. As they got closer, Mike tried to decipher what they were on about.

"No, there's no way!" Kyle said firmly. His eyes narrowed, and his shoulders pulled back. "It's not happening. It doesn't work, I won't let you. I don't care, Izzie!"

His sister murmured something, and Kyle fell silent. They stopped right before Mike. Izzie tilted her head at him, tucking a strand of her brown hair behind her ear. Her cloudy blue eyes rimmed with yellow were guarded, constantly darting around with a hand on her sword's hilt. She was shaken. As was her brother.

Pushing off the wall, Mike studied their expressions. The slight rasp in his voice returned, "You guys good?"

Izzie gave a small smile, sneaking a glance at Kyle. "We're fine. You look worse, Mike. Have you gotten any sleep?"

"Long enough." His body did feel heavy. Thinking about Zack didn't do him any good. He noted the bags under their eyes. "You should both rest."

She sighed, but didn't move. "I will."

"Hey, I've been meaning to ask…" Kyle jumped in, shifting his weight. The edges of his lips twitched downward, and he scratched the back of his head. "When will we have Zack's funeral?"

Mike stiffened. He took a deep breath and nodded. "After we win, we'll give him and others the funeral they earned."

"Okay." Kyle lowered his head, but the tension in his

shoulders didn't ease. "I don't want him to think we forgot."

Stepping forward, Izzie wrapped her arms around Kyle from the side. "We could never forget Zack."

Mike looked away. They stayed there for several minutes, but eventually Izzie let go and left. He fell in step with Kyle as they went back inside.

. . .

IZZIE

Why haven't I told anyone about these dreams yet? I sat at the edge of my bed, kicking my legs back and forth. *Then again, Kyle's already in denial about what I want to do in the battle...Telling him would make him hate it more. The brothers would be against it.*

I lay down, staring at the clock. *What time would the Nemesis come?* Tension filtered throughout the building, with many constantly on watch. *Maybe if I go to sleep, will I get another vision...?*

I shut my eyes, unable to fall asleep until much later.

>>>

My eyes flew open, a scream on the tip of my tongue. Another nightmare— I held my cold hand to my forehead, focusing on my breathing to calm my racing heart. *They're getting worse. How is that even possible?*

Thunder growled outside, rain pelted, and wind howled against the walls. Hopefully, it'll slow the Nemesis down. And by chance, the weather will calm down if they arrive.

I rolled out of bed. In the corner, a girl about twenty slept on another bed. *There probably weren't enough rooms.*

262

I carefully get dressed and do a ponytail. I walked out, closing the door behind me. The lights in the halls flicker, yearning for the end of their lives.

When I made it halfway, a siren blared on, paired with red lights. That meant one thing. Nemesis was here. Or, two, they upgraded security. Well, at least I strapped my sword on before I left.

I sprinted to the stairs, my sword swinging side to side, taking them two at a time. Others joined side by side, rushing to get outside. Shouts and clashing metal and gunshots fill the halls.

At the bottom, I caught up with Luke in the middle of the crowd, pushing through the door. I followed him out, despising the light rain pelting my face. Cheering took over the thunder of the storm. *How did it start so fast? How did Nemesis get in?*

I forced my way closer to the field, exiting the mountain. Trees bent under the force of the wind, and on the other side, a hill led to a lake and more land. Across the grasslands, the Nemesis charged. Every minute they got closer and closer, and people were already clashing.

Should I find Mike and his brothers? Or Kyle?

Most of XXS widened their stances, preparing for the brunt of it, holding weapons tightly. Archers with specialized bows and guns were stationed at the top of the mountain, hidden in the illusion. *Atticus should be up there with them.*

Dread coiled in my stomach. This battle will end in a massacre. My plan had to be initiated. I don't think this is as straightforward as the brothers or the Clans think. Both sides were trying to survive for different reasons. *How had this battle come into place?* I balled my hands in fists.

It's a battle, not a war. What did I miss? My eyes narrowed. *The vision I had of Jane with that man. That man wasn't wearing Nemesis's colors. Could it be…? Another enemy. We had to have another enemy. Could the writing on his cuff, Nemesis Dark Hope, be it?* I needed to stop the fight. *They* wanted us to fight, kill, and capture each other as prisoners. Like they did with the Ikris.

Ikris… Where had I heard that name before? Who did the Ikris fight against?

Wait, the man from Nemesis Dark Hope… is it possible that he… planned all of this?

Screaming disrupted my thoughts. The battle raged. Was I too late to stop it?

Chapter 20

IZZIE

Someone rammed into my back. Lifting my sword, I spun to face a girl with horns sprouting from her head, lips curled in a snarl. A shaggy tan torso dragged over her shorts. She waited; knees bent, then lunged with a wavy dagger aimed straight at my neck. I sidestepped, watching her crash onto the floor into a smooth roll. In one fluid motion, I got on her, my shoe pressed on her chest, sword inches from her throat.

"Tell me, are you Nemesis or Dark Hope?" I shouted. I pressed the blade closer to her throat. *She was not that hard to beat, and that's saying something. Why did they send her out to fight?*

She hissed, spitting dirt from her mouth. "Yes. Of course, I am Nemesis. Why don't you kill me on sight as you do the rest of us? You monsters."

"Because we don't do that." I leaned away, relieving most of the pressure of my sword. "We're the good guys." Stepping off her, I let her get up. "I don't kill until you give me no choice. Or if you threaten my brother and friends."

The girl stared at me in shock, then she tilted her

head. "Are you that—?"

I ran. There must be a place to stop this. To stop all this chaos. I skimmed the battlefield, smoke brushing my nose. *The hill. No one is on top of that hill.* I ducked, avoiding two swords clashing and weaving around the melee. There is a cliff at the edge of it, but that won't stop me.

Luke blurred, fighting side-by-side with Ryan, who cursed. The three Umbra soldiers held well against them, parrying and covering each other's backs. But the brothers kept up, even advancing at times.

Will this idea work? Was I going to my death?

No, it had to. This was the only way I was able to help, not be another useless tool. To repay and protect the brothers, XXS, and Kyle. Nothing will stop this bloodbath except for what I might be able to do. Or I will seriously injure myself from the fall, but the damage will already be done.

Wind passed by me. Out of the corner of my eye, I saw Mike take down a hybrid of a cat squirrel, its squirrel face scrunched and bleeding as it bolted.

Kyle's going to hate me.

Swinging my sword over my arm, I hiked the hill. *This is about my new family and finally leaving my 'mother' behind.* A new energy, not just adrenaline, broke from hiding inside me and seeped through my veins. Similar to that of the facility, but not painful. The connection reached out to me, ready.

In another part of the moors, my twin darted towards an injured fighter, helping them stand with one hand while keeping the dagger raised in the other. My twin looked up, eyes immediately drawn to me.

Almost there.

"Izzie!" Kyle shouted. *No, please.* Lightning struck nearby, the crack of thunder nearly deafening. The fighting below didn't cease, full of thousands of people. I reached the top, the edge of the cliff looming before me. "Stop!" My twin's voice grew closer, pleading. I stiffened but widened my stance, overlooking the edge.

There's no turning back. I have to do this. I stood at the edge, the world below was chaos. Flames, smoke, screams, all of it blended into a roar. *It has to work. I'm sorry, Kyle... You'll hate me for this, but I hope you understand.*

"It ends today," I whispered.

With one last burst of energy, I leaped from the cliff, sword raised above my head and visible light swirling around me. That flicker of energy surged to life.

And everything shifted into slow motion.

. . .

MIKE

Mike angled his sword, blocking a soldier with a gun. It was a multi-use tool that could render one useless if they didn't know what they were doing.

"You think this is about control? We're saving humanity from monsters like you! If you had your way, the whole world would burn." Aiming the gun at Mike, the guard grinned.

Why can't they understand we're not like that? He lifted his hand but hesitated, seeing movement from the

267

corner of his eye. Izzie jumped off the edge of the cliff, sword overhead. *What is she doing?!*

"No, stop!" he yelled, thrusting out his hand to make the wind stop her. Someone rammed into the guard, knocking the gun out of his hand, which slid to his feet. It was Luke who pinned him, hair wild, a grin on his face. But Mike focused on Izzie, frozen as she quickly fell. The wind wasn't listening and raged on with the clouds. *STUPID STORM!*

I can't save her.

A cold blue wave rippled out, flipping the air around as a soundwave traveled the area. The fighting ceased as all eyes gradually turned towards her, almost like the wave forced them to. She impaled the sword through the ground, a blinding blue light exploding out.

Her wings were back, glowing with white tips. A ring of red light shone briefly above her head, fading. Her skin reflected the light, creating this aura of blue.

Mike opened his mouth in awe. The fog, this kind of veil over his memories, lifted. It hit him like a thunderbolt. He remembered *who* she was. Who *they all* were. His long-lost siblings, the young twins, playing with *wings* bright against the sky. He and his brothers, laughing, with *wings.* The lies they were fed… the exile to Earth to be mere humans for treason.

Izzie and Kyle were his lost siblings. All this time they were here, fighting alongside him. He had them back. And he somehow didn't realize it.

What kind of brother was he?

Below her, he saw Jane next to a man with his neck

adorned with tattoos. Both of them stared at his sister, Jane, with her mouth open and the man with narrowed eyes. They stood amid the crowd, hands at their sides, unbothered by the blood. Far behind them stood Irous and Lucas, wide-eyed.

Flapping her wings, his sister took off. Circling, Izzie, no her Ikris name, Isaiah, ended up hovering over her sword. Her glowing eyes darted around, pausing on Mike—Michalis for a moment.

"In the name of the Ikris, I command you to cease fire!" Another ripple of wind swept across the field. *How did she do it?* She extended her hand. *"They took my family, and they lied to yours. Each side is trying to do the right thing and survive, fighting a war we never needed. This ends now."*

Weapons dropped as people stared, some exchanging glances, others tilting their heads as if perplexed.

"There's another evil neither of us sees. One who knew and wanted this to happen. One who wants power, for us to destroy each other. They killed the Ikris and made us extinct. But the Ikris are no longer a memory—we're a promise that as long as there's darkness, someone will stand to fight it. Forget fighting each other, we should be against them. These people will do anything to win. They manipulated all of us. They fear us. You."

Stiffly lifting her gun, Jane furrowed her eyebrows and shakily aimed it at his sister. But the man swatted it back down, looking as if he reprimanded her.

Izzie flapped her wings, circling. *"As one of the last knights of dark and light, being stripped from the power of an Ikris I have regained once more, I say in the name of my ancestors that we join forces to defeat this threat. They are Nemesis Dark Hope. We must succeed or we will all be destroyed."*

Another flash of light blinded Michalis as thunder echoed. His sister dropped, switching back to her human form before she struck the ground. Dirt and bruises covered her body with blood streaking from her mouth.

Snapping from his trance, he ran towards her, but the crowd became thick, blocking his way and his line of sight. People wanted to see her; it was chaotic.

"Izzie!" Mike shoved, struggling to get around. More people flooded in between them. Dark smoke swirled from where she was, and angry shouts erupted. *No-no-no.*

Kyle and Luke arrived as Mike reached the spot where Izzie landed. More footsteps signaled the arrival of Ryan, then eventually Whitney and Atticus.

The area was vacant, an indent of her sword left within the singed ground. He stared at the empty space, no trace of his sister left. *Izzie-Isaiah's gone. Why couldn't I have reached her in time?*

Kyle crumpled to his knees, soaked, rain mixing with the tears streaking down his face. He reached a hand to the soaked earth, his voice strangled between an angered scream and a sob, "No, no, no. Why do you keep doing this, Iz?"

Luke knelt beside him, placing a hand on Kyle's back. "We'll get her back," he promised, his hand curling into a fist. "We'll get *our* sister back. I will not watch another sibling die."

270

Mike stared, clenching and unclenching his hand. *No, don't be gone. Not like Zack. I can't lose someone else.*

"FIND HER!" Mike commanded, wiping the rain out of his eyes.

He glanced around furiously, seeing Jane and the man gone, but Irous and Lucas stayed. Lucas met his gaze, his expression throwing Mike off guard. His lips parted open, ears drawn back, and he dropped his weapons.

Izzie's gone.

The realization punched him in the chest. His siblings needed him to lead, but how could he if he couldn't protect them or keep them safe? Mike forced his breathing to steady as the battlefield slowly emptied.

"We're going to find her," Mike agreed firmly, placing a hand on Kyle's other shoulder.

Breathing in deeply, his little brother straightened, eyes sharp and voice terse. "I don't care what it takes, I won't be away from her again."

Ryan came up to Mike's side. "And when we do, they will regret everything they've put us through."

The rain-slick earth where his sister had pierced still had a burned indent of her sword. The storm raged, but all he could hear was the echo of her voice. He turned his neck, trying to loosen the tension.

The Hyphenx's were Ikris.

Kyle stood. He looked down at the charred mark where his sister had vanished and took a breath. "We won't lose her too," he whispered. "Zack never gave up on family. Neither will I."

Mike glanced at Kyle, Ryan, Luke, and the rest of XXS and Nemesis as they helped out those injured or moved those who died.

It took a decade, but he found them. He finally found his little siblings.

Kyle stepped forward, lifting his sword and touching the dirt. Together, they turned from the smoke and walked back into XXS.

Nemesis Dark Hope declared war on the wrong family.

Epilogue

It's done. I did it. After years of torment, of trying to escape. We had survived her. I found my family.

Am I dead? My senses faded in and out. I lay there, motionless, unable to speak. *What have I done?* The details were a blur, slipping away like sand through my fingers. My original form resided with me. *Ikris.*

My brothers… Kyle was right. We had siblings. I was with them all this time. I did this for them.

I winced, a sharp pain lancing through my chest. My ribs must be broken. That drop hadn't done it well at all. Light-headedness crept in as the weight of it came so fast. Everything hurts. The light hurt.

Now they're back, I have to take on what's next. For them. I'm not only surviving anymore. I have to…

Cold stone touched my skin as I rolled over. *Am I in a tomb?* A groan escaped my lips as I struggled to open my eyes. They feel like they're glued shut, nailed closed.

What happened to the woman who raised us?

I try again, straining against the effort. The ceiling was black, dampness lingering in the air. *Where am I? How much time has passed?*

"Hello, Izzie," a familiar man's voice said. "Miss me?"

Acknowledgments

Whoa, this is what it is like to be here. This is insane. After creating it, I would like to thank some people.

Hint: That's weird. Why is the 'L' on page 181 bolded? Or the 'B' on 182. Huh, must've been a mistake.

First off, Anilee Briscoe, my sister. Thank you for always being there to give *insightful* tips, comments, and helping me to learn how to write. Your input and love for writing inspired me in more ways than one. And thanks for the cover :)

My English Teachers, I loved being in your classes. Thanks so very much for helping me write, figure out ideas, and learn. You all had such a passion for literature or other careers that I strive to live by.

E. Walsh, if it wasn't for you, I don't think I would've ever come up with this idea of Izzie and her brother(s) in the first place. In fact, I began this book because of you. I know it's been years, but thanks for being a part of my life.

Jade Crandell, thank you for supporting me. You always got me to try again, even if I thought it was a complete failure. You're amazing and the best friend I could ask for. Don't ever forget your worth.

My other friends, Sarah Tholen, Porter Stone, Kali Jeffery, Holly Peterson, the actors in my book trailer, and more. Thanks a lot for giving me new ideas, tips, and suggestions. You guys helped so much with this and supported me all the way. Thank you for putting up with me and being willing to help me out.

Special thanks to Rebekah Adams, Jarren Briscoe, Julie Briscoe, La'Rue Briscoe, (etc.), for proofreading.

Dude Random Number (Jesse Sorenson), thank you for helping me live to get here. I don't know if I ever would've made it without you. Your help has never gone unnoticed.

Thanks to the critiquing website I used for pointing out my inconsistencies and wording. That's actually the main reason I added like, 25k words (not exaggerating).

And to my first readers/beta readers, thanks for reading. Your comments are always welcome to give any insight into my book or the next. I am happy you took the time to read this!

Thank You again! Live life, you only have one chance. Make it worth it and help others. Good luck.

About the Author

Lórien Briscoe—yes, named after Lord of the Rings—wrote Magic's Escape: Wingless at fifteen and re-edited it at nineteen. She's been a storyteller since kindergarten.

In the United States, she multitasks between sports (Basketball, Softball, Soccer, Wrestling, Fencing), art, percussion, filming and editing videos or live streams, or scribbling story ideas in the margins of her notes. Lórien's studying toward her B.A. in Film and Media Arts with five minors and one certificate at the University of Utah.

Fans of underdog heroes, fractured families, and philosophical "what ifs," will feel right at home in her morally tangled universes—with no romance—where not every hero saves the world… some just save their family.

Stay tuned, because Lórien is revising the second in the duology "Magic's Escape: Shadow of the Ikris", and her next standalone, "In Between the Lines to Villainy", a villain origin story which dares to ask: Is conflict necessary for advancement?

www.ingramcontent.com/pod-product-compliance
Lightning Source LLC
Chambersburg PA
CBHW060622260626
47161CB00008B/2778